After Words

Conanical Correspondence
from the World of Sherlock Holmes
& Dr. Watson

Thomas W. Campbell

Publishing Information

The fictional letters found in this book are based on the characters and stories created by Sir Arthur Conan Doyle. While drawing inspiration from Doyle's original characters and Victorian London setting, all events, dialogue, and character interactions depicted herein are products of the author's imagination and should not be construed as historical fact or canonical representations of Doyle's original works. The author utilized spell check, grammar check, sentence composition tools, and artificial intelligence during the writing of this book.

AfterWords
First Edition: October 1, 2025
ISBN: 979-8-218-79155-1

Published by:

Sherlock Holmes Society USA
P. O. Box 347
Carolina Beach, NC   28428

Contact:
SHolmesSociety@gmail.com

Printed in the United States of America

Introduction

Every solved case leaves loose ends—and letters to be written.

When Sherlock Holmes closed a case, life didn't simply stop. A grateful client would put pen to paper. A grieving family would send condolences. A convicted criminal would scratch out bitter words from his cell. A witness would feel compelled to set the record straight. These *afterwords*—the human responses that naturally follow extraordinary events—are what Arthur Conan Doyle never showed us.

AfterWords presents what happened next: the correspondence that would inevitably have followed each of Holmes's sixty recorded adventures. Here are the thank-you notes and angry letters, the updates and clarifications, the expressions of gratitude and demands for justice that such dramatic interventions would naturally provoke.

This collection contains such correspondence—each flowing directly from the canonical events Doyle recorded, each representing the routine human need to reach out after significant events touch our lives. There is nothing extraordinary about these letters themselves. They are simply what people do: they write, they seek connection, they look for understanding or closure.

Together, these *afterwords* complete the picture of each case, revealing not just what Holmes solved, but how those solutions rippled through the lives he touched. Because the story never really ends with Watson's final sentence—it continues in the words that people feel compelled to write afterward.

For the optimal reading experience, I recommend approaching this book by starting with a story from the original Canon, then turning to the corresponding letters contained within these pages. This method will deepen your appreciation and comprehension of the narrative in ways that would hopefully meet with Sir Arthur Conan Doyle's approval.

Conanical or Canonical?

The sub-title on the cover of this book describes it as being "Conanical Correspondence from the World of Sherlock Holmes & Dr. John Watson."

The term **conanical** is a play on the author's surname that describes expansions or elaborations of the 60 existing canonical stories—filling in details, exploring loose threads, or developing implications that Doyle himself might have pursued with greater space, time, or narrative inclination. This form of writing remains faithful to Doyle's established characters, settings, and distinctive narrative voice.

Unlike the traditional pastiche, which introduces new adventures, characters, or locations, **conanical** writing operates strictly within the boundaries of Doyle's existing imaginative framework. It seeks to maintain the authentic texture and sensibility of the canonical works.

AfterWords is **conanical** because it comes as close to being canonical as possible without actually having been written by Sir Arthur Conan Doyle himself.

Table of Contents

To Watson From Murray (STUD)

My Dear Dr. Watson,

I hope this letter finds you in better health than when we last parted at those dreadful field hospitals near Peshawar. You may be surprised to hear from your old orderly after all these years, but not a day passes that I don't think of that terrible business at Maiwand and wonder how you've fared.

I pray the shoulder has mended properly, sir. That Jezail bullet made a right mess of things, and I still wake some nights thinking of the blood and the way you looked so pale when I got you across that packhorse. The Ghazis were closing in something fierce, and I thought we were both done for. But you always were made of stronger stuff than most, Dr. Watson.

I've been back home in Wales these past months, working my father's farm and trying to forget the sound of those Afghan winds. It's peaceful here, but sometimes too quiet for a man who's heard the thunder of battle. I ran into Corporal Jenkins from our old unit last week at the market in Bangor. He told me you'd been invalided out and were living in London now. It took some doing, but I managed to get your address from Colonel Hayter, who remembered you fondly.

I hope you don't mind my writing, sir. I've often wondered if you think poorly of me for not staying in touch. The truth is, I wasn't sure you'd want to hear from the likes of me, what with you being a proper doctor and gentleman.

Are you practicing medicine again? I do hope your wounds haven't prevented you from continuing your calling. You were the finest medical officer I ever served under, sir, always putting the men's welfare before your own.

If you're ever in Wales, you'd be most welcome at our farm. My wife makes the finest Welsh cakes this side of Snowdonia, and she's heard me

tell the story of Maiwand so many times, she feels she knows you herself.
I remain, as always, your faithful servant,

Private William Murray
Late of the 66th (Berkshire) Regiment of Foot

To Murray from Watson (STUD)

My Dear Murray,

Your letter was the most welcome surprise I have received in many months. Please, dispense with the formalities—after what we endured together, you have certainly earned the right to call me simply Watson, as a friend would.

I am delighted to hear you have returned safely to Wales and to your family. Your courage at Maiwand saved not only my life but my sanity, for I often wonder what would have become of me in the hands of those Ghazis. I have never forgotten your loyalty, and I confess I have often wondered about your fate as well.

You ask about my condition—I am pleased to report that while my shoulder still aches in damp weather and my constitution remains somewhat weakened, I have largely recovered. I was indeed invalided out of the service, as Jenkins correctly reported, and returned to London to resume civilian life.

The most remarkable turn in my circumstances, however, has been my recent acquaintance with an extraordinary individual named Sherlock Holmes. We have become flatmates here at Baker Street, and I find myself serving as something of an assistant in his work as a consulting detective. He solves the most baffling mysteries with methods that seem almost supernatural, though he insists they are merely the application of logical deduction.

I have begun chronicling some of our adventures together, thinking they might be of interest to the reading public. It is strange how life takes unexpected turns—from the dusty plains of Afghanistan to the fog-shrouded streets of London, pursuing criminals instead of treating bullet wounds.

Thank you, my good fellow, for reaching out. Your grateful friend,

John H. Watson, M.D.

To Watson from Stamford (STUD)

My Dear Watson,

I trust this letter finds you in the very best of health and spirits on this most blessed of Christmas Days. Please accept my heartiest compliments of the season, and may this day bring you all the joy and contentment that the occasion merits.

I fear I must begin with a most sincere apology for my unconscionable delay in writing to you. It has been far too long since we last corresponded, and I am quite ashamed that I have allowed such a lengthy silence to persist between us. The truth is, my dear fellow, that I have been so consumed with my studies and the various trials that accompany the pursuit of our noble profession that I scarcely knew where to begin in renewing our correspondence.

You will, I am certain, be pleased to learn that I have at long last achieved that which we both pursued with such determination during our days at Barts. Yes, Watson, I can now proudly sign my name as Doctor Stamford, having successfully completed my examinations and received my Doctor of Medicine degree this past spring. It has been a considerably longer journey than I had initially anticipated—as you well predicted, being some four years behind you proved to be quite the obstacle to overcome—but perseverance has finally been rewarded.

I often think back with great fondness to those days when I served as your dresser at St. Bartholomew's. Your patience with my inexperience and your willingness to share your knowledge were instrumental in shaping whatever competence I may now possess. I daresay those early lessons in practical medicine, learned at your side while attending to patients, proved more valuable than many a lecture hall discourse.

I have followed your career with great interest, and I understand that your service as an army surgeon has taken you to some rather exotic and, I fear, dangerous corners of the Empire. I do hope that your experiences, however challenging they may have been, have added to your store of medical knowledge and personal character.

As we stand on the threshold of a new year, I find myself hoping that we might renew the friendship we once enjoyed. If your schedule permits, and if the notion appeals to you, I should be delighted if you would join me for drinks at the Criterion Bar sometime in the coming weeks. It would give me the greatest pleasure to hear of your adventures and to share what news I have of our mutual acquaintances from the old days.

I remain, my dear Watson, with the warmest regards and the sincerest hopes for your continued success and happiness,

Your devoted friend and colleague,

Doctor Stamford

To Stamford from Watson (STUD)

My Dear Stamford,

What a delightful surprise your letter proved to be! I confess that when Mrs. Hudson handed me the correspondence bearing your familiar hand, a flood of memories came rushing back to those early days at Bart's Hospital. How vividly I recall our chance encounter in the laboratory, and how little I could have imagined the extraordinary turn my life would take following your kind introduction to that singular fellow, Sherlock Holmes.

I must extend my heartiest congratulations on your elevation to the ranks of the medical profession proper. The transition from dresser to doctor is no small achievement, and I have no doubt that your patients are fortunate indeed to benefit from your skill and dedication.

Your proposal that we should meet at the Criterion is most welcome. Indeed, I find myself quite eager to renew our acquaintance and to hear of your adventures in the years since our paths diverged. There is much I should like to share with you as well—though I suspect you may have already read some account of my experiences with Holmes.

I shall be at the Criterion this coming Thursday evening at seven o'clock, if that time suits you. I suggest we take our usual table by the window—assuming, of course, that you remember our old preferences as clearly as I do.

It occurs to me that I owe you a debt far greater than I have ever properly acknowledged. Had you not taken pity on a somewhat lost army surgeon that day, introducing him to your curious acquaintance, my life might have taken a very different and far less remarkable course.
I look forward with genuine pleasure to our reunion and to hearing all your news. Your devoted friend,

John H. Watson, M.D.

To Holmes from John Rance (STUD)

Dear Mr. Holmes,

I trust this letter finds you in good health, though I confess I write not out of courtesy but from a sense of duty—duty to myself and to the uniform I have worn with pride these past seven years.

Your recent remarks regarding my capabilities as a police constable, particularly your prediction that I "will not rise in the force," have caused me considerable distress. While I acknowledge your reputation for keen observation and deductive reasoning, I believe your assessment of my character and professional abilities to be both hasty and unjust.

You criticized my handling of the Lauriston Gardens incident, suggesting that I had failed to secure the scene properly. I would remind you, sir, that when I discovered that ghastly scene, I was alone in the dark hours before dawn. The sight that greeted me would have unsettled men of far greater experience than myself. Yet I maintained my composure, secured the premises, and immediately sent word to my superiors.

Furthermore, you made light of my encounter with the intoxicated man near the scene. I will grant that the fellow appeared to be merely another drunkard, but I followed proper procedure in moving him along. How was I to know that this shambling inebriate might have been connected to the crime? You speak as though such insights should be obvious, yet even you required considerable time and investigation to unravel the mystery.

I have served faithfully in Brixton for these many years, and my record speaks for itself. I have apprehended seventeen pickpockets, broken up countless street fights, and have never once been found wanting in courage when duty called. My superior officers have commended my diligence and reliability. Inspector Gregson himself has noted my thoroughness in official reports.

You may possess extraordinary gifts of observation, Mr. Holmes, but that does not grant you license to dismiss the honest efforts of those who serve the public good in more conventional ways. Not every man can peer at a scene and divine its secrets as you claim to do. We common constables must rely on methodical police work, attention to regulations, and dogged persistence. These are not failings, sir—they are the very foundations upon which law and order rest.

I do not write seeking an apology, for I suspect your pride would not permit such a gesture. Rather, I write to inform you that your harsh judgment has only strengthened my resolve to prove myself worthy of advancement. Perhaps one day you will have occasion to revise your opinion of Constable John Rance.

Until such time, I remain committed to my duties and to the protection of Her Majesty's subjects, with or without your approval.

I have the honour to be, sir,

Your obedient servant,

John Rance
Police Constable 426H
Metropolitan Police

Post Scriptum: Should you require the assistance of the Metropolitan Police in future investigations, please be assured that I shall perform my duties with the same dedication I have always shown, regardless of your personal opinion of my abilities.

To Holmes from Jonathan Small (SIGN)

Dear Mr. Holmes,

I write to you from my cell, where I have had much time to reflect upon the events that brought us together and the terrible crimes for which I now pay the price. I know you are a man who values truth above all else, and so I hope you will receive this letter in the spirit in which it is intended—as a genuine expression of remorse from a man who has finally come to understand the full weight of his actions.

When I first told you my tale in that cab, I spoke with anger and justification, believing myself wronged by fate and by Major Sholto. I told myself that the treasure was rightfully mine, that I had earned it through suffering and sacrifice. I convinced myself that my pursuit of it was just, even noble. How wrong I was.

The death of poor Bartholomew Sholto weighs most heavily upon my conscience. Though it was Tonga's dart that ended his life, I know that I bear the greater responsibility. I brought my faithful friend into this dark business, and in his loyalty to me, he committed an act I never intended but for which I am truly culpable. That young man died for treasure— mere gold and jewels that now lie at the bottom of the Thames, as worthless as they always truly were.

I have come to realize that my wooden leg was not the only part of me lost to that crocodile in the Ganges so many years ago. Somewhere in those dark waters, I also lost my moral compass, my sense of right and wrong. The years on the Andaman Islands, the bitterness, the obsession with the treasure—they all conspired to make me forget the man I once was.

Tonga died because of me, Mr. Holmes. Shot down like a wild animal while trying to serve what he believed was my cause. He was a simple soul who showed me kindness when I had nothing, and I repaid that kindness by leading him to his death. This knowledge tortures me more than any physical pain I have ever endured.

I know that my confession came too late to save lives or undo the harm I caused. I know that expressing remorse now, from the safety of my prison cell, may seem hollow or self-serving. But I want you to know that I understand the true nature of my crimes. I was not a victim of circumstance seeking justice—I was a criminal driven by greed and obsession, willing to destroy innocent lives for treasure that ultimately meant nothing.

I have asked the prison chaplain to help me write to Mrs. Bernstone and to young Mr. Thaddeus Sholto, to express my deepest regrets for the pain I have caused their family. I know my words cannot bring back Bartholomew or ease their grief, but perhaps they might provide some small measure of closure.

You showed me more consideration and fairness than I deserved during our encounter. You listened to my story without judgment and treated me as a human being rather than merely a criminal to be apprehended. For that courtesy, I am grateful.

I pray that in time, I might find some way to atone for my sins, though I know that such redemption may be beyond my reach. I can only hope that by acknowledging the full truth of my guilt and the terrible consequences of my actions, I might begin the long journey toward becoming the man I should have been all along.

I remain, sir, your humble and repentant correspondent,

Jonathan Small
Prisoner No. 47839

P.S. - I hope Dr. Watson is in good health. Please give him my regards and my thanks for the medical attention he provided to my wounded leg. Even in pursuit of a criminal, he showed the compassion that marks a true physician.

To Holmes from Mary Morstan (SIGN)

Dear Mr. Holmes,

I hope this letter finds you well and perhaps enjoying a brief respite from the demands of your profession. I write to express my most heartfelt gratitude for the extraordinary service you have rendered in resolving the mystery that has haunted me these many years.

When I first appeared at your door in Baker Street, clutching that peculiar letter and those lustrous pearls, I was filled with both hope and trepidation. The annual gifts had provided comfort, yet the uncertainty surrounding my dear father's disappearance had cast a shadow over my entire adult life. I could never have imagined that your remarkable powers of observation and deduction would so completely illuminate the dark corners of this puzzle.

Learning the truth about Papa's fate, though painful, has brought me a peace I had not dared to hope for. To know that Major Sholto acted out of greed rather than malice toward my father personally provides some small comfort. While the circumstances of Papa's death remain tragic, understanding that he was not abandoned or forgotten, but rather fell victim to the corrupting influence of the Agra treasure, allows me to finally lay my questions to rest.

The knowledge that Jonathan Small and his companion have been apprehended and will face justice for their crimes provides additional solace. That they can harm no other innocent families brings me satisfaction, even as I feel some sympathy for the circumstances that first set Small upon his dark path.

As for the treasure itself, I must confess that its loss to the Thames troubles me not at all. The true treasure I sought was the truth about my father, and that you have delivered in full measure.

I must also thank you for the companionship of Dr. Watson throughout this adventure. His presence provided both comfort and courage during those uncertain and sometimes frightening moments. His gentle nature and steadfast character proved invaluable, and I find myself grateful for his friendship—a friendship I hope may, in time, develop into something even more precious.

Please know that your name will always be spoken with the highest regard in my household. Should you ever have need of assistance, or should you simply wish the company of those who appreciate your remarkable gifts, you will always find a warm welcome at my door.

With deepest gratitude and respect,

Miss Mary Morstan

P.S. - I have taken the liberty of enclosing a small token of my appreciation. It is but a modest gesture, yet I hope you will accept it as a symbol of my sincere thankfulness for all you have done.

To Watson from Mrs. Forrester (SIGN)

My Dear Dr. Watson,

I hope this letter finds you in the best of health and spirits. I felt compelled to write and express my most heartfelt gratitude for your invaluable assistance in resolving the extraordinary matter concerning our dear Mary Morstan.

When I first suggested that Mary consult with your esteemed colleague Mr. Holmes, I could never have imagined the remarkable adventure that would unfold. The revelation of her father's fate, though tragic, has at last brought her the peace that comes with certainty. After so many years of uncertainty and worry, she can finally lay those troubling questions to rest.

I must say, Doctor, that your courage and dedication throughout this perilous affair have not gone unnoticed. Mary has spoken of your conduct with such warmth and admiration that even my usually unobservant husband has remarked upon the particular glow that lights her countenance whenever your name is mentioned in conversation. Indeed, she seems to find endless opportunities to speak of your "steadfast bravery" and "gentle consideration" during those dangerous days.

Only yesterday, while arranging flowers in the morning room, Mary was moved to observe—quite unprompted—how fortunate any lady would be to have such a companion as yourself through life's trials. The sentiment was accompanied by such a becoming blush that I fear my youngest daughter, Evangeline, felt compelled to tease her governess about "secret admirers."

I do hope you will not think me presumptuous in noting that Mary has seemed rather melancholy since the conclusion of the affair. While she maintains her usual cheerful demeanor with the children, I have observed her gazing wistfully from the windows of late, and she has declined two perfectly pleasant invitations to take tea with neighbors. When pressed, she merely sighs and speaks of how quiet life has become after such "stimulating company."

Should you find yourself with leisure time, I know that Mary—and indeed our entire household—would be delighted to receive a visit from the hero of the Agra treasure affair. Perhaps you might join us for dinner this Sunday? Mary has expressed particular interest in hearing more of your military experiences in Afghanistan, though I suspect any tales you might share would be warmly received.

With deepest appreciation for your service to our dear girl, and hoping we may have the pleasure of your company soon,

I remain, most sincerely yours,

Mrs. Cecil Forrester

P.S. - Mary has asked me no fewer than three times whether I thought it proper for a young lady to write a letter of thanks to a gentleman. I assured her that such correspondence would be entirely appropriate given the circumstances, yet she seems to lack the confidence to take up her pen. Perhaps a word of encouragement from you might ease her hesitation?

To Mrs. Turner from Mrs. Hudson (SCAN)

My Dear Mrs. Turner,

I hope this letter finds you in the very best of health and spirits. I have only just returned from my visit with my sister's family in Brighton, and I wanted to write to you immediately to express my most heartfelt gratitude for the admirable manner in which you managed my household during my absence.

Mr. Holmes himself took the unusual step of mentioning—without any prompting from myself—how excellently you had maintained the rooms and attended to both his and Dr. Watson's needs. Coming from a gentleman who rarely notices such domestic arrangements unless they fall considerably short of his expectations, this is praise indeed! He was particularly complimentary about the cold beef and glass of beer you had served him, as well as the way you prepared his afternoon tea, noting that you had somehow divined his preference for the brew to be considerably stronger than most people find agreeable.

Dr. Watson, ever the gentleman, was even more effusive in his commendations. He mentioned that your cooking reminded him fondly of his days in Afghanistan, though I suspect he meant this as the highest form of compliment regarding hearty, sustaining fare rather than any comparison to military rations! He also expressed his appreciation for the quiet efficiency with which you managed the household, allowing him to continue his writing without disruption.

I understand from our neighbor next door that you handled Mr. Holmes's rather irregular hours with admirable composure, including the occasion when he returned at three in the morning with what she described as "a most peculiar assortment of scientific apparatus." I can only imagine the state of the sitting room, and I am doubly grateful that you managed to restore it to proper order by morning.

I do hope that my tenants' sometimes eccentric habits did not prove too trying for you. As I mentioned before my departure, Mr. Holmes is rather particular about his correspondence being left undisturbed on the mantelpiece, and his chemical experiments in the corner require a wide berth. I trust he remembered to warn you about the occasional small explosions from his laboratory work—they are generally quite harmless, though they do tend to rattle the china.

Please find enclosed a small token of my appreciation for your exceptional service. I do hope we might call upon your assistance again should the need arise, as it is such a comfort to know that 221B Baker Street is in such capable hands when duty calls me away.

With my sincerest thanks and warmest regards,

Mrs. Hudson
Landlady, 221B Baker Street

P.S. - I trust you found Mr. Holmes's violin practice tolerable. I have learned over the years that his midnight serenades are often a sign that he is working through a particularly challenging case—though I realize this knowledge provides little comfort when one is attempting to sleep!

To Holmes from John the Cabman (SCAN)

Dear Mr. Holmes,

I hope this letter finds you in good health and spirits. My name is John, and I am writing to you as the late cabman in the employ of Miss Irene Adler—or rather, as she became, Mrs. Norton.

You may recall me, though we never spoke directly. I was the cabman who served Mrs. Norton faithfully during her time in Serpentine Avenue. She was a most reliable employer, requiring my services daily with her regular schedule of departures and returns. For this constancy of work, she compensated me most generously.

I write to inform you that Mrs. Norton and her new husband have departed England permanently for the continent, as I believe you may already know. Before her departure, she took the liberty of explaining to both myself and her housekeeper the nature of your recent... investigations. She mentioned your rather clever impersonation of a groom when you spoke with the stable hands to gather information about her habits and movements, and also about your impersonation of the old clergyman who visited her the night that the plumber's smoke rocket was thrown into her sitting room. Quite ingenious, if I may say so, sir.

With Mrs. Norton's departure, I find myself in rather reduced circumstances. Having lost my primary source of income, I am now seeking new employment. As I own my own hansom cab and have many years of experience navigating the streets of London at all hours, I wondered if you might know of any gentlemen or establishments in need of a reliable cabman's services.

I take particular pride in my driving abilities and knowledge of London's streets. On one memorable occasion, Mrs. Norton required urgent transport to the church of St. Monica in the Edgware Road, requesting that I accomplish the journey in twenty minutes—a considerable challenge given the distance and traffic. Through expert navigation of lesser-known routes and skillful handling of my cab, I delivered her to the church steps with time to spare. Such promptness and reliability have been hallmarks of my service throughout my career.

I am also particularly skilled at discretion—a quality I imagine might be valued in your line of work, Mr. Holmes. Mrs. Norton often required journeys of a... shall we say, confidential nature, and I learned never to inquire about destinations or passengers beyond what was necessary for my duties.

Should you know of any situations requiring an experienced cabman who can be trusted to ask no questions and remember even less, I would be most grateful for your consideration or recommendation. I am available at any hour and can provide references as to my character and driving abilities.

I remain, sir, your humble servant,

John
Licensed Cabman

Post Scriptum: I do hope Mrs. Norton's photograph served its intended purpose in your dealings with her. She seemed quite pleased with her arrangements before departing.

To Holmes from Jabez Wilson (REDH)

Dear Mr. Holmes,

I hope this letter finds you in good health and spirits. I write to you with a heart full of gratitude, though I confess it is somewhat tempered by a peculiar sense of loss that I feel compelled to share.

First and foremost, I must express my most sincere thanks for your remarkable deduction in the matter of the Red-Headed League. When Dr. Watson first brought you to my humble shop, I thought you a rather odd fellow—if you'll forgive my saying so—with your intense scrutinizing and peculiar questions about my assistant Vincent Spaulding. Little did I know that behind those keen eyes lay a mind capable of unraveling such an extraordinary deception.

Your swift action in alerting Inspector Jones and positioning yourselves in the bank vault was nothing short of brilliant. To think that while I was innocently copying out the Encyclopedia Britannica, believing myself to be engaged in legitimate employment, that scoundrel John Clay—for that was Spaulding's true name, as you revealed—was beneath my very feet, tunneling his way toward the City and Suburban Bank! The audacity of it still takes my breath away.

I am profoundly grateful that you prevented what would surely have been a most heinous crime. The thought that my shop served as the staging ground for such villainy fills me with horror, and I shudder to think what might have befallen me had I stumbled upon their scheme accidentally. No doubt my safety, and indeed my very life, hung in the balance without my knowing it.

However, Mr. Holmes, I must confess to you a certain melancholy that has settled upon me since the resolution of this affair. While I am immensely relieved that justice has been served and that Clay and his accomplice Duncan Ross are safely behind bars, I cannot help but feel a profound disappointment at the loss of my position with the Red-Headed League.

Four pounds a week, Mr. Holmes! Four whole pounds for the simple task of copying articles from the encyclopedia. In all my years as a pawnbroker, I have rarely seen such generous compensation for such agreeable work. The morning hours spent in that pleasant office on Pope's Court had become the brightest part of my day. There was something quite satisfying about the methodical copying of knowledge, from "Abbots" through "Archery" and beyond. I had such hopes of reaching "Azygous" by Christmas!

I know it sounds foolish—indeed, my wife has told me as much—but I had grown quite fond of my routine. The walk to Fleet Street, the quiet hours with my pen and ink, the satisfaction of a job well done, and of course, the reliable weekly income that allowed us small luxuries we had not enjoyed in years. Mrs. Wilson was already making plans for new curtains in the parlor.

I understand, of course, that the League was nothing but an elaborate fiction designed to keep me away from my shop during the crucial hours of Clay's excavation work. I bear no ill will toward you for exposing this truth—quite the contrary, as I've stated. Yet I cannot help but wonder if somewhere in London there might not be a legitimate organization in need of copying services? A fellow with neat handwriting and a methodical disposition?

Should you ever find yourself in need of any item that might be found in a respectable pawn shop, I hope you will consider Wilson's establishment. It would be my pleasure to serve the man who saved both my reputation and quite possibly my life.

With deepest gratitude and highest respect,

Jabez Wilson
Proprietor, Wilson's Pawn Shop

P.S. - I have taken the liberty of copying out several articles on "Detective" and "Detection" from the encyclopedia, thinking they might interest you. Should you care for them, I would be delighted to send them along.

To Holmes from John Clay (REDH)

My Dear Mr. Holmes,

How utterly delightful it was to make your acquaintance in the vault of
the City and Suburban Bank! I must confess, your timing was
impeccable—though I suspect you would prefer to call it "deduction"
rather than mere coincidence. How very like you to take credit for what
any observant gentleman with a modicum of intelligence might have
pieced together.

Bravo, Mr. Holmes! Bravo! Your reputation as London's foremost
consulting detective is clearly well-deserved. The way you unraveled our
little enterprise with the Red-Headed League was truly... adequate. I
particularly admired how you connected the dots between dear Mr.
Wilson's conspicuous absence from his shop and our modest excavation
project. Elementary, as I'm sure you would say.

I do hope you enjoyed your dramatic moment in the vault, crouching
there in the darkness with Inspector Jones and his constables like
schoolboys playing at hide-and-seek. The look of satisfaction on your
face when you sprang your little trap was almost worth the inconvenience
of these iron bars. Almost.

You see, Mr. Holmes, while you may fancy yourself the master of this
particular game, I fear you've made one rather significant miscalculation.
You seem to believe that catching John Clay is the same as defeating him.
How charmingly naive. This minor setback—for that is all it truly is—has
provided me with the most valuable commodity a man in my profession
can possess: intimate knowledge of my adversary's methods.

Prison, I've discovered, offers remarkable opportunities for reflection
and planning. The days are long, the nights longer still, and a man has
ample time to consider his next moves. I've been thinking of you quite
often, Mr. Holmes. Studying your techniques. Learning your patterns.
Contemplating the most... educational ways to renew our acquaintance.

So by all means, enjoy your moment of triumph. Read about your cleverness in the papers. Accept the grateful handshakes of bank directors and the admiration of Scotland Yard. But do remember this, my dear detective: lightning rarely strikes the same place twice, and a wise man does not depend upon luck indefinitely.
For make no mistake—there will be a next time. And when that time comes, I suspect you'll find me a rather more challenging opponent. After all, I've had the distinct advantage of watching you work, while you've only seen me fail.

Until we meet again—and we most certainly shall—I remain,

Your devoted adversary,

John Clay
Graduate of Eton and Oxford
Temporarily detained at Her Majesty's pleasure

P.S. - Do give my regards to Dr. Watson. His chronicle of our little adventure was quite flattering, though I feel he may have undersold my organizational abilities. Perhaps next time he'll have opportunity to write a more... comprehensive account.

To Holmes from Mary Sutherland (IDEN)

Dear Mr. Holmes,

I hope this letter finds you in good health and that you will forgive my boldness in writing to you after such a considerable time has passed since our meeting. I confess that I have been greatly troubled by the silence that has followed our consultation regarding my dear Hosmer's mysterious disappearance, and I find myself compelled to reach out to you once more.

It has been several weeks now since I had the honour of visiting your chambers in Baker Street, and I must admit that I had rather hoped to hear from you before this time. When I left that day, I felt certain that a gentleman of your remarkable reputation and extraordinary abilities would surely uncover the truth behind my beloved's vanishing. Yet as the days have turned to weeks, and the weeks begin to feel like months, I find myself growing increasingly anxious and disappointed.

I do not wish to appear impatient or presumptuous, Mr. Holmes, but I cannot help but wonder whether you have discovered any clues as to what became of my dear Hosmer Angel. Has your investigation yielded any results? Have you perhaps uncovered some trace of where he might have gone, or what circumstances led to his sudden disappearance on what should have been the happiest day of our lives?

I remain as faithful to him as ever, just as I promised I would be. Indeed, his final words to me—that I should remain true to him no matter what might happen—ring in my ears each day. I take comfort in the solemnity of that vow, for it assures me that whatever has befallen him, our bond remains unbroken. Surely a man who would exact such a promise from his intended bride would not abandon her without the gravest of reasons.

I continue to believe, Mr. Holmes, that some terrible misfortune must have overtaken poor Hosmer. Perhaps he has met with an accident, or fallen victim to some criminal enterprise. The very thought fills me with dread, yet I cannot abandon hope that he lives still and that circumstances beyond his control prevent him from returning to me.

Might he be injured somewhere, unable to communicate his whereabouts? Could he be held against his will by persons unknown?

I have searched my memory countless times for any detail that might provide a clue to his fate. I have re-read his letters until the paper has grown thin from handling, hoping to find some hidden meaning that might illuminate his whereabouts. Yet I remain as mystified as ever by his disappearance.

If you have made any progress in your investigation, I beseech you to share what you have learned, no matter how painful the truth might be. The uncertainty is becoming unbearable, and even the most dreadful news would be preferable to this terrible suspense. If, however, you have found no trace of him, I wonder whether you might suggest other avenues of inquiry that a woman of limited means and connections might pursue.

I remain hopeful that your superior intellect and extensive experience in such matters will yet reveal the solution to this mystery. Indeed, I believe that you are perhaps the only person in all of London capable of discovering what has become of my dear Hosmer.

I eagerly await your response and remain, with the greatest respect and gratitude for your consideration of my case,

Your most obedient servant,

Miss Mary Sutherland

P.S. - I should mention that I have taken to walking past the church of St. Saviour's each Sunday, in the hope that I might encounter some person who witnessed unusual events on the morning of our intended wedding. Thus far, my inquiries have yielded nothing, but I felt you should know of my continued efforts in this regard.

To Holmes from Mrs. Etherege (IDEN)

My Dear Mr. Holmes,

I trust this letter finds you in good health and spirits. I write to you with some urgency regarding Miss Mary Sutherland, whom I had the honour of recommending to your professional services some weeks past.

As you may recall, it was through your exceptional skill and dedication that my own dear husband was restored to me after his most troubling disappearance last spring. The relief and gratitude I felt upon his safe return cannot be adequately expressed in mere words, and it was with the utmost confidence that I directed poor Miss Sutherland to your door when she found herself in similar distressing circumstances.

I have since had occasion to speak with the dear girl, and I confess myself somewhat puzzled by her current disposition. While she speaks of you with the highest regard and mentions that you took up her case with your customary thoroughness, she remains as bereft as ever regarding the fate of her beloved Mr. Hosmer Angel. Indeed, she seems to have settled into a most melancholy resignation, speaking of waiting faithfully for his return as though it were her sacred duty.

I cannot help but wonder, Mr. Holmes, whether perhaps the matter of your fee has presented an obstacle to the full resolution of this case. Miss Sutherland, though possessed of a comfortable independence, is not a lady of extensive means, and I fear she may have been too delicate to discuss financial arrangements with you directly.

If such is the case, I should be most honoured to remedy this situation immediately. The sum of fifty guineas is at your disposal, with the promise of an additional fifty upon the successful location of Mr. Angel. I assure you this is offered not from any want of confidence in your methods, but purely from my desire to see justice done for a most deserving young woman who has already suffered far too much uncertainty.

Miss Sutherland is a gentle soul who deserves either the joy of reunion with her intended or, at the very least, the comfort of knowing his fate with certainty. Her current state of perpetual waiting seems most unhealthy for one so young.

I should be grateful for any communication you might provide regarding the progress of this matter, as my concern for Miss Sutherland grows daily. She has become quite dear to me, and I find I cannot rest easy knowing she remains in such distress.

I remain, with the highest esteem and confidence in your abilities,
Your most obedient servant,

Mrs. Etherege

P.S. - Should you require any additional resources or assistance in pursuing this matter, please do not hesitate to call upon me. I have several acquaintances who might prove useful should wider inquiries become necessary.

To Holmes from Miss Turner (BOSC)

My Dear Mr. Holmes,

I hope this letter finds you and Dr. Watson in excellent health and spirits. As I write to you on this beautiful summer evening, exactly one year has passed since you came to our aid in Boscombe Valley during those dark and terrible days that seemed to threaten the very foundations of my world.

I find myself compelled to write to you once more, not merely to express my gratitude—though that remains as profound as ever—but to share with you news that I believe will bring you considerable satisfaction.

James and I have decided to marry. Our engagement, which once seemed so impossibly shadowed by tragedy and suspicion, has blossomed into something beautiful and certain. We have set the date for the 3rd of August, and I write to formally invite both you and Dr. Watson to join us in celebrating this joyous occasion. It would be the greatest honor to have present the man whose remarkable powers of observation and deduction not only saved an innocent man from the gallows, but restored to me the future I had feared was lost forever.

The past year has been one of healing for both James and myself. We have learned to carry the weight of our families' histories without allowing them to burden our own hearts unduly. As you so wisely understood, some truths are meant to rest in peace with those who carried them, and we have found great comfort in your decision to let sleeping sorrows lie.

James has proven himself to be everything I believed him to be—kind, honorable, and possessed of a strength that has only grown through adversity. He speaks often of the day you visited him in that dreadful cell, and how your confidence in his innocence gave him hope when all seemed lost. "Holmes saw something in me that even I had begun to doubt," he says, and I know he would be deeply honored by your presence at our wedding.

Dr. Watson, too, holds a special place in our hearts for his steadfast loyalty to you and his gentle kindness during those difficult days. We should be delighted to welcome you both as our most honored guests.

The ceremony will take place at St. James Church in Boscombe at two o'clock in the afternoon, followed by a celebration at Turner Lodge. Should your detective work permit, we would be overjoyed to see you there.

I remain, as always, your most grateful and devoted friend,

Miss Alice Turner

P.S. - I have heard tales of your recent adventures from the London papers, and I confess that James and I often find ourselves wondering what fascinating mysteries currently occupy your brilliant mind. Perhaps, if you honor us with your presence, you might regale us with an account or two that Dr. Watson has not yet seen fit to publish!

To Holmes from Savannah Chief (FIVE)

Dear Mr. Holmes,

I write to acknowledge receipt of your urgent communication dated 3rd of November, which reached our offices on the 12th instant via the regular Atlantic mail service. Your letter, warning of the imminent arrival of dangerous criminals aboard the merchant vessel *Barque Lone Star*, was received with the utmost seriousness and immediate action was taken pursuant to your detailed intelligence.

Upon receiving your correspondence, I personally briefed my most trusted officers regarding the three individuals you described—members of that abominable organization whose initials you dared not fully spell out in your missive, though their meaning was perfectly clear to this office. We had already received disturbing reports from our colleagues in other Southern ports regarding the activities of such men, and your warning confirmed our worst suspicions about their intended operations in our jurisdiction.

I deployed a full complement of officers to monitor the harbor approaches and had arranged for customs officials to conduct a thorough inspection of the *Lone Star* upon her anticipated arrival. Additional men were stationed at the railway depot and principal hotels, armed with the descriptions you so helpfully provided.

However, I must now report that our preparations, though thorough, proved unnecessary due to the intervention of Divine Providence—or perhaps, as some of my more superstitious officers would have it, the justice of the Almighty working through the forces of nature.

The *Barque Lone Star*, which our harbor master's records indicate departed Liverpool on the 7th of November, was expected to make port by the 14th instant. However, she failed to arrive as scheduled, and we can only presume that she fell victim to the terrible gale that struck our coast during the night of the 13th—one of the most violent storms in recent memory.

While no vessel reported sighting the *Lone Star* during the tempest, compelling evidence of her fate was discovered on the morning of the 15th instant. The fishing vessel *Mary Catherine*, working the waters some twenty miles southeast of our harbor, recovered a piece of wreckage that proved most significant—the shattered sternpost of a vessel, bearing the carved letters "L. S." upon its weathered surface.

Acting upon this discovery, I immediately dispatched our most capable rescue boats to conduct a thorough search of the area where this grim evidence was found. Despite their diligent efforts over the course of two full days, combing the waters in ever-widening circles, no trace of survivors could be located. The violence of the storm and the treacherous currents in those waters lead us to conclude that all souls aboard have been claimed by the sea.

While I cannot say that I mourn the loss of men whose intentions toward our community were so clearly malevolent, I am nevertheless duty-bound to report that justice, in this instance, appears to have been administered by a Higher Court than our own.

I wish to express my profound gratitude for your warning, Mr. Holmes. Your reputation as a consulting detective has reached even these shores, and your assistance in this matter demonstrates the finest cooperation between our respective nations in the pursuit of justice. Should you ever find yourself in our fair city, please know that you would be most warmly received at our headquarters.

I remain, sir, your most obedient servant,

Colonel James R. Whitmore
Chief of Police
City of Savannah, Georgia

P.S. — I have taken the liberty of forwarding copies of this correspondence to the appropriate Federal authorities in Washington, as well as to our colleagues in Charleston, Mobile, and New Orleans, that they might be apprised of the resolution of this matter.

To Major Prendergast from Holmes (FIVE)

My Dear Major,

It is with the gravest regret that I must write to inform you of the tragic fate that has befallen young John Openshaw, whom you so thoughtfully referred to my attention some days past. As you were instrumental in directing him to seek my counsel, I feel it incumbent upon me to apprise you of the melancholy conclusion to this most sinister affair.

Mr. Openshaw called upon me on the evening of September 29th, bearing a tale of such singular menace that even my experience with the criminal classes had scarcely prepared me for its implications. As you doubtless suspected when you advised him to consult me, the matter concerned the mysterious deaths of both his uncle Elias and his father Joseph, each preceded by the receipt of a letter containing five orange pips and bearing the ominous initials "K.K.K."

The young man had himself received such a communication, accompanied by instructions to surrender certain papers from his uncle's possession. Though every instinct rebelled against yielding to such coercion, I advised him to comply with the demands, recognizing that we were dealing with an organization of ruthless determination and far-reaching influence.

Alas, my counsel proved insufficient to preserve his life. Mr. Openshaw was discovered the following morning at Waterloo Station, having fallen—or been pushed—from the platform into the path of an approaching train. The papers he carried had vanished.

I am pleased to report, however, that justice, though delayed, has been served. Through careful investigation, I was able to identify the perpetrators as members of that most pernicious American secret society, the Ku Klux Klan, who had pursued the Openshaw family to England to recover documents that could have exposed their criminal activities during the late American conflict. The murderers had taken passage aboard the barque *Lone Star*, bound for Savannah.

Though they escaped my immediate reach, Providence itself has rendered the final judgment. I have received word from the maritime authorities that the *Lone Star* foundered in a severe gale off the Goodwin Sands, with the presumed loss of all hands. The sea has claimed those whom earthly justice might have struggled to reach.

I confess that this case weighs heavily upon my mind, Major. Had I possessed fuller knowledge of the ruthless nature of our adversaries, I might have counseled different precautions. Yet I take some comfort in knowing that the deaths of the Openshaw family have not gone unavenged, and that this particular branch of a most evil organization can claim no further victims.

I remain, as always, grateful for your confidence in referring this matter to my attention, despite its tragic conclusion.

I am, sir, your most obedient servant,

Sherlock Holmes
Consulting Detective

To Holmes from Mrs. St. Clair (TWIS)

My Dear Mr. Holmes,

I write to you with a heart full of gratitude and, I confess, no small measure of curiosity regarding the recent events surrounding my husband's mysterious disappearance.

First and foremost, I must express my deepest appreciation for your tireless efforts in attempting to locate dear Neville during those dreadful days when I feared the worst. Your dedication to the case, despite the peculiar circumstances and the initial lack of promising leads, provided me with considerable comfort during what was undoubtedly the most distressing period of my life.

I am delighted to inform you that Neville has returned home safely, though I must admit that his account of recent events has left me somewhat perplexed. He tells me that after I glimpsed him at that dreadful establishment on Upper Swandam Lane, he suffered some sort of episode—perhaps brought on by the noxious fumes of that den of iniquity—which caused him to lose consciousness.

When he finally recovered his faculties, he found that several days had passed, and he was in an unfamiliar part of the city with little recollection of the intervening time. Being a man of considerable pride and not wishing to cause me further distress, he chose to make his own way home rather than involve the authorities or seek assistance.

While I am, of course, overjoyed at his safe return, I cannot help but wonder about certain aspects of the investigation. The police mentioned discovering blood near the window, and there was talk of his coat being found in the Thames. Neville seems reluctant to discuss these particulars, claiming that his memory of those lost days remains frustratingly unclear.

I find myself curious, Mr. Holmes, about what exactly transpired during your investigation. Did you perhaps uncover any details that might illuminate this strange affair? I have the distinct impression that there are elements to this story that remain untold, though I cannot quite put my finger on what they might be. Your involvement seems to have concluded rather abruptly, and I wondered if you had discovered something that led you to believe the case was resolved.

Please do not mistake my inquiry for anything other than natural curiosity. Neville is home, he appears to be in good health, and we are gradually returning to our normal domestic routine. I simply find myself pondering the mysterious circumstances and your role in bringing about this happy resolution.

Should you ever find yourself in our neighborhood, please do not hesitate to call upon us.

With sincere appreciation and warmest regards,

Mrs. Neville St. Clair

P.S. I do hope that your investigation, though it may have seemed to end without a clear resolution, was not entirely without value to your professional endeavors. I have heard it said that even cases which do not conclude as expected can provide valuable insights for future investigations.

To Holmes from Neville St. Clair (TWIS)

My Dear Mr. Holmes,

I write to you with a heart full of gratitude and relief, emotions that I fear mere words can scarcely convey. Your remarkable discretion in the recent matter concerning my... unfortunate circumstances... has preserved not only my reputation but the very foundation upon which my family's happiness rests.

When you discovered the truth behind Hugh Boone's identity in that squalid cell at Bow Street, I feared that my secret would become the talk of all London society. By your silence, you have allowed me to maintain my standing in our community, sparing my dear wife and children the humiliation that would surely have followed such a revelation.

I am deeply ashamed that my desperate pursuit of financial gain led me down such a degrading path. What began as a momentary expedient during my days as a struggling reporter became, through its very success, a terrible trap.

Your intervention has given me the opportunity to abandon this deception forever. I have already secured more respectable employment through a friend's recommendation, and though the income may be modest, it comes with the invaluable gift of self-respect.

I understand that your services are often required by those of considerable means, and I am acutely aware that my case has cost you both time and trouble. Please find enclosed the sum of one hundred pounds, which I hope will serve as some small compensation for your efforts on my behalf.

I remain, sir, your most grateful and devoted servant,

Neville St. Clair

P.S. - I have taken the liberty of destroying all remnants of my former disguise. Hugh Boone shall trouble the streets of London no more.

To Watson from Kate Whitney (TWIS)

My Dear Dr. Watson,

I find myself compelled to take up my pen this morning to express my most heartfelt gratitude for your extraordinary kindness yesterday evening. When I approached you in such distress, fearing for dear Isa's welfare, I could never have anticipated the lengths to which you would go to ensure his safe return.

Your immediate willingness to venture into that dreadful establishment on Upper Swandam Lane, despite the obvious dangers and unsavory nature of such a place, speaks volumes of your noble character. I confess that when the hours stretched on without word, I feared the worst—that perhaps both you and my poor husband had fallen victim to some terrible fate in that den of iniquity.

How my heart leaped when I heard the wheels of the Hansom cab upon our street, and saw you personally ensuring that Isa was delivered safely to our door! Your consideration in seeing him properly settled, and your discrete words of reassurance to me regarding his condition, demonstrated not only your skill as a physician but your compassion as a gentleman.

I am deeply conscious that this unfortunate episode has placed you in a most awkward position, and I can only hope that your own evening's adventure concluded more favorably than it began.

Please give my fondest regards to your dear wife, and know that both she and you will forever have our most sincere friendship and gratitude.

I remain, with deepest appreciation, your most obliged and grateful friend,

Kate Whitney

To Henry Baker from Peterson (BLUE)

Dear Sir,

I trust this letter finds you in good health and spirits as we approach the close of this most eventful year. I write to extend to you and yours the compliments of the season, and to wish you a most prosperous and joyful New Year. Mr. Sherlock Holmes gave me your address, with the promise that I did not abuse it.

You will no doubt recall the curious circumstances involving your hat and goose, which I had the fortune to recover following that unfortunate altercation in Goodge Street. As I am sure you already know, the matter has been resolved most satisfactorily, thanks to the remarkable deductive powers of Mr. Sherlock Holmes, whose reputation for unraveling the most perplexing mysteries continues to astound all who witness his methods.

As a consequence of these extraordinary events, I have been the fortunate recipient of a substantial reward, which I feel, in all good conscience, I cannot keep entirely for myself. The recovery of your property was merely my duty as a citizen and servant of the public, yet it has led to benefits far beyond what any reasonable man might expect.

Therefore, I am delighted to enclose herewith a bank draft for the sum of One Hundred Pounds (£100), which I hope you will accept as a token of my goodwill and as some small compensation for the inconvenience you suffered. I trust you will find this modest gift useful in whatever manner best suits your circumstances.

Perhaps you might consider the purchase of a fine new hat—one that might prove more resilient to the rough handling of street ruffians. Or, if you are so inclined, you might procure another goose for your table, though I daresay you may wish to ensure it contains nothing more extraordinary than a proper Christmas dinner! Should domestic concerns press upon you, as they do upon us all in these times, you might find it practical to settle such matters as having your gas service restored, that you might enjoy the comfort and convenience of proper lighting during these dark winter months.

Whatever use you make of this gift, please know that it comes with my sincere hopes for your continued happiness and prosperity. The season of goodwill reminds us that fortune, when it smiles upon us, is best shared with our fellow men.

I remain, Sir, with the greatest respect and warmest wishes for the season,

Your most obedient servant,

Peterson
Commissionaire

P.S. - My wife has asked me to convey her compliments and to express her hope that you have recovered fully from your ordeal. She also wishes you to know that the remaining portions of your goose made for a most excellent Christmas dinner, seasoned as they were with the satisfaction of a good deed accomplished.

To Holmes from Breckinridge (BLUE)

Dear Mr. Holmes,

I hope this letter finds you in excellent health and spirits. I am writing to express my most sincere gratitude for the extraordinary turn of fortune your recent visit to my humble establishment has brought upon my business.

When you first approached my stall some weeks ago with your peculiar inquiries about geese—particularly those fine birds I had sold to the Landlord at the Alpha Inn—I confess I took you for nothing more than another persistent customer with an unusually keen interest in the provenance of his Christmas dinner. Your persistent questioning about my suppliers, especially old Mrs. Oakshott from Brixton Road, struck me as rather odd, though I answered as best I could.

It was not until I read the account in the newspapers of your brilliant resolution of the Blue Carbuncle affair that I realized the true nature of your visit. To think that I had the honour of assisting the great Sherlock Holmes himself in one of his investigations! Had I known your identity at the time, I would certainly have been more accommodating and less brusque in my responses.

Since word has spread throughout Covent Garden that the famous detective made inquiries at my stall, my business has flourished beyond my wildest expectations. Much like the Landlord at the Alpha Inn, who I understand has seen a considerable increase in patronage since being mentioned in connection with your case, I too have benefited enormously from this association.

Customers arrive daily, eager to purchase fowl from "the very establishment where Sherlock Holmes solved the mystery of the stolen gem." Some even request to see the exact spot where you stood while making your inquiries!

I have had to take on an additional assistant to manage the increased trade, and my wife declares that we have sold more poultry in these past few weeks than in the entire previous quarter. The ladies particularly seem delighted to purchase their Christmas birds from a shop with such distinguished detective connections.

In recognition of your inadvertent but most welcome contribution to my prosperity, I should be delighted to offer you the finest bird in my establishment, free of charge, the next time you find yourself in the vicinity of Covent Garden. Whether your visit is for business or pleasure, you need only mention your name, and my finest goose, duck, or fowl shall be yours with my compliments.

I remain, sir, your most grateful and humble servant,

Breckenridge
Proprietor, Breckenridge & Sons

P.S. - I have taken the liberty of ensuring that all my birds are thoroughly inspected before sale. One never knows what valuable items might find their way into a bird's crop, and I should hate for any of my customers to experience the shock that poor Mrs. Peterson must have felt when preparing her unexpected Christmas dinner!

To Holmes from Bradstreet (BLUE)

Dear Mr. Holmes,

It is with considerable displeasure that I write to you regarding the recent matter of the Blue Carbuncle and your handling of the case involving one James Ryder, formerly chief of staff at the Hotel Cosmopolitan.

I have been made aware through my investigations that you not only identified Mr. Ryder as the true perpetrator of the theft of the Countess of Morcar's precious stone, but that you subsequently allowed him to depart the country without informing the proper authorities. This action, Mr. Holmes, constitutes nothing short of obstruction of justice and aiding in the escape of a known criminal.

While I acknowledge that your intervention ultimately led to the exoneration of the innocent Mr. John Horner—who was wrongfully accused and arrested—this does not excuse your flagrant disregard for proper legal procedure. The fact that justice was served for one man does not grant you the authority to dispense your own brand of mercy to another, regardless of your personal assessment of his character or circumstances.

I was, I confess, sorely tempted to present myself at your lodgings with a warrant for your arrest on charges of harboring a criminal and perverting the course of justice. The only considerations that stayed my hand were the inevitable waste of public funds that such proceedings would entail, and your occasional—though irregular—assistance to this department in matters where official channels have proven insufficient.

However, let this correspondence serve as an unequivocal warning: Scotland Yard will not tolerate further instances of your taking the law into your own hands. Your reputation for brilliance in detection does not place you above the law, nor does it grant you judicial powers that rightfully belong to Her Majesty's courts alone.

Should you discover evidence of criminal activity in future cases, you are duty-bound to report such findings to the appropriate authorities immediately. Any failure to do so will result in your prompt arrest and prosecution to the fullest extent of the law, regardless of past services rendered.

The recovery of the Blue Carbuncle and the vindication of Mr. Horner are indeed satisfactory outcomes, but they were achieved through means that cannot and will not be overlooked again.

I trust this matter is now clearly understood between us.

Your servant,

Inspector G. Bradstreet
Metropolitan Police
Scotland Yard

P.S. - I trust the £1,000 reward distributed to Peterson was done through proper channels, as befits an honest citizen's service to justice.

To Holmes from James Ryder (BLUE)

Dear Mr. Holmes,

I write to you with a heart both heavy with shame and light with gratitude. The events of yesterday evening have left me a changed man, and I feel compelled to express my deepest thanks for the extraordinary mercy you have shown me.

When I stood trembling in your rooms, caught in my web of lies and facing the certainty of prison, I expected nothing but the justice I deserved. That you chose instead to offer me redemption—to give me a second chance when the law would have shown no such compassion—is a kindness I shall never forget nor take lightly.

Your words ring constantly in my ears: that you are not retained by the police to supply their deficiencies, and that perhaps it is better that a man should be driven to reform than driven to ruin. These words have pierced my soul more deeply than any judge's sentence could have done. You have seen something in me worth saving, when I could see nothing in myself but a common thief and coward.

I write now to solemnly reaffirm the promise I made to you: I shall leave England within the week, and I give you my sacred word that I will never again stain my hands with crime. The terror and remorse of these past days have shown me the true cost of dishonesty—not merely the risk of punishment, but the corruption of one's very soul. I have gazed into that abyss and found it wanting.

You spoke of this being the season of forgiveness, and indeed, your mercy has given new meaning to the Christmas spirit for me. Though I go into exile, I go with hope rather than despair, and with a determination to prove worthy of the trust you have placed in me.

I cannot undo the wrong I did to poor John Horner, though I am grateful beyond measure that he has been cleared of all charges. I pray that time will heal the damage my actions have caused, and that my departure might bring some small measure of peace to those I have wronged.

Mr. Holmes, you have given me not merely my freedom, but my chance at redemption. I swear to you, as God is my witness, that I shall not squander this precious gift. The James Ryder who stole the Countess of Morcar's blue carbuncle dies today; the man who begins anew tomorrow shall be someone you need never regret having spared.

With profound gratitude and the utmost respect,

Your humble and reformed servant,

James Ryder
Former Commissionaire, Hotel Cosmopolitan

P.S. - I have arranged passage on the steamship "Canterbury" bound for New York, departing January 2nd. By the time you read this, I shall be making final preparations for my new life. Thank you again for believing that such a life is possible.

To Maggie Oakshott from Ryder (BLUE)

My Dearest Sister Margaret,

I write to you with a heavy heart and trembling hand, for I must confess to you a terrible thing I have done—something that has brought shame upon our family name and nearly destroyed an innocent man's life.

You will no doubt hear of this matter in the newspapers within the day, but I could not bear for you to learn of it from strangers' words rather than from my own pen. Margaret, I am the one who stole the Blue Carbuncle from the Countess of Morcar at the Cosmopolitan Hotel.

I know how this must shock you, dear sister. You who have always known me as steady and reliable, if perhaps too ambitious for my own good. But greed and desperation clouded my judgment so completely that I convinced myself I could take that precious stone and begin a new life, free from the financial pressures that have plagued me these past months.

In my foolishness, I allowed suspicion to fall upon John Horner, the poor plumber who was merely doing his work. I gave testimony against him, knowing full well he was innocent. This weighs most heavily upon my conscience—that I would see an honest working man imprisoned for my own crime.

When I realized the theft would be discovered, I panicked. I came to you for one of your geese, thinking to hide the stone within it until the immediate danger passed. You were so kind, so trusting, never questioning why your brother needed a Christmas goose so urgently. I chose the largest of your birds and forced the carbuncle down its throat, meaning to retrieve it later. But fate intervened, and the goose found its way to Mr. Henry Baker, and from there to the very man I should have feared most—Mr. Sherlock Holmes.

Margaret, I have today experienced something I did not think existed in this world: true mercy. Holmes uncovered my crime with that brilliant mind of his, laid bare every detail of my scheme. I stood before him expecting arrest, transportation, perhaps worse. But after hearing my full confession, this remarkable man looked upon me with what I can only call compassion. "Ryder," said he, "I am not retained by the police to supply their deficiencies. It is the season of forgiveness. Chance has put a most singular and whimsical problem into my hands, and its solution is its own reward."

He then advised me most earnestly to make a fresh start elsewhere, warning me that should our paths cross again under similar circumstances, I would not find him so lenient. The carbuncle has been returned to its rightful owner, and Mr. Horner has been released without charge, the case against him having collapsed entirely.

I am taking Mr. Holmes's advice and will be departing soon. I have enough saved to begin modestly somewhere else, perhaps in farming or some honest trade. I swear to you, Margaret, by our dear mother's memory, that I will never again allow greed or ambition to lead me astray. This brush with ruin has shown me the value of an honest name and a clear conscience.

I do not know when I might see you again, but I promise you this: the brother who next embraces you will be a better man than the one who writes this letter. I will work hard, live honestly, and perhaps in time earn back some small measure of the respect I have forfeited.

Give my love to your children, and please remember me not as the fool I have been these past weeks, but as the brother who loved you always, even when he had forgotten how to love himself.

Your repentant brother,

James Ryder

P.S. - I have left what money I could spare with Mrs. Hudson at 221B Baker Street, with instructions that it be given to Mr. Horner as some small compensation for the suffering I caused him. It is far less than he deserves, but it is all I can manage while still having enough for passage to the colonies.

To John Horner from Ryder (BLUE)

Dear Mr. Horner,

I write to you from a place of profound shame and regret, knowing full well that no words can undo the terrible injustice I have caused you. By the time you receive this letter, I shall have departed England, never to return—a self-imposed exile that is but a fraction of what my crimes deserve.

You know by now, I am certain, that it was I who stole the blue carbuncle from the Countess of Morcar's rooms at the Cosmopolitan Hotel. Worse still—and this weighs most heavily upon my conscience— it was I who bore false witness against you, an innocent man going about his honest work. In my cowardice and desperation, I allowed you to be arrested, to face the magistrate, to endure the shame and fear of imprisonment, all to save my own wretched skin.

There can be no excuse for such villainy. You have a family who depends upon you, a reputation built through years of honest labor, a life that I nearly destroyed with my lies. When I think of the sleepless nights you must have endured in that cell, of your wife's tears, of your children's confusion at their father's absence—I am consumed with a remorse that gnaws at me day and night.

Mr. Sherlock Holmes, in his wisdom and perhaps his Christmas charity, has seen fit to let me go free rather than see me face the full consequences of my actions. I do not understand this mercy, nor do I feel I deserve it, but I am determined not to squander this unexpected gift of redemption. I swear to you, upon whatever honor I may yet possess, that I shall spend the remainder of my days in honest work and righteous living, that this shameful chapter might be the last dark deed of my life.

I do not ask for your forgiveness—I have no right to such a request, and I know that my betrayal cuts too deep for such healing. I ask only that you know the depth of my repentance and my fervent hope that time will ease the wounds I have inflicted upon you and your family.

As a small gesture toward the massive debt I owe you, I have left a sum of money with Mrs. Hudson at 221b Baker Street, marked for your family's use. It cannot restore your peace of mind or repair your suffering, but perhaps it may provide some small comfort in the difficult days ahead. Mrs. Hudson has been instructed to ensure it reaches you without delay.

Please give my apologies to your dear wife and children. Tell them that they have my solemn promise that the man who wronged their father so grievously will trouble them no more.

I remain, in deepest shame and sincere contrition,

James Ryder
Former Upper Attendant
Hotel Cosmopolitan

P.S. I have also written to the Countess of Morcar and to the hotel management, providing full confession of my crimes and absolute exoneration of your character. Whatever small good my testimony might now accomplish, it is yours.

To Holmes from the Alpha Inn (BLUE)

Dear Mr. Holmes,

I trust this letter finds you and Dr. Watson in the best of health and spirits as we approach the close of another eventful year.

I write to you today with a heart full of gratitude and an establishment bustling with more customers than I have seen in my twenty-three years as landlord of the Alpha Inn. Word of your remarkable investigation into the affair of the Blue Carbuncle has spread throughout London like wildfire, and I find myself in the peculiar but most welcome position of being at the center of one of your celebrated cases.

Since the particulars of Mr. Henry Baker's misadventure and your brilliant deductions became common knowledge, my humble public house has been quite transformed. Gentlemen of all stations call daily, eager to hear the tale firsthand and to examine the very premises where you conducted your inquiries regarding the Christmas geese. I have had scholars from the British Museum, clerks from the City, and even a delegation of constables from Scotland Yard, all requesting to see "the establishment that helped the great detective solve the Carbuncle mystery."

My wife and I have taken to regaling our patrons with her recollections of your visit, particularly your methodical questioning about our goose suppliers and your keen interest in our ledger books. She has become quite the storyteller, though I assure you she embellishes nothing—your reputation requires no enhancement from our humble quarters.

The increased trade has been a blessing beyond measure, Mr. Holmes. Where once we served perhaps a dozen customers of an evening, we now see thrice that number, all hoping to drink where the famous consulting detective once stood. I have even had to engage an additional barmaid to assist with the custom.

It is for this reason that I write to extend a most earnest invitation to you and Dr. Watson to honor us once again with your presence. I should be delighted to provide you both with the finest ales in my cellar, entirely at the house's expense, as a small token of my appreciation for the prosperity your investigation has brought to our establishment.

Should you find yourselves in Bloomsbury, perhaps while pursuing another of your fascinating cases, please know that the Alpha Inn stands ready to welcome you with the warmest hospitality. I have already selected a choice bottle of our finest port for the occasion, whenever that may be.

I remain, with the deepest respect and gratitude,

Your most obliged servant,

Landlord, The Alpha Inn

P.S. I have taken the liberty of framing the newspaper clipping that mentioned our establishment in connection with your case. It now hangs with pride above the bar, drawing no small amount of attention from our curious visitors.

To Mrs. Farintosh from Holmes (SPEC)

My Dear Mrs. Farintosh,

I trust this letter finds you in the best of health and spirits. I write to you today with a heart both relieved and grateful, for it is through your kind intervention that a most grievous tragedy has been averted.

You will recall that some days ago, you were so good as to direct Miss Helen Stoner to my humble consulting rooms, following what I understand was a most distressing conversation regarding her unfortunate circumstances. I am delighted to inform you that Miss Stoner's case has been brought to a complete and satisfactory resolution, though I confess the matter proved to be far more sinister than even my initial investigations had suggested.

Without divulging those details which must remain confidential out of respect for Miss Stoner's privacy, I can tell you that the young lady was indeed in the most immediate and mortal peril. The mysterious death of her sister Julia, which had so troubled Miss Stoner's peace of mind, was no accident of nature or quirk of fate, but rather the result of a most calculated and diabolical scheme. Had you not possessed the wisdom and compassion to direct her to seek professional assistance, I have little doubt that Miss Stoner would, within a matter of days, have suffered the identical fate that befell her poor sister.

The perpetrator of these heinous acts has, by the curious workings of Providence, met with his own demise through the very instrument of death he had so cunningly employed against others. Justice, though arriving by an unexpected route, has been thoroughly served. Miss Stoner is now safe, her inheritance secure, and her future bright with the prospect of the matrimonial happiness that was so nearly denied her.

I cannot adequately express my admiration for your perspicacity in recognizing that Miss Stoner required assistance beyond what conventional channels might provide. Your recommendation quite literally saved her life. In my long experience, I have observed that it is often the intervention of thoughtful individuals such as yourself that

prevents the gravest of tragedies from reaching their intended
conclusion.

Dr. Watson joins me in expressing our sincere gratitude for your role in
bringing this matter to our attention. It is consulting work of this
nature—where we are able to preserve innocent life and see justice
properly administered—that provides the greatest satisfaction in our
professional endeavors.

Should you ever again encounter circumstances where my particular
methods might prove beneficial, I hope you will not hesitate to make the
appropriate recommendation. The knowledge that there are individuals
such as yourself, possessed of both keen observation and genuine
concern for the welfare of others, provides considerable comfort in a
world that can often seem indifferent to the sufferings of the innocent.

Miss Stoner has asked me to convey her deepest gratitude for your
kindness during her darkest hour. She speaks of you with the warmest
affection and hopes to call upon you personally when her present
circumstances have settled into their new and happier arrangement.

I remain, dear Mrs. Farintosh, your most obliged and grateful servant,

Sherlock Holmes
Consulting Detective

*P.S. - Dr. Watson wishes me to add that he was most favorably impressed by your
practical wisdom in this matter, and hopes that your own health continues to benefit
from the constitutional remedies he had occasion to recommend during your previous
consultation.*

To Percy Armitage from Holmes (SPEC)

My Dear Mr. Armitage,

I write to you in the strictest confidence regarding Miss Helen Stoner, your intended bride. Recent events at Stoke Moran have concluded satisfactorily, though not without considerable strain upon Miss Stoner's constitution.

Without divulging details that must remain between these pages, I can assure you that the immediate danger which threatened Miss Stoner has been permanently resolved. The malevolent influence that claimed her dear sister Julia has been eliminated through what I can only describe as a most fitting turn of justice. You need harbour no fears for her physical safety going forward.

However, I must impress upon you that Miss Stoner has endured a shock of no small magnitude. The events of the past few days have tested the very limits of human endurance, and though she possesses a spirit of remarkable fortitude—as evidenced by her courage in seeking my assistance—she will require your utmost patience and tender consideration in the weeks to come.

I remain confident that Miss Stoner will emerge from this ordeal stronger than before, and that your approaching union will provide her with the security and happiness she so richly deserves after enduring such tribulations.

Should you require any further counsel in this delicate matter, please do not hesitate to call upon me.

I remain, sir, your most obedient servant,

Sherlock Holmes
Consulting Detective

To Watson from Victor Hatherley (ENGR)

My Dear Dr. Watson,

I trust this letter finds you in the best of health and spirits. As I sit here in my modest lodgings, my hand—though somewhat diminished—moves across the page with surprising steadiness, and I am compelled to write to express my most heartfelt gratitude for your exceptional kindness during that most extraordinary night when fate delivered me, bloodied and bewildered, to your doorstep.

Your swift and skillful treatment of my wounded hand undoubtedly saved me from far worse consequences than the loss of a single digit. The wound has healed remarkably well under your care, and I am pleased to report that the absence of my thumb proves to be far less of an impediment to my engineering work than I had initially feared. Indeed, I find that my remaining fingers have adapted with remarkable alacrity, and my ability to handle delicate instruments and manipulate mechanical components remains largely unimpaired. It seems the human hand, like the human spirit, possesses a wonderful capacity for adaptation in the face of adversity.

But perhaps even more significant than your medical ministrations was your decision to escort me to Baker Street and introduce me to your esteemed colleague, Mr. Sherlock Holmes. At the time, I confess I was still reeling from my ordeal and scarcely knew what to make of the great detective's penetrating questions and remarkable deductions. Yet I now understand that his involvement, though it came too late to apprehend the villainous Colonel Stark and his confederates, provided a most valuable service in unraveling the mystery that had so nearly cost me my life.

Mr. Holmes's explanation of the counterfeiting operation and his swift action in pursuing the matter to Eyford—even though we arrived to find only smoldering ruins where once stood that accursed house—brought a clarity to my experience that has proven most therapeutic. There is something to be said for understanding the nature of the danger one has escaped, rather than living forever in puzzled terror of shadowy threats.

I must confess, with perhaps a touch of dark humor, that I find myself oddly grateful for what Mr. Holmes called my "experience." Though I would hardly recommend such an adventure to any fellow engineer seeking excitement, it has given me a perspective on life—and on the value of one's limbs—that no amount of comfortable routine could provide. I have gained stories that will serve me well in conversation for years to come, and a healthy skepticism regarding any future employment offers that require excessive secrecy or midnight travels to isolated locations.

The newspapers have since reported the apprehension of several individuals connected to the counterfeiting ring, though I understand the principals—including the mysterious Colonel Stark and poor Elise, whose warning likely saved my life—remain at large. I take some small satisfaction in knowing that their profitable operation has been thoroughly disrupted, even if justice has not yet fully run its course. I hope that my small contribution to your collection of cases has proven worthy of your chronicling efforts.

Please extend my continued gratitude to Mr. Holmes, and know that should either of you ever require the services of a hydraulic engineer— for entirely legitimate purposes, I should specify—you need only call upon me.

With the deepest appreciation and warmest regards,

Your most grateful patient,

Victor Hatherley

P.S. I have enclosed a small token of my appreciation—a precision instrument of my own design that I thought might interest Mr. Holmes in his investigative work. My nine remaining fingers proved quite adequate to its construction.

To Robert St. Simon from Holmes (NOBL)

My Dear Lord St. Simon,

I trust this letter finds you in better spirits than when you departed my lodgings yesterday evening. I write not as the consulting detective who unraveled the mystery that so profoundly affected your life, but as one gentleman to another, compelled by a sense of human decency to offer what consolation words might provide.

I am acutely aware that my revelation of Miss Doran's—or rather, Mrs. Moulton's—true circumstances brought you considerable distress. While the facts of the case demanded exposition, I cannot help but reflect upon the personal cost to yourself. To lose a wife on one's wedding day is a tragedy; to discover that she was never truly yours to lose compounds that tragedy with a peculiar species of humiliation that few men are called upon to endure.

Your reaction yesterday evening was entirely comprehensible, and I harbour no ill feeling toward the manner of your departure. When a man's world is suddenly inverted, when what he believed to be joy transforms instantaneously into loss, courtesy naturally yields to the more pressing demands of wounded pride and genuine sorrow. Please know that I take no satisfaction in having been the instrument of this revelation.

Should you ever have need of my services again, under what I trust would be happier circumstances, please do not hesitate to call upon me. In the meantime, I remain,

Your obedient servant,

Sherlock Holmes
Consulting Detective

To Holmes from Arthur (BERY)

Dear Mr. Holmes,

I write to you with a heart both heavy with shame and light with gratitude. Your remarkable investigation has freed me from the shadow of criminal accusation, yet it has also laid bare the foolishness of my actions and the misguided nature of my silence.

When my father first mentioned engaging your services, I confess I felt a mixture of hope and dread. Hope, because I knew you might uncover the truth that I dared not speak; dread, because that same truth would reveal the extent of my failure to protect those I held dear.

You have shown the world that I am no thief, and for that I am eternally grateful. Yet I cannot help but feel that my vindication comes at a terrible price - the exposure of poor Mary's tragic entanglement with that villain Burnwell. My misguided attempt to shield her reputation through my silence nearly cost my father his career and certainly caused him tremendous anguish. I see now how foolish it was to believe that my sacrifice could somehow preserve her honor while allowing the truth to remain buried.

I had thought myself noble in protecting Mary's secret, even as I stood accused of theft and faced the prospect of imprisonment. But your investigation has revealed the hollowness of such nobility when it is built upon deception. My loyalty to Mary, though born of genuine affection and family duty, blinded me to the greater harm my silence was causing. My poor father suffered sleepless nights believing his own son capable of such betrayal.

When I discovered Mary in the garden that night, passing the coronet to Burnwell, every instinct screamed at me to cry out, to raise the alarm. Instead, I chose to grapple with that scoundrel in silence, hoping to retrieve the coronet without exposing Mary's shame. The coronet bent and broke in our struggle, and three beryls were lost - yet still I remained silent when discovered, allowing suspicion to fall entirely upon me.

I understand now that my actions, however well-intentioned, served only Burnwell's interests. My silence gave him time to dispose of the stolen beryls and escape justice, while an innocent man - myself - faced the consequences of his crime. Worse still, it allowed him to continue his manipulation of Mary, leading to their eventual flight to the Continent.

Your brilliant deduction of the truth from mere footprints in our garden fills me with admiration, even as it humbles me. What I could not bring myself to speak, you read in the very earth beneath our feet. You have shown me that sometimes the greatest loyalty lies not in protecting someone from the consequences of their actions, but in ensuring that the truth comes to light.

I am profoundly grateful that your investigation has restored my reputation and eased my father's mind. The knowledge that he no longer views me as a thief and a betrayer of his trust means more to me than my freedom itself. Yet I am chastened by the realization that a simple, honest account of that night's events would have achieved the same result with far less suffering for all concerned.

I pray that Mary, wherever she may be, will someday find the strength to break free from Burnwell's influence. As for myself, I am resolved to prove worthy of the faith my father has maintained in me, and to ensure that my actions in future are guided by truth rather than misguided discretion.

Please accept my deepest gratitude for your services, not merely in clearing my name, but in teaching me a valuable lesson about the true nature of loyalty and honor.

With sincere appreciation and respect,

Arthur Holder

Post Scriptum: I hope that my ordeal might serve as a cautionary tale to any other young man who believes that silence in the face of wrongdoing constitutes nobility.

To Holmes from Holder (BERY)

My Dear Mr. Holmes,

I find myself compelled to take pen to paper, though I fear no words can adequately convey the depth of my gratitude for your extraordinary services in the matter of the beryl coronet. Your remarkable deductive powers have not only preserved my professional reputation but, more importantly, have revealed truths that have fundamentally altered my understanding of my own household.

When I first arrived at your lodgings in Baker Street, I was a man consumed by despair, convinced that my own son had betrayed the sacred trust placed in me by one of England's most distinguished personages. The weight of that £50,000 loan, secured by such a priceless national treasure, seemed destined to crush both my career and my family's honor. How wrong I was in my assumptions, and how grateful I am for your willingness to look beyond the obvious.

Your fee of £4,000, though substantial, represents but a fraction of what this resolution has meant to me. The recovery of the three missing beryls for £3,000, plus the additional £1,000 you so generously provided as reward to the pawnbroker, has restored the coronet to its original magnificence. More precious still is the restoration of my son's reputation and the revelation of his noble character.

I confess that Arthur's willingness to accept disgrace and imprisonment rather than expose Mary's indiscretions demonstrates a strength of character I had failed to recognize. That he should have pursued Sir George Burnwell through our garden in a desperate attempt to retrieve the coronet, suffering injury and suspicion in the process, speaks to a courage I am ashamed to have doubted. Your astute reading of the footprints in the garden revealed a tale of sacrifice that brings tears to my eyes even now.

As for my niece Mary, while I cannot condone her actions with that scoundrel Burnwell, I understand now the web of manipulation in which she found herself ensnared. Your suggestion that she has since departed for the Continent with her seducer removes a source of potential future scandal, though I cannot help but pity her fate.

The coronet now rests safely in my strong room, awaiting its return to its rightful owner, completely restored and with its integrity intact. My professional reputation remains unblemished, and my son stands vindicated before the world. These outcomes seemed impossible mere days ago, yet your singular talents have achieved what I deemed miraculous.

I have taken the liberty of recommending your services to several of my most distinguished clients, though I suspect your reputation requires no enhancement from a humble banker such as myself. Should you ever require the services of my institution, you need only present this letter as introduction.
Please accept not only my payment in full, but also my profound and lasting gratitude for services rendered with such discretion, brilliance, and expedition.

I remain, with the highest respect and admiration,

Your most obliged servant,

Alexander Holder
Senior Partner
Holder & Stevenson, Private Banking

Post Scriptum: I have arranged for a small token of appreciation to be delivered to Mrs. Hudson, recognizing her patience during my rather dramatic late-evening visit to Baker Street.

To Mr. & Mrs. Fowler from Watson (COPP)

My Dear Mr. and Mrs. Fowler,

It is with the greatest pleasure that I take up my pen to offer you both my most heartfelt congratulations on your recent marriage. Holmes and I were delighted to receive word of your nuptials, and I must confess that few unions have given me such satisfaction to contemplate, knowing as I do the extraordinary circumstances that preceded your happiness.

When we first encountered this most peculiar case through the brave Miss Violet Hunter's account, I little imagined that we would witness such a triumph of true love over the most unscrupulous of schemes. Mrs. Fowler, your courage during those dark months of imprisonment at the Copper Beeches was nothing short of remarkable, and Mr. Fowler, your unwavering devotion in the face of such mysterious circumstances speaks to the nobility of your character.

I trust that the memory of that dreadful house near Winchester grows dimmer with each passing day, replaced now by the bright prospect of your life together. Miss Hunter, that exemplary young woman whose quick wit and determination proved so instrumental in your liberation, has written to inform us that she has taken a position as head governess at a distinguished school in Yorkshire.

Holmes, in his characteristically reserved manner, has asked me to convey his satisfaction at the successful resolution of the case. Between you and me, I believe he was particularly pleased that justice prevailed without the loss of life—even that of the misguided Mr. Rucastle, who I am told is recovering well from his injuries, though I understand his perspective on paternal authority has undergone considerable revision. Mrs. Watson joins me in sending our warmest wishes for your continued happiness and prosperity.

Most sincerely yours,

John H. Watson, M.D.

To Miss Stoper from Holmes (COPP)

Dear Miss Stoper,

I write to you in the aftermath of a most disturbing case that has recently concluded—one that could have resulted in tragedy for a young woman under your professional care. The matter of Miss Violet Hunter and her placement with Mr. Jephro Rucastle at The Copper Beeches demands serious examination of your agency's practices.

It is abundantly clear that your investigation into Mr. Rucastle's character and circumstances was woefully inadequate. A man who offers wages so exorbitant as to be suspicious, coupled with demands so peculiar as to border on the bizarre—requiring a governess to cut her hair and wear specific clothing—should have aroused immediate concern in any conscientious placement agent. Yet you appear to have been so dazzled by the prospect of your commission that you failed entirely in your duty.

Had you exercised even the most elementary precautions—a visit to the household, inquiries among the local community, or investigation into the mysterious absence of Mr. Rucastle's eldest daughter—you would have discovered the sinister truth.

Your negligence nearly resulted in Miss Hunter becoming an accessory to kidnapping, and she was placed in considerable physical danger. The presence of a savage mastiff, the isolation of the house, and Mr. Rucastle's evident instability created a situation that could have proved fatal.

I trust this unfortunate affair will serve as a sharp reminder that your responsibilities extend far beyond the mere matching of employer and employee.

I remain, with grave disapproval of your methods,

Sherlock Holmes
Consulting Detective

To Violet Hunter from Watson (COPP)

My Dear Miss Hunter,

I trust this letter finds you in the best of health and spirits as you embark upon your new endeavors in Yorkshire. Holmes and I have been most gratified to learn of your appointment as head governess at such a distinguished institution—a position that, I am certain, will benefit greatly from your remarkable courage and keen intelligence.

It has been some weeks now since the curious affair at The Copper Beeches reached its dramatic conclusion, and I felt compelled to write and express, once again, how thoroughly impressed we both were by your conduct throughout that most trying ordeal. Your quick wit in recognizing the deception being practiced upon you, and your presence of mind in summoning our assistance, undoubtedly prevented a far more tragic outcome for poor Miss Alice Rucastle.

Holmes has often remarked that the most valuable quality in any person is the ability to observe keenly and act decisively when circumstances demand it. In you, Miss Hunter, we found these qualities in abundance. Your willingness to place yourself in considerable danger to uncover the truth of what was transpiring at that isolated Hampshire estate speaks to a strength of character that I have rarely encountered, even in my years accompanying Holmes on his various investigations.

I confess that when we first received your telegram requesting our urgent attendance at Winchester, I feared we might be too late to prevent some terrible mischief. The sight of you, unharmed and resolute despite the frightening circumstances in which you found yourself, was a considerable relief to us both. Your detailed observations of the household's peculiar arrangements—the insistence upon the blue dress, the positioning by the window, and most crucially, your discovery of the locked wing—provided Holmes with precisely the intelligence required to unravel Mr. Rucastle's elaborate deception.

The revelation that you had been employed not merely as a governess, but as an unwitting participant in a scheme to convince Miss Alice's devoted fiancé that she had abandoned him, was as ingenious as it was despicable. That you maintained your composure even after discovering the existence of the hidden chamber speaks volumes about your fortitude.

I am pleased to report that young Mr. Fowler and Miss Alice Rucastle are now happily settled in their new life together, having safely escaped her father's tyrannical control. They have asked me to convey their deepest gratitude for your role in securing their freedom. Without your courage in contacting us when you did, their story might have concluded far differently.

As for Mr. Rucastle himself, I understand he has made a full recovery from his unfortunate encounter with his own mastiff, though I am told the experience has considerably tempered his disposition. Mrs. Rucastle has taken their young son and removed to relatives in the north, and the house itself now stands empty.

Holmes joins me in wishing you every success in your new position. Should you ever find yourself in London, please do not hesitate to call upon us at Baker Street. The world of education has gained a most remarkable practitioner in you, Miss Hunter, and we consider ourselves fortunate to have played some small part in ensuring that your talents were not lost to Mr. Rucastle's schemes.

With our warmest regards and best wishes for your continued success, I remain, most sincerely yours,

John H. Watson, M.D.

P.S. - Holmes has asked me to remind you that should you ever encounter another situation requiring our particular expertise, you need only send word. As he put it in his characteristic manner: "Miss Hunter has proven herself to be an admirable ally in the pursuit of justice—we should be honored to assist her again, should the need arise."

To Holmes from Colonel Ross (SILV)

My Dear Holmes,

I find myself compelled to put pen to paper to express my most profound gratitude for your extraordinary work in resolving the perplexing matter of Silver Blaze's disappearance and the tragic death of my trainer, John Straker.

When Inspector Gregory first suggested consulting you, I confess I harbored some skepticism about whether even your renowned methods could unravel such a bewildering case. The circumstances seemed so contradictory—a champion racehorse vanished without trace, a trusted trainer found dead upon the moor, and young Ned Hunter drugged senseless while on watch. The appearance of that suspicious character, Fitzroy Simpson, seemed to provide an obvious culprit, yet something about the whole affair felt incomplete.

Your methodical examination of the evidence, however, revealed truths that would have remained forever hidden from lesser minds. The significance of the curried mutton, the peculiar knife found with poor Straker, and most remarkably, your deduction about the true purpose behind that fateful midnight expedition—these insights demonstrated the remarkable power of logical reasoning applied with precision.

I am particularly grateful for your discretion in handling the more delicate aspects of this case. That Straker had been leading a double life, supporting a mistress in London while betraying the trust I had placed in him, was a bitter revelation. To learn that he intended to lame my prize horse—the very animal whose victories had brought him fame and comfortable employment—in order to profit from betting against Silver Blaze, strikes me as the basest form of treachery.

Your diplomatic negotiations with Silas Brown at Mapleton were masterful. That he had discovered our horse wandering on the moor and concealed him in his own stables, disguised and hidden, might have remained our secret forever had you not approached the matter with such tact. His cooperation in returning Silver Blaze unharmed, and indeed in prime condition for the Wessex Cup, speaks to your persuasive powers.

The irony that Silver Blaze himself delivered justice to his would-be mutilator is not lost upon me. That single, fatal kick saved not only the horse's career but prevented a grave injustice from being perpetrated. As you so memorably observed, it was indeed "the curious incident of the dog in the night-time"—or rather, the horse that did not cry out—that provided the key to the entire mystery.

Silver Blaze's subsequent victory in the Wessex Cup was all the sweeter knowing that justice had been served and that my faith in the horse's abilities was vindicated. The odds were quite favorable, as I recall, and I trust your own modest wager proved profitable.

I remain, my dear Holmes, deeply in your debt. Your methods may occasionally perplex those of us with more conventional minds, but your results speak with undeniable authority. Should I ever again find myself in need of such exceptional detecting skills, I shall not hesitate to call upon your services.

With renewed thanks and highest regards,

I remain, most gratefully yours,

Colonel Ross
Proprietor, King's Pyland Stables

P.S. - I have taken the liberty of sending along a small token of my appreciation—a bottle of the finest whiskey from my personal collection. I trust it will prove suitable for those long nights when you find yourself pondering the criminal mind.

To Ned Hunter from Colonel Ross (SILV)

My Dear Ned,

I write to you today with a heart full of gratitude and admiration for the courage and loyalty you displayed during that dreadful night when our Silver Blaze disappeared. Though the events that transpired were far more complex than any of us could have imagined at the time, your steadfast commitment to your duties as stable boy proved invaluable.

When that scoundrel Fitzroy Simpson appeared at our stables with his suspicious manner and wild theories, you showed remarkable judgment in refusing to be swayed by his talk. Your instincts to chase him off and your determination to hold your ground, even when faced with what we now know was a deliberate attempt to drug you, demonstrate the finest qualities of character and dedication.

I am told by Inspector Gregory that despite being overcome by the sleeping draught, you fought against its effects for as long as you could, showing a devotion to Silver Blaze and our stables that goes far beyond what duty requires. You are indeed a good lad, Ned, and I am proud to have you in my employ.

As a token of my appreciation for your faithful service and courage, you will find an additional sum in your next week's wages. Consider it a small recognition of your worth to our establishment and my personal thanks for your unwavering loyalty to Silver Blaze.

I trust this unfortunate episode has not dampened your spirits, and I look forward to many more years of your reliable service at King's Pyland. With sincere gratitude and respect,

Colonel Ross
Proprietor, King's Pyland Stables

To Silas Brown from Holmes (SILV)

My Dear Brown,

I trust this letter finds you in better spirits than when we last spoke at your stables. I write to you now not as the consulting detective who unraveled your unfortunate entanglement in the Silver Blaze affair, but as one gentleman addressing another on matters of considerable importance to your future welfare.

You are, I believe, a man of sufficient intelligence to appreciate how remarkably fortunate you have been in this entire business. When I discovered Silver Blaze concealed in your stables, disguised by your amateur but adequate efforts at altering his distinctive markings, I could easily have summoned Inspector Gregory at once. The good Inspector, I can assure you, would not have been inclined toward the lenient view I ultimately chose to take.

Consider your position had Gregory made the discovery himself: conspiracy, theft of valuable property, obstruction of justice, and fraud—charges that would have seen you transported or, at the very least, enjoying an extended residence at Her Majesty's pleasure. Your career in racing would have been finished, your reputation destroyed, and your livelihood swept away like morning mist on Dartmoor.

Instead, I chose to view your actions through the lens of opportunity rather than malice. You found a valuable horse wandering the moors, and in a moment of poor judgment, you saw a chance to prevent Colonel Ross's champion from competing. I understand the pressures of your profession, Brown—the constant struggle to gain advantage in a sport where fortunes rise and fall with each race. But I trust you also understand that such pressures can never justify the path you nearly chose to follow.

More importantly, I have kept your involvement in this affair entirely to myself. Neither Inspector Gregory nor Colonel Ross knows the full extent of your actions. As far as they are concerned, you were merely cooperative in facilitating Silver Blaze's return to racing condition. This silence on my part shall continue indefinitely—provided, of course, that I hear no whispers of further mischief from your direction.

You have been granted what few men receive in such circumstances: a second chance, untainted by public scandal or criminal prosecution, with your secret safe in the hands of one who chooses discretion over exposure.

This brings me to the crux of my letter, Brown. You have witnessed firsthand where dishonesty leads. John Straker, driven by financial desperation and moral bankruptcy, attempted to lame the very horse entrusted to his care. His deception cost him his life and nearly destroyed the animal he was meant to protect. Your own brief flirtation with deception brought you to the very edge of ruin.

Honesty, my dear fellow, is not merely a moral virtue—it is the most practical policy a man can adopt, particularly in the racing world where reputation is everything and trust is the foundation of all dealings. The turf has little tolerance for those who breach its codes, and even less mercy for those caught in the act.

You have been given an extraordinary opportunity to begin again with your reputation intact and your future secure. I strongly advise you to embrace absolute honesty in all your future dealings. The racing world needs men of integrity, Brown. Be one of them. Your brush with disaster should serve as a permanent reminder that the temporary gains of dishonesty pale beside the lasting rewards of an honest reputation.

I remain, with hopes for your continued success and integrity,

Sherlock Holmes
Consulting Detective

P.S. - Should you ever find yourself tempted to stray from the path of honesty, I suggest you recall our conversation in your stable and the uncomfortable proximity of Inspector Gregory's handcuffs to your wrists. The memory should prove most instructive.

To Holmes from Grant Munro (YELL)

My Dear Mr. Holmes,

I write to you with a heart overflowing with gratitude and joy, though I confess I scarcely know where to begin in expressing my thanks for your involvement in what I had feared was a most distressing domestic matter.

When I first approached you at Baker Street, I was, as you well observed, a man consumed by alarm and suspicion. The strange behavior of my beloved Effie had filled me with such dread that I feared our marriage itself was under threat. The mysterious circumstances surrounding that cottage, the unexplained need for money, and those peculiar nocturnal wanderings had convinced me that some terrible secret lay between us.

How wrong I was, and yet how right you were to encourage me to approach the matter with an open heart! Though your initial theory of blackmail proved incorrect—and I daresay this may be one of the few occasions where you will admit to having been mistaken—your guidance led us to a truth far more beautiful than I could ever have imagined.

My dear Holmes, I cannot adequately express the joy that now fills our home. Little Lucy—for that is her name—has brought such light and laughter to our lives that I wonder how we ever managed without her sweet presence. She is a remarkable child, bright and affectionate, and I find myself marveling daily at Effie's wisdom in protecting her so carefully all these years. What I initially mistook for deception was, in truth, the most selfless love a mother could show.

Effie herself has been transformed by the lifting of this burden she carried so long in silence. The woman I married has returned to me in full, and with her comes this precious addition to our family. I can honestly say, Mr. Holmes, that we are now happier than we have ever been. Our cottage rings with the sound of Lucy's laughter, and I discover new depths to my capacity for love each day.

I must also confess that this experience has taught me much about the dangers of hasty judgment and the paramount importance of trust within marriage. Had I followed my initial instincts and confronted this matter with suspicion rather than seeking your counsel, I shudder to think what damage might have been done.

Please know that you will always be welcome in our home, and I hope that you might find time to visit us soon. Lucy has heard much about the famous detective who helped bring our family together, and I believe she would be delighted to meet you. Effie, too, wishes to express her gratitude for your understanding and discretion throughout this delicate matter.

With the deepest appreciation and warmest regards,

Your most grateful client and friend,

Grant Munro

P.S. - I have enclosed a small photograph of our family, taken just last week in the garden. I thought you might appreciate seeing the happy conclusion to what began as such a troubling mystery.

To Holmes from Hall Pycroft (STOC)

My Dear Mr. Holmes,

I trust this letter finds you and Dr. Watson in excellent health. I write to express my most profound gratitude for your extraordinary intervention in what I can only describe as the most bewildering and distressing episode of my life.

When I first approached you with my peculiar tale of the Franco-Midland Hardware Company and those confounding Pinner brothers, I confess I was uncertain whether my observations about their identical gold fillings warranted the attention of London's most celebrated consulting detective. How foolish I would have been to dismiss such details as mere coincidence! Your remarkable ability to perceive the significance in what others might consider trifling has once again proven itself invaluable.

I shudder to think what might have transpired had you not accompanied Dr Watson to Birmingham that fateful day. The discovery of that wretched man's attempt upon his own life was shocking enough, but the revelation of the brothers' criminal enterprise—using my very identity to gain access to Mawson & Williams for purposes of burglary and murder—has left me quite overwhelmed by the magnitude of their deception.

I am pleased to report that the ordeal has concluded more favorably than I dared hope. Despite the criminal use of my name and credentials, the partners at Mawson & Williams have demonstrated remarkable understanding of my predicament. Indeed, they have honored their original offer of employment, recognizing that I was as much a victim of this elaborate scheme as they themselves. I am to begin my position as clerk on Monday next, at the agreed salary of two pounds per week.

The irony is not lost upon me that in rejecting their legitimate offer for the false promise of Arthur Pinner's three pounds weekly, I nearly lost everything to men who sought to use my reputation for the most nefarious purposes. Your swift action not only prevented a great crime but preserved my character and professional standing.

I find myself reflecting often on your methods, Mr. Holmes. Your insistence that we observe every detail, however minute, and your ability to construct from seemingly unrelated facts a complete picture of criminal intent, continues to astound me. That you could deduce from my simple account the true nature of the conspiracy speaks to abilities that seem almost supernatural, though I know them to be the product of keen observation and logical deduction.

Dr. Watson's steadfast companionship throughout the affair was equally appreciated. His calming presence and medical expertise were invaluable during those tense moments when we discovered the unfortunate Pinner in such desperate straits.

I hope that one day I might have the opportunity to repay your kindness, though I suspect my humble skills as a financial clerk would prove of little use in your remarkable cases. Nevertheless, should you ever require assistance in matters of accounting or commercial practice, you have but to call upon me.

With the deepest respect and gratitude,

Your most obliged servant,

Hall Pycroft

P.S. I have taken the liberty of enclosing a small token of my appreciation—a bottle of the finest cognac I could afford. I thought it might serve as a suitable accompaniment to your evening pipe and contemplations.

To Mawson & Williams from Holmes (STOC)

Dear Sir,

I write to you upon a matter of some delicacy concerning one of your recent appointments, Mr. Hall Pycroft, whom I understand you engaged as a clerk prior to the recent unfortunate incident involving an attempted deception at your establishment.

Having had occasion to observe Mr. Pycroft closely during the investigation of what has come to be known as the Franco-Midland Hardware affair, I feel compelled to offer my professional assessment of his character and conduct. It is my considered opinion that your original decision to employ this young man was entirely sound and reflects well upon your judgment in matters of personnel.

Mr. Pycroft demonstrated several qualities that speak highly of his integrity and practical intelligence. When presented with what appeared to be an exceptionally generous offer from the fraudulent Arthur Pinner, he maintained a healthy skepticism despite the considerable financial temptation. More significantly, when he observed certain peculiarities in his supposed new employers—specifically, the identical dental work of the two men claiming to be brothers—he possessed both the observational acuity to note such details and the wisdom to seek counsel regarding his suspicions.

It was this same discernment that ultimately led him to consult me, a decision that proved instrumental in preventing what would have been a serious criminal enterprise directed against your firm. Had Mr. Pycroft been of lesser character, he might have been easily duped into the conspiracy, or worse, become a willing participant in exchange for monetary gain. Instead, his actions directly contributed to the apprehension of the criminal and the protection of your establishment.

During our interactions, I found Mr. Pycroft to be forthright, methodical in his thinking, and possessed of that rare combination of loyalty and independence of mind that marks the superior employee. His conduct

throughout this trying affair has been exemplary, and I believe he would
serve your company with distinction.

I trust this assessment may be of some value to you in your future
dealings with Mr. Pycroft. I would be most grateful if you would regard
this communication as entirely confidential. The young man is unaware
that I have taken this liberty, and I believe it would serve no useful
purpose to burden him with knowledge of this correspondence.

I remain, sir, your obedient servant,

Sherlock Holmes
Consulting Detective

Private and Confidential

To Holmes from Victor Trevor (GLOR)

My Dear Holmes,

I find myself compelled to take pen to paper, though I confess the words come with some difficulty. The events of these past months have left me profoundly shaken, yet simultaneously grateful for your remarkable assistance during our family's darkest hour.

When I first invited you to spend that month with us here at Donnithorpe, I could never have imagined the tragic circumstances that would unfold. Your keen observation and deductive reasoning—qualities I had glimpsed during our time at university but never fully appreciated—proved invaluable in helping me comprehend the terrible burden that had haunted my poor father for so many years.

The revelation that our family name was not truly Trevor, that my father had once been James Armitage, and that his past included such desperate circumstances aboard the Gloria Scott, has been a shock from which I am still recovering. Yet I cannot express how much comfort your presence brought during those final, agonizing days of father's life. Your ability to piece together the fragments of his confession and Hudson's malevolent influence provided me with the understanding I so desperately needed.

I know now why father lived in such constant anxiety, why certain names or chance encounters would cause him to pale and withdraw. The weight of carrying such secrets, the fear of exposure, and the shame of his youthful transgression—though born of desperation rather than malice—had slowly consumed him. That Hudson should have exploited this for his own gain makes the wretch's ultimate fate seem almost fitting, though I pray we shall never know the full truth of what transpired between him and poor Beddoes.

Your insight into human nature and your methodical approach to unraveling the mystery has given me peace where there might have been only confusion and torment. For this, Holmes, I am eternally in your debt.

I hope most sincerely that you will consider returning to Donnithorpe when time permits—though I trust that any future visit will be under far more pleasant circumstances. Perhaps we might enjoy those long walks across the Norfolk countryside without the shadow of tragedy hanging over us, and you could indulge your interest in the local flora without the distraction of human drama. The shooting season will soon be upon us, and I recall you mentioning an appreciation for the countryside's quieter pursuits.

Please know that you will always find a warm welcome here, and that your friendship during these trying times has been a source of strength I shall not forget.

With deepest gratitude and warmest regards,

Your devoted friend,

Victor Trevor

P.S. - I have taken the liberty of forwarding the documents father left regarding his time in Australia to his solicitors, as you suggested. The estate matters are proceeding as smoothly as can be expected under the circumstances.

To Holmes from Reginald Musgrave (MUSG)

My Dear Holmes,

I find myself compelled to take pen to paper this evening, though words seem inadequate to express the profound gratitude I feel toward you for your extraordinary work in unraveling the dreadful mystery that has haunted Hurlstone these past months.

When I first approached you with the peculiar circumstances surrounding Brunton's disappearance—and that of our maid, Rachel Howells—I confess I harboured little hope that the truth would ever come to light. The whole affair seemed so inexplicable, so removed from any rational explanation. A trusted butler of seven years simply vanishing, along with a young woman who had served our family faithfully, leaving behind only the most bizarre of clues and a bag of seemingly worthless trinkets dredged from our lake.

Your revelation that our family ritual—that quaint verse which we had recited for generations without thought—was in fact an elaborate cipher has left me quite astounded. To think that what we considered mere tradition was actually a map, carefully preserved through centuries, leading to treasure beyond imagination! The crown of the martyred King Charles I, hidden by my ancestors during those dark days of the Commonwealth, lying beneath our very feet all this time.

Yet even as I marvel at your deductive brilliance in solving this ancient puzzle, I find myself deeply troubled by the human tragedy you have uncovered. Poor Brunton—however misguided his actions may have been—did not deserve such a fate. To think that he lay trapped beneath that massive stone slab in our cellar while we searched the grounds above, calling his name. The horror of his final moments haunts me still.

And Rachel Howells—that she could have committed such a deed speaks to the terrible power of betrayal and wounded love. I had no inkling of the romantic entanglement between them, nor of Brunton's callous abandonment of her affections. Her revenge was swift and merciless, yet

I cannot help but feel a measure of pity for the pain that drove her to such desperate action.

Your explanation of how she managed the deed—using the tackle from the old well-house to lift the stone, then allowing it to fall once she had secured her share of the treasure—demonstrates not only her cunning but the depths of her fury. That she should have fled with the ancient crown, leaving her accomplice to perish, shows how thoroughly love had curdled into hatred.

I have given much thought to whether we should alert the authorities to pursue her, but I confess myself uncertain. She has no doubt fled far from England by now, and the crown—while historically precious—has been lost to our family for two centuries already. Perhaps it is enough that we know the truth of what transpired. Justice, in its way, may already have been served through the torment she must carry for her actions.

The knowledge you have provided brings both closure and disquiet. I am grateful beyond measure to understand at last what became of Brunton and why he met his end, yet I cannot help but reflect on the terrible secrets that may lie dormant within any family's history, waiting for the right combination of ambition, desperation, and betrayal to bring them to light.

Please know that your services in this matter will never be forgotten by the Musgrave family. Your singular ability to perceive patterns where others see only chaos, to find meaning in the most obscure of clues, marks you as truly exceptional in your chosen profession.

Should you ever find yourself in West Sussex, you would be most welcome at Hurlstone.

With deepest gratitude and highest regard, I remain, your most obliged servant,

Reginald Musgrave
Master of Hurlstone Manor

To Janet Tregellis from Holmes (MUSG)

My Dear Miss Tregellis,

I trust this letter finds you bearing up as well as can be expected under the most trying circumstances. Mr. Reginald Musgrave has informed me that he has shared with the household staff the tragic details of Brunton's fate, and I can only imagine the profound shock and grief this revelation must have caused you.

Having concluded my investigation into this most distressing affair, I felt compelled to write and express my deepest sympathies for your loss. Though I encountered Brunton only in death, it was evident from my inquiries that he was a man of considerable intelligence and determination - qualities that, tragically, led him into the very peril that claimed his life.

The callous betrayal by Rachel Howells makes his death all the more grievous. That she should abandon him to such a fate, driven by jealousy over his affection for you, speaks to a cruelty of spirit that defies comprehension. No matter what disappointment she may have suffered, nothing could justify her monstrous actions.

I know that words can provide little comfort in the face of such loss, yet I hope you may find some small solace in knowing that justice will be pursued. The wretch who left poor Brunton to perish must answer for her crime.

To that end, I must make a request of you. Should you hear any word of Rachel Howells's current whereabouts, I beseech you to communicate such information immediately to myself at the above address or to the local constabulary.

With my most sincere condolences and respect,

Sherlock Holmes
Consulting Detective

To Colonel Hayter from Holmes (REIG)

My Dear Colonel Hayter,

I find myself compelled to express my most sincere gratitude for your generous hospitality during my recent sojourn at your charming residence in Reigate. Watson's prescription of country air and quiet companionship proved, as usual, to be precisely what the physician ordered—though I suspect neither of you anticipated quite the degree of "excitement" that Surrey would provide during my convalescence.

Your home offered exactly the peaceful sanctuary I required after the rather taxing affair of apprehending Colonel Sebastian Moran and dismantling the remnants of the late Professor Moriarty's organization. The comfortable quarters, excellent library, and your stimulating conversation on military strategy in Afghanistan provided the perfect tonic for my overwrought nerves.

I must confess that when the Reigate burglaries first came to our attention, I feared my rest would be entirely interrupted by the call to duty. How wrong I was! The mental exercise of unraveling the Cunningham affair proved to be precisely the sort of gentle intellectual stimulation that aided, rather than hindered, my recovery. There is something wonderfully restorative about a case that presents itself so conveniently at one's doorstep, requiring no arduous journeys through London's fog-shrouded streets or lengthy vigils in uncomfortable hiding places.

The revelation that old Acton's "burglary" was merely a cover for the Cunninghams' desperate attempt to retrieve that incriminating document provided exactly the sort of logical puzzle that serves to clear the mental cobwebs without overtaxing one's faculties. And I must say, the discovery of young Alec Cunningham's distinctive handwriting in that torn scrap of paper was most satisfying—a delightful reminder that the criminal mind, however cunning, invariably provides the very evidence of its own undoing.

Poor Kirwan's fate was regrettable, of course, though his attempt at blackmail demonstrated a fatal lack of understanding regarding the ruthless nature of his employers. Still, justice has been served, and Inspector Forrester seemed quite pleased to add the Cunninghams to his growing collection of apprehended malefactors.

I hope you will forgive the rather dramatic conclusion to my stay, particularly the unfortunate scene in the Cunninghams' study. I fear my methods occasionally appear somewhat theatrical to the untrained observer, but I assure you that allowing them to attempt my strangulation was a calculated risk designed to secure their complete confession. Watson's timely intervention with the constables was, as always, impeccable.

Your patience with these proceedings, and your gracious insistence that the entire affair only added to the interest of my visit, speaks to your character as both a gentleman and a former military officer accustomed to unexpected developments. I departed Reigate feeling more refreshed and invigorated than I have in months.

Please extend my regards to your excellent housekeeper, whose culinary skills rival those of Mrs. Hudson herself—no small compliment, I assure you. Should you ever find yourself in London and in need of any small service that my peculiar talents might provide, you need only call upon me at Baker Street.

I remain, my dear Colonel, your most grateful and devoted friend,

Sherlock Holmes
Consulting Detective

P.S. - Watson asks me to convey his particular thanks for your patience in listening to his rather embellished accounts of our various adventures. I fear retirement has made him even more prone to dramatic storytelling than usual.

To Holmes from Forrester (REIG)

Dear Mr. Holmes,

I write to express my most sincere gratitude for your invaluable assistance in the recent criminal matters that have plagued our district. Your intervention in what initially appeared to be separate incidents of burglary and murder has proven instrumental in bringing justice to our community.

When I first learned of your presence in Reigate, recovering at Colonel Hayter's residence, I confess I had little expectation that your convalescence would be interrupted by such grave matters. Yet your willingness to apply your remarkable deductive abilities, despite your need for rest, speaks to both your character and your dedication to justice.

The case of the Acton burglary had left us quite perplexed, particularly given the apparent lack of valuable items taken. Your insight that this was no ordinary theft, but rather a calculated attempt to obtain specific documents, transformed our entire understanding of the crime. Without your guidance, I fear we would have continued pursuing the wrong leads entirely.

The tragic murder of William Kirwan presented us with what seemed a straightforward case—a coachman killed by the same band of burglars who had been terrorizing the neighborhood. The testimony of the Cunninghams themselves appeared to confirm this theory. How wrong we were, and how brilliant your deduction that they were not witnesses, but perpetrators.

Your discovery that old Mr. Cunningham and his son Alec were themselves the "burglars," seeking to destroy evidence in their property dispute with the Actons, was nothing short of remarkable. That poor Kirwan had witnessed their crime and foolishly attempted blackmail, sealing his own fate, was a connection only your keen mind could have made.

I must particularly commend your courage when the Cunninghams, realizing their exposure, turned violent and attempted to destroy the crucial evidence in your possession. Their assault upon your person could have had tragic consequences had Dr. Watson and I not arrived promptly. Your quick thinking in preserving that vital scrap of paper, despite their desperate attempts to destroy it, ensured their conviction.

The arrest of both Cunninghams has restored peace to our district and brought justice for poor Kirwan. The community of Reigate owes you a debt that cannot easily be repaid. Your methods, though sometimes unconventional, have once again proven superior to standard police procedure.

I hope your recovery continues smoothly and that this excitement has not overly taxed your strength. Should your travels ever bring you to Surrey again under more pleasant circumstances, you will find a warm welcome at our station.

With the highest regard and deepest appreciation,

Inspector Forrester
Surrey Constabulary
Reigate Division

To Nancy Barclay from Holmes (CROO)

My Dear Mrs. Barclay,

I trust this letter finds you in improved health and that the dreadful shock of recent events has begun to diminish, though I am well aware that such traumatic experiences leave marks upon the soul that time alone must heal. I write to you not as the consulting detective who investigated the circumstances surrounding your husband's death, but as one human being extending compassion to another who has endured unimaginable tribulation.

I must inform you that I have had occasion to speak at length with Mr. Henry Wood. Through this conversation, the full and tragic history has been revealed to me—a history spanning twenty years, encompassing betrayal, imprisonment, suffering, and ultimately, a most unfortunate reunion. I now understand the complete circumstances that led to that fateful evening in your sitting room, and I wish to assure you that the truth of the matter reflects no dishonor upon your character.

The revelation that your husband's death was neither murder nor suicide, but rather the consequence of shock upon seeing a figure from his guilty past, must provide some measure of relief amidst your grief. That he fell and struck his head upon the hearth in his moment of overwhelming surprise speaks to the weight of conscience he had carried these many years.

I feel compelled to share with you an observation regarding Mr. Wood, gleaned from our discourse. Should you find yourself inclined to renew acquaintance with him—and I make no presumption as to whether such contact would be welcome or advisable—I believe you should know that his feelings toward you remain unchanged by the passage of time and the cruelties he has endured. Yet I observed in him something quite remarkable: a man who, despite having suffered grievously due to another's betrayal, harbors no wish to burden you with his own pain or to complicate your path forward. His affection for you, which I perceive burns as steadily as ever it did in your youth, is tempered by a selfless desire for your peace and happiness above his own.

In short, Mrs. Barclay, Mr. Wood loves you still, but loves you enough to step aside should his presence bring you further sorrow. It is a rare quality in this world—to possess the strength to relinquish what one most desires for the welfare of the beloved.

I offer no counsel as to your future course, for such decisions rest solely with you. I merely thought it proper that you should understand the true nature of the man's character, as it has been shaped by both suffering and enduring devotion.

Please accept my sincere wishes for your recovery and eventual peace. Should you ever have need of my services, you have but to call upon me.

I remain, Madam,

Your most obedient servant,

Sherlock Holmes
Consulting Detective

To Simpson from Holmes (CROO)

My Dear Simpson,

I write to express my sincere gratitude for your invaluable assistance in the matter of Colonel Barclay's death. Your keen observations and timely information proved most instrumental in unraveling the true circumstances surrounding this tragic affair.

The case has now been satisfactorily resolved, with the real truth of Henry Wood's involvement coming to light. Without your help, I fear the mystery of the locked room and the strange footprints might have remained unsolved for considerably longer.

I should be most pleased if you would call upon me at Baker Street at your earliest convenience. There is a small token of appreciation awaiting you—something rather more substantial than mere thanks, and far better suited to acknowledge the value of your contribution to this investigation.

I remain, with the highest regard for your assistance,

Yours very truly,

Sherlock Holmes
Consulting Detective

To Holmes from Percy Trevelyan (RESI)

My Dear Holmes,

I write to you now with a matter of considerable urgency regarding the unfortunate affair that brought us together—the tragic case of my late benefactor, Mr. Blessington.

As you will recall, the investigation you so masterfully conducted revealed that the man I knew as Blessington was, in reality, one Sutton—a former member of the notorious Worthingdon Bank Gang who had turned Queen's evidence against his former associates. Your brilliant deduction of the circumstances surrounding his death at the hands of Biddle, Hayward, and Moffat has been vindicated by subsequent events, though justice came too late for the poor wretch.

I find myself now in a most peculiar and distressing situation. Following Blessington's death, I have been informed by the authorities that his entire estate—including the Brook Street premises where I maintained my medical practice—has been declared *bona vacantia* and has consequently passed to the Crown. The Treasury Solicitor now holds authority over all of Blessington's former possessions.

You will remember that my arrangement with Blessington was most unusual. Having completed my medical studies with distinction but lacking the capital to establish my own practice, I was entirely dependent upon his generosity. He provided not merely the premises and equipment for my consulting rooms, but also my very lodgings and sustenance. In return, I was to remit to him three-quarters of my professional earnings—an arrangement that, while onerous, allowed me to practice medicine and serve my patients.

For three years, I fulfilled this obligation faithfully, building a modest but respectable practice while living under his roof. The premises became, in every practical sense, my professional home and the foundation of my medical career. Indeed, many of my patients continue to seek me out at that address, unaware of the recent tragic developments.

I am now preparing to submit a formal claim to the Treasury Solicitor, requesting that the Crown grant me ownership of the medical practice and the Brook Street property. My argument rests upon the substantial investment of time, professional reputation, and labor I have contributed to the establishment, as well as the fact that my livelihood was entirely dependent upon the arrangement Blessington himself had initiated and encouraged.

However, I fear that my word alone may carry insufficient weight with the Treasury Solicitor. The bureaucratic machinery of government can be impersonal and unmoved by individual circumstances, no matter how compelling they may appear to those directly affected.

This is where I must humbly request your assistance, dear Holmes. Your reputation for precision, your intimate knowledge of the facts of this case, and your standing in official circles could prove invaluable. Would you be willing to compose a letter to the Treasury Solicitor, detailing the circumstances of the case as you discovered them?

I am particularly hopeful that your account might emphasize how I was, in effect, an unwitting victim of Blessington's deception—a young physician whose only crime was accepting what appeared to be a generous benefactor's assistance in establishing a medical practice. The arrangement was formalized and conducted entirely above board, with regular financial records that demonstrate my compliance with our agreement.

Should you be willing to assist me in this matter, I would be forever in your debt. I await your response with considerable anxiety, as the Treasury Solicitor has indicated that all claims must be submitted within a relatively brief period.

I remain, with the deepest gratitude for your past assistance and in hope of your future aid,

Your most obedient servant,

Percy Trevelyan, M.D.

To Treasury Solicitor from Holmes (RESI)

Sir,

I write to you in my professional capacity regarding the estate of the late Mr. Blessington of Brook Street, which has come under your jurisdiction as *bona vacantia* following his recent death under circumstances that required my investigative services.

I understand that Dr. Percy Trevelyan has submitted a claim for ownership of the Brook Street premises and the medical practice established therein. Having conducted a thorough investigation into the circumstances surrounding Mr. Blessington's death, and being intimately familiar with Dr. Trevelyan's situation, I write to provide you with material facts that I believe strongly support Dr. Trevelyan's claim.

My investigation revealed that the deceased, known to Dr. Trevelyan as Mr. Blessington, was in reality one Sutton, a member of the Worthingdon Bank Gang who had turned Queen's evidence against his former associates. Dr. Trevelyan was entirely ignorant of this criminal history and knew the deceased only as a seemingly respectable gentleman who had offered to sponsor his medical practice.

The arrangement between Dr. Trevelyan and the deceased was established approximately three years ago under the following terms: the deceased provided medical consulting rooms, complete with equipment and furnishings, as well as residential quarters and sustenance for Dr. Trevelyan. In return, Dr. Trevelyan was to remit three-quarters of his professional earnings to the deceased while retaining one-quarter for his personal expenses.

This arrangement was conducted with complete propriety and transparency. Dr. Trevelyan maintained detailed financial records and fulfilled his obligations with scrupulous honesty throughout the entire period. I have personally examined these records and can attest to their accuracy and completeness.

During the three years of this arrangement, Dr. Trevelyan established a legitimate and growing medical practice. His professional reputation, built through competent and conscientious service to his patients, became inextricably linked to the Brook Street premises. Many of his patients continue to seek his services at that location.

More significantly, Dr. Trevelyan's professional investment in the practice extends far beyond mere occupancy. He has:

- Established patient relationships that constitute the primary value of any medical practice
- Built professional reputation associated specifically with the Brook Street location
- Invested his time and expertise in developing the practice for three years
- Generated all income that supported both himself and the deceased through his medical skills
- Created the goodwill that gives the practice its commercial value

It is crucial to note that without Dr. Trevelyan's professional services, the medical practice would have had no value whatsoever. The deceased possessed no medical qualifications and contributed nothing to the practice beyond the initial capital investment in premises and equipment. I submit that several principles support Dr. Trevelyan's claim:

- First, the principle of equitable contribution: Dr. Trevelyan's labor and professional skill were the essential elements that created and maintained the value of the medical practice. While the deceased provided capital, Dr. Trevelyan provided the expertise, reputation, and professional relationships that constituted the practice's worth.
- Second, the doctrine of unjust enrichment: To deny Dr. Trevelyan's claim would result in the Crown receiving the benefit of three years of his professional labor and expertise without compensation, while simultaneously destroying his livelihood.
- Third, considerations of public policy: Dr. Trevelyan's patients, many of modest means, depend upon his continued practice.

Disrupting these established medical relationships serves no beneficial purpose and may cause genuine hardship to members of the public who rely upon his services.
- Fourth, the innocent party principle: Dr. Trevelyan was entirely deceived as to the true character and history of the deceased. He entered into the arrangement in good faith, believing he was dealing with a legitimate benefactor. It would be inequitable to punish him for deception practiced upon him by another.

My investigation established that the deceased met his death at the hands of his former criminal associates, who had tracked him down following their release from prison. The deceased's accumulation of property was directly related to his criminal activities and his subsequent betrayal of his accomplices.

Dr. Trevelyan was not merely ignorant of these criminal connections—he was, in effect, an unwitting victim of the deceased's elaborate deception. The deceased deliberately sought out a young, inexperienced physician who could be induced to enter into an arrangement that would provide both legitimate income and respectable cover for his activities.

Based upon my investigation and analysis of the facts, I respectfully submit that Dr. Trevelyan's claim possesses both legal merit and equitable justice. The arrangement, while unusual, was legitimate and above board. Dr. Trevelyan fulfilled his obligations with complete integrity and was entirely innocent of any wrongdoing.

I therefore recommend that the Crown exercise its discretionary authority to grant Dr. Trevelyan's application for ownership of the Brook Street premises and the medical practice established therein.

I have the honour to be, Sir, your obedient servant,

Sherlock Holmes
Consulting Detective

To Holmes from Tanner (RESI)

Dear Mr. Holmes,

I find myself compelled to put pen to paper to express my most sincere gratitude for your invaluable assistance in the recent matter concerning Dr. Percy Trevelyan and the tragic death of his so-called "resident patient," Mr. Blessington.

I must confess that when I first arrived at Brook Street to investigate what appeared to be a straightforward case of suicide, I was somewhat skeptical of your involvement. My fellow inspectors at the Yard—Lestrade, Bradstreet, and others—had often spoken of your... unconventional methods, and I admit I harboured doubts about the efficacy of such approaches. However, having now witnessed firsthand your remarkable powers of deduction and observation, I understand completely why they hold you in such high regard.

Where I saw merely a man who had taken his own life in a fit of despair, you perceived the subtle signs that pointed to murder most foul. Your ability to discern that the supposed suicide was, in fact, a carefully staged execution by Blessington's former confederates was nothing short of extraordinary. The way you unraveled the victim's true identity as Sutton, the notorious informant whose testimony had sent his accomplices to the gallows and prison, demonstrated a level of analytical thinking that I fear is quite beyond the reach of conventional police work.

Your deduction that the recent "cataleptic" patients who had so disturbed poor Dr. Trevelyan were none other than Blessington's former gang members—come to exact their long-delayed revenge—was particularly brilliant. The manner in which you traced their movements and identified their method of gaining access to the house showed an understanding of criminal psychology that proved instrumental in bringing this dark affair to light.

I am particularly impressed by your compassion toward Dr. Trevelyan, who found himself an unwitting accomplice to Blessington's deception.

Your handling of this delicate aspect of the case showed not only your intellectual prowess but also your understanding of human nature.

I now understand why my colleagues speak so highly of your assistance, and I hope that should Scotland Yard require your expertise in future matters, you will look favorably upon our requests. The Metropolitan Police is indeed fortunate to have such a consulting detective willing to aid in the pursuit of justice.

With my deepest appreciation and professional respect,

I remain, sir,

Your obedient servant,

Inspector G. Tanner
Metropolitan Police
Scotland Yard

P.S. - Please extend my regards to Dr. Watson, whose medical knowledge and steadfast companionship clearly contribute greatly to your investigative successes.

To Mr. J. Davenport from Holmes (GREE)

My Dear Mr. Davenport,

I write to express my most sincere gratitude for your invaluable assistance in the recent matter concerning Mr. Melas, the Greek interpreter. Your prompt response to our advertisement in the morning papers, and more crucially, your provision of the Beckenham address, proved instrumental in preventing what would undoubtedly have been a most tragic conclusion to an already dark affair.

As I observed during our brief encounter, you displayed a keen interest in the particulars of the case, and I confess that your perspicacity in matters of deduction was not lost upon me.

The case, as you will recall, centered upon the coercion of one Paul Kratides by Harold Latimer and his confederate Kemp, with the unwilling assistance of a woman known to us only as Sophy. What emerged during our investigation was a web of greed and familial betrayal that would have done credit to the most sordid of Greek tragedies.

Paul Kratides, as we discovered, was Sophy's brother, separated by circumstances unknown to us for many years. The property in question—substantial holdings in Greece—rightfully belonged to both siblings. Latimer and Kemp, through means both legal and decidedly illegal, had gained influence over Sophy and sought to use her to compel her brother's cooperation in signing away his inheritance.

The reunion of brother and sister, witnessed by poor Melas during that fateful translation session, appears to have awakened in Sophy a conscience long dormant. Whether through genuine remorse for her part in her brother's persecution, or perhaps simply the rekindling of familial affection, she found herself torn between her criminal associates and her blood.

Your timely information led us to the Beckenham house just as Kratides and Melas faced mortal peril from their captors' growing desperation. Though we succeeded in rescuing Mr. Melas, Paul Kratides had been too grievously injured to survive his ordeal—a fact that sealed the fate of his tormentors.

As you may have read in the morning papers some days later, both Latimer and Kemp were discovered deceased, each having suffered multiple stab wounds. The local constabulary initially suspected a robbery gone wrong, but the evidence suggested a more personal motive. Nothing of value was taken, and both men bore wounds that spoke of methodical rather than frantic violence.

I have little doubt that Sophy, driven by grief over her brother's death and perhaps guilt over her own complicity, sought her revenge upon the men who had manipulated her and destroyed her family.

As for Sophy herself, she has vanished as completely as morning mist. Whether she has fled to the Continent, returned to Greece, or met some other fate entirely, remains unknown. In truth, I confess to a certain reluctance to pursue her further. While I cannot condone vigilante justice, I find it difficult to summon much enthusiasm for bringing to account one who has already paid so dearly for her crimes through the loss of her brother.

The case serves as a reminder that the bonds of blood, however strained or forgotten, often prove stronger than the ties of criminal enterprise. Sophy's transformation from willing accomplice to avenging sister illustrates the powerful influence of conscience when stirred by genuine emotion.

I hope this explanation proves satisfactory to your inquiring mind. Your assistance was truly invaluable, and I should be most pleased to hear from you should you ever encounter any matter that might benefit from my particular methods.

I remain, sir, your most grateful servant,

Sherlock Holmes
Consulting Detective

To Percy Phelps from Holmes (NAVA)

My Dear Phelps,

Now that the matter of the naval treaty has been brought to its satisfactory conclusion and the document safely restored to Her Majesty's government, I find myself compelled to share an observation that may prove instructive for future security arrangements at the Foreign Office.

Upon reflection of the entire sequence of events, it strikes me that this regrettable incident might have been entirely prevented had one individual simply performed his duties with the vigilance expected of his position. I refer, of course, to the commissionaire who was on duty that fateful evening.

The chain of causation, when examined logically, reveals itself to be remarkably simple: The commissionaire fell asleep at his post. Consequently, when your coffee was ready, there was no one available to bring it up to you as would have been the normal procedure. This negligence forced you to leave the security of your office and descend to collect the refreshment yourself. It was during this brief absence—an absence that should never have been necessary—that the treaty was abstracted from your desk.

Had the commissionaire remained alert and performed his customary duty of delivering your coffee, you would never have left your office, and the document would have remained secure. The entire elaborate scheme orchestrated by Joseph Harrison would have been thwarted by something as simple as an old man staying awake. I venture to suggest that you might wish to bring this matter to the attention of your superiors.

I trust this observation may prove useful in preventing similar incidents in the future. I remain, my dear Phelps, your most obedient servant,

Sherlock Holmes
Consulting Detective

To Holmes from Annie Harrison (NAVA)

Dear Mr. Holmes,

I find myself quite at a loss for words adequate to express the profound gratitude that Percy and I feel toward you for your remarkable service in recovering the stolen naval treaty. Your extraordinary deductive powers and unwavering determination have not merely solved a puzzling crime, but have restored my dear fiancé's honor and secured his future with the Foreign Office.

When Percy first fell ill from the shock and worry of that dreadful night when the treaty was stolen from under his very nose, I feared we might never see him restored to his former health and spirits. The weight of responsibility he bore, knowing that such a vital document had been entrusted to his care, was nearly crushing his gentle nature. Each day that passed without the treaty's recovery seemed to dim the light in his eyes a little more.

Your arrival at Briarbrae brought with it the first glimmer of hope we had experienced since that terrible evening. Though I confess I was initially mystified by some of your methods—your examination of the back stair, your particular interest in the Tangeys, and especially your insistence that I remain in Percy's room while you spirited him away to London—I now see the brilliant design behind each step of your investigation.

The night when that villainous intruder crept into Percy's chamber with a knife will frighten me. The terror I imagined seeing that desperate figure silhouetted against the moonlight was matched only by my amazement at how perfectly your preparations had anticipated such an attempt. That you had foreseen Joseph's desperate gambit to retrieve the treaty from its hiding place speaks to a mind of extraordinary penetration.

Dr. Watson has been kind enough to apprise me of the details of the final confrontation—how you discovered Joseph Harrison's perfidious role in this affair, and how you engaged him in physical combat to wrest the precious document from his grasp. That my own future brother-in-law should prove to be the author of Percy's misfortune is a bitter revelation, yet I am grateful beyond measure that his treachery has been exposed before any permanent damage could be done to England's interests.

Percy's recovery has been nothing short of miraculous since the treaty's return. The color has returned to his cheeks, his appetite has been restored, and most wonderfully, he has regained his confidence in himself and his abilities. Lord Holdhurst's kind reassurances regarding Percy's future prospects have completed what your efforts began.

I hope you will not think it presumptuous of me to say that in solving this case, you have not merely recovered a document—important though it was—but have preserved the happiness and future of two people who will be forever in your debt. Percy speaks of you in terms that border on hero-worship, and I must confess that I find myself quite in agreement with his assessment.

Please know that you will always be a most welcome guest at our future home, and that the name of Sherlock Holmes will be spoken with reverence and gratitude in our household for as long as we both shall live.

With the deepest appreciation and warmest regards,

I remain, most gratefully yours,

Miss Annie Harrison

P.S. - Percy has asked me to convey his particular thanks for the discretion you showed in handling this delicate matter. The knowledge that the affair has been resolved without unnecessary publicity has been an enormous comfort to him.

To Holmes from Lord Holdhurst (NAVA)

My Dear Mr. Holmes,

I write to you with a heart full of gratitude and relief that words can scarcely express. Your extraordinary success in recovering the stolen naval treaty has not only saved my career from certain ruin, but has preserved the security interests of Her Majesty's Government at a most critical juncture.

When young Phelps first brought this terrible matter to my attention, I confess I feared the worst. The thought that such a vital document—one whose contents could have compromised our naval strategies and endangered countless lives—might fall into foreign hands filled me with dread. The potential damage to Britain's position in European affairs was incalculable.

Your methodical investigation and brilliant deductive reasoning have once again demonstrated why your reputation as our nation's foremost consulting detective is so richly deserved. The speed and discretion with which you unmasked the true culprit—Joseph Harrison, that serpent who had wormed his way into poor Phelps's confidence—was nothing short of remarkable. That he should have been the very brother of Phelps's own fiancée makes his treachery all the more despicable.

I am particularly grateful for your absolute discretion throughout this affair. That you were able to recover the treaty without any word of its temporary disappearance reaching the press or our European neighbors is a testament to your professionalism and understanding of the delicate nature of diplomatic matters. The Prime Minister himself has asked me to convey his personal thanks for your service to the Crown.

The physical courage you displayed in confronting Harrison during that final encounter at Briarbrae was admirable, though I confess I should have preferred you to have summoned the authorities rather than risk personal injury. Nevertheless, your swift action prevented any possibility of the document's destruction or further concealment.

I trust that young Phelps has now fully recovered from both his illness and the terrible strain this affair placed upon him. His devotion to duty, even whilst gravely unwell, reflects the finest traditions of the Foreign Office, and I am pleased to report that his position remains secure and his future prospects bright.

Please find enclosed a token of the Government's appreciation for your invaluable services. While no monetary consideration can adequately reflect the magnitude of what you have accomplished, I hope you will accept this as a small measure of our profound gratitude.

With the highest regard and deepest appreciation,

I remain, sir, Your most grateful servant,

The Right Honourable Lord Holdhurst
Secretary of State for Foreign Affairs

Private & Confidential

To Watson from Annie Harrison (FINA)

My Dear Dr. Watson,

It is with the heaviest of hearts that I take up my pen to write to you in this, your darkest hour. Percy and I have only just received the devastating news of Mr. Holmes's tragic fate at the Reichenbach Falls, and I felt compelled to reach out to you immediately, knowing as I do the profound bond that existed between you and your remarkable friend.

Though our acquaintance was brief during that troubling affair of the Naval Treaty, I was struck then by the evident devotion and loyalty that characterized your partnership with Mr. Holmes. It was clear to anyone who observed you together that yours was not merely a professional relationship, but a friendship built upon mutual respect, shared danger, and an unshakeable trust. In those few days when Percy's career and indeed his very sanity hung in the balance, I witnessed firsthand how Mr. Holmes's brilliant mind worked in harmony with your steady presence and medical expertise.

I cannot pretend to comprehend the magnitude of your loss, Dr. Watson. To lose such a friend—one who had been your constant companion through countless adventures, who had shared with you the thrill of the chase and the satisfaction of justice served—must create a void that no words of comfort can truly fill.

Percy joins me in expressing our deepest sympathies. He speaks often of how Mr. Holmes not only saved his professional reputation but restored his peace of mind when all seemed lost. Please know that you are in our thoughts and prayers during this difficult time. Should you find yourself in need of quiet companionship or simply a change of surroundings, you would be most welcome at our home.

With deepest sympathy and warmest regards,

Mrs. Annie Harrison
née Phelps

To Watson from Colonel Hayter (FINA)

My Dear Dr. Watson,

It is with the heaviest of hearts that I take up my pen to write to you in this, your darkest hour. The dreadful news of Mr. Holmes's fate at Reichenbach has only just reached me through the morning papers, and I confess I can scarcely credit what I have read.

Though my acquaintance with your remarkable companion was but brief, the memory of those few days he spent recovering at my estate remains vivid in my mind. I witnessed firsthand not only his extraordinary powers of observation and deduction during that unfortunate business with the Cunninghams, but also—and perhaps more meaningfully—the profound bond of friendship and mutual respect that existed between you both.

I remember how you watched over him with such devoted care during his convalescence, and how his eyes would brighten whenever you entered the room. It was clear to me then that yours was no ordinary partnership, but a friendship forged in shared dangers and tempered by absolute trust. That such a partnership should end in this terrible manner seems a cruel mockery of Providence.

Please know that you have my deepest sympathies in this time of unimaginable loss. Mr. Holmes was, without question, a singular man whose like we shall not see again.

I can only hope that in time, the pain of your loss may be softened by pride in having been the trusted companion of such an extraordinary individual, and by the knowledge that through your chronicles, his memory and methods shall live on to inspire future generations.

With profound sympathy and respect, Your servant,

Colonel Hayter

To Watson from Colonel Ross (FINA)

My Dear Dr. Watson,

I have only just learned of the terrible tragedy that befell you and your remarkable companion at the Reichenbach Falls. The news has struck me with profound sorrow, and I felt compelled to write to you immediately to express my deepest condolences.

Though my acquaintance with Mr. Holmes was brief, confined as it was to that troubling affair of Silver Blaze, I was left with an indelible impression of his extraordinary capabilities and noble character. In the space of those few days, he demonstrated not only his unparalleled powers of deduction but also his unwavering commitment to justice and truth. The manner in which he unraveled the mystery surrounding my prize stallion revealed to me a man of exceptional integrity.

I can only imagine the depth of your grief at losing such a friend and colleague. From what I witnessed of your partnership, it was clear that you shared not merely professional collaboration but a bond of genuine mutual respect and affection.

The loss to our nation, indeed to all of civilized society, is immeasurable. Professor Moriarty's evil machinations have been brought to an end, but at what cost! That such a brilliant mind as Mr. Holmes should be sacrificed to rid the world of that criminal mastermind seems a cruel irony of fate.

I pray that time will ease your sorrow, and that you will find solace in the knowledge that Mr. Holmes's sacrifice was not in vain. The criminal empire of Professor Moriarty has been shattered, and countless future victims have been spared through his courageous action.

With deepest sympathy and highest regard,

Colonel Ross
King's Pyland Stables

To Watson from Grant Munro (FINA)

My Dear Dr. Watson,

I have only just learned of the terrible tragedy that befell you and Mr. Holmes at the Reichenbach Falls. Words seem utterly inadequate to express the profound shock and sorrow I feel upon hearing this devastating news.

Though my acquaintance with Mr. Holmes was brief, centered around that peculiar matter of my wife Effie and the mysterious occupant of our cottage, I shall never forget the extraordinary man who solved what seemed an impossible puzzle.

I recall how gently he handled the revelation about little Lucy, and how his wisdom helped preserve my marriage when lesser men might have seen only scandal. In those few hours of our association, I witnessed not merely a brilliant detective, but a man of genuine humanity and moral courage.

My dear Doctor, I can scarcely imagine the depth of your grief. The partnership you shared with Holmes was evident even to one who knew you both so briefly. Please know that you are in my thoughts and prayers during this darkest hour. If there is anything—anything at all—that Effie and I might do to ease your burden, you have but to ask. We shall never forget our debt to Mr. Holmes, and by extension, to you.

The world has lost a giant among men. Take comfort in knowing that his legacy—and yours as his chronicler—will inspire others to pursue justice and truth for generations to come.

With deepest sympathy and respect,

Grant Munro

P.S. — Effie sends her fondest regards and wishes me to convey that little Lucy often speaks of the kind gentleman who ensured she could remain with her loving mother.

To Watson from Miss Helen Stoner (FINA)

My Dear Dr. Watson,

I pray this letter finds you in better spirits than I fear it shall, though I confess I write to you from the depths of my own despair. The dreadful news of Mr. Holmes's fate at the Reichenbach Falls has reached even our quiet corner of Surrey, and I find myself quite unable to comprehend the terrible reality of it.

Can it truly be so? Can that brilliant mind, those keen grey eyes that saw through the darkest mysteries, that steady hand that never trembled in the face of danger—can they all be silenced forever beneath those merciless Swiss waters? My heart rebels against accepting such a cruel turn of fate.

You must forgive my presumption in writing to you during what I know must be your own period of profound grief. Yet I felt compelled to reach out, for you alone can truly understand the magnitude of this loss—not merely to the world of justice, but to those of us whose very lives were saved by his extraordinary gifts.

I shall never forget that terrible April morning when I came to your lodgings at 221B Baker Street, trembling with fear and certain that death stalked me as it had taken my poor dear Julia. How desperate I was, how utterly without hope! And yet Mr. Holmes listened to my tale with such patience and attention, his penetrating mind already at work unraveling the sinister web my stepfather had woven.

That night at Stoke Moran, when Dr. Roylott's vile scheme was finally exposed, I witnessed Mr. Holmes's courage firsthand. While I cowered in terror, he faced that dreadful serpent—that "speckled band" that had claimed my sister's life and nearly claimed my own. His quick thinking and fearless action saved me from a fate too horrible to contemplate.

I owe him my life, Dr. Watson. More than that—I owe him my future, my happiness, my very existence. Through his intervention, I was able to marry my dear Armitage and find the peace and contentment that had seemed forever beyond my reach. Every day of joy I have known since that terrible night is a gift from Mr. Holmes's dedication to justice.

And now to learn that this noble soul, who preserved so many others from harm, could not preserve himself from the clutches of that arch-villain Moriarty! The irony is too bitter to bear. That such a mind should be snuffed out in the prime of life, dragged down by the very evil he fought so tirelessly to defeat!

I cannot—I will not—believe that this is truly the end. Surely a man who solved the impossible, who saw what others could not see, who cheated death so many times before—surely he has found some way to survive even this? Perhaps even now he rests somewhere, recovering, planning his return to confound us all with his resurrection?

Forgive me these wild fancies, dear Doctor. I know you are a man of science and medicine, and such desperate hopes must seem foolish to your rational mind. Yet I find I cannot reconcile myself to a world without Sherlock Holmes in it. The very foundations of justice seem shaken without his presence to uphold them.

I know that you shared the closest friendship with Mr. Holmes, that you were his constant companion in danger and his chronicler in triumph. Your grief must be beyond words, and I do not wish to add to your burden. Yet I felt I must tell you how profoundly his loss affects even those of us who knew him but briefly, how his memory burns bright in the hearts of all whose lives he touched.

Please accept my deepest condolences and know that you are in my prayers during this darkest hour.

With profound sympathy and enduring gratitude,

Miss Helen Stoner
(Mrs. Percy Armitage)

To Watson from Mr. Henry Baker (FINA)

My Dear Dr. Watson,

I hope this letter finds you in as good health as circumstances permit, though I fear my words may only add to the profound grief that must already weigh so heavily upon your heart.

The dreadful news of Mr. Sherlock Holmes' fate at the Reichenbach Falls has reached even my humble corner of London, and I find myself compelled to write to you, though we have had but the briefest of acquaintances. You see, Dr. Watson, I am Henry Baker—perhaps you may recall the rather embarrassing affair of my lost hat and Christmas goose some years ago, which led to that extraordinary business with the blue carbuncle.

I confess that incident, which might have landed me in the most serious trouble through no fault of my own, has remained vivid in my memory not merely for its remarkable conclusion, but for the extraordinary kindness and keen intellect that Mr. Holmes displayed throughout. Here was a man who could have dismissed me as just another unfortunate soul fallen on hard times, yet he treated me with dignity and saw through to the truth with that miraculous mind of his.

Dr. Watson, I cannot—I will not—believe that such a brilliant light has been extinguished. The newspapers speak of his struggle with that villain Professor Moriarty, and while I understand the evidence may seem conclusive, surely a man capable of unraveling the most impossible mysteries might find a way to survive even the most impossible circumstances?

I keep remembering how Mr. Holmes examined my old felt hat with such care, drawing conclusions that seemed like magic to my simple understanding. A man who could read an entire life story from a few scratches on a hat brim—could such a man truly be defeated by mere physical peril? My heart rebels against the notion.

If the worst has indeed come to pass, then London—nay, all of England—has lost its greatest defender against the criminal classes. But you, dear Dr. Watson, have lost something far more precious: a true friend and companion. I can only imagine the anguish you must feel, having been witness to this terrible event.

Please know that even those of us who knew Mr. Holmes only briefly were deeply touched by his nobility and genius. He was, in the truest sense, a gentleman—one who used his extraordinary gifts in service of justice and the protection of the innocent. The memory of his kindness to a struggling clerk who had merely lost his hat will remain with me always.

I remain, with deepest sympathy and the faintest hope that this tragedy may yet prove to be merely another of Mr. Holmes' ingenious deceptions,

Your most humble and sorrowful correspondent,

Henry Baker

P.S. - I have kept the hat Mr. Holmes returned to me all these years. Strange to think that it was touched by hands that could solve any puzzle save, perhaps, the final one.

To Watson from Holder (FINA)

My Dear Dr. Watson,

It is with the deepest sorrow and profound shock that I have learned of
the tragic fate that has befallen our mutual friend, Mr. Sherlock Holmes.
The news of his apparent death at the Reichenbach Falls, locked in
mortal combat with that most sinister of criminals, Professor Moriarty,
has left me quite shaken.

I feel compelled to write to you, knowing as I do the extraordinary bond
of friendship that existed between yourself and the great detective. While
my own acquaintance with Mr. Holmes was brief—limited to that most
distressing affair of the beryl coronet—it was sufficient to reveal to me
the true nobility of his character and the powers of his intellect.

I shall never forget how, in my darkest hour, when my own son stood
accused and my faith in him wavered, Mr. Holmes saw through to the
truth with such clarity and compassion. He not only recovered my
precious coronet but, more importantly, restored my family's honor and
my son's good name. The debt I owe him can never be repaid, and his
loss is felt most keenly in this household.

Should you find yourself in need of anything during this difficult time—
be it assistance of a practical nature or merely the companionship of one
who held Mr. Holmes in the highest regard—please do not hesitate to
call upon me.

I remain, with deepest condolences and highest respect, Your most
obedient servant,

Alexander Holder
Senior Partner
Holder & Stevenson Private Banking

To Watson from Inspector Lestrade (FINA)

My Dear Dr. Watson,

I pen these words with the heaviest of hearts, having received the dreadful news from Switzerland regarding the fate of our mutual friend, Mr. Sherlock Holmes. Though the official reports have reached us here at the Yard, I confess I struggle to accept the reality of what has transpired at those accursed Reichenbach Falls.

I will not pretend that Holmes and I always saw eye to eye on matters of procedure and method. Many a time I found his unconventional approaches... well, let us say they tested my patience considerably. Yet I would be the meanest of men if I did not acknowledge, now that he is gone, what London—indeed, what all of England—has lost in his passing.

The truth is, Watson, that man possessed a mind unlike any I have encountered in my twenty-three years with the Metropolitan Police. Where we saw confusion, he found clarity. Where we stumbled in darkness, he struck a light that illuminated the very heart of the mystery. I cannot count the number of cases that would have remained forever unsolved were it not for his remarkable faculties of observation and deduction.

I recall, with particular clarity, the Boscombe Valley affair, when I was certain young McCarthy was guilty as sin. Holmes not only proved the lad's innocence but delivered the true perpetrator into our hands. "You see, but you do not observe, Lestrade," he told me that day. How those words sting now, knowing I shall never hear his voice again—neither in reproach nor in that peculiar satisfaction he took when unraveling the most complex of puzzles.

The men here at Scotland Yard speak of him with a respect that was perhaps not always evident during his lifetime. Even Inspector Bradstreet, who often bristled at Holmes's methods, admitted yesterday that "London will be a good deal less safe without that consulting detective prowling about."

But it is not merely the professional loss that weighs upon me, my dear fellow. In his own singular way, Holmes was a friend. Though he could be insufferably superior and maddeningly secretive, there was an essential decency in the man that I came to rely upon. He fought not for glory or reward, but for justice itself—a quality rarer than one might hope in our profession.

I know that his loss must be particularly grievous for you, having shared his lodgings and his adventures these many years. The partnership between you both was remarkable to witness, and I hope you will find some small comfort in knowing that his memory is honored by all who knew his work.

The newspapers are full of speculation about Professor Moriarty, this "Napoleon of crime" as Holmes termed him. I confess we at the Yard knew precious little of this mastermind until Holmes brought him to our attention. That such evil should have claimed so noble a spirit seems a cruel jest of Providence.

Please know that you have my deepest sympathies, and should you require anything—whether assistance with arrangements or simply the ear of one who also mourns his passing—you need only call upon me.

The criminal classes of London may celebrate tonight, but their victory is hollow. Sherlock Holmes may be gone, but the light he brought to our darkest mysteries will not be so easily extinguished.

I remain, with sincere condolences and lasting respect for our fallen friend,

Your obedient servant,

G. Lestrade
Inspector, Criminal Investigation Department
Scotland Yard

To Watson from Irene Adler Norton (FINA)

My Dear Dr. Watson,

I write to you from the warmth of the Mediterranean coast, yet I find myself chilled to the very bone by the dreadful news that has reached me here. The papers speak of a tragedy at the Reichenbach Falls, of two men locked in mortal combat who plunged together into those merciless waters. They say that one of those men was Sherlock Holmes.

I confess, Doctor, that I cannot bring myself to believe it. Not him. Not the man whose mind moved like quicksilver, who could unravel the most intricate puzzles with such elegant precision. How can it be that such a brilliant flame has been extinguished? The very notion seems to violate the natural order of things.

You knew him better than anyone, dear Watson. You were his constant companion, his chronicler, his truest friend. If anyone can comprehend the magnitude of this loss, it is you. I have read your accounts of his methods, his extraordinary deductions, his unfailing commitment to justice. Through your words, I came to understand that beneath his sometimes cold exterior beat the heart of a man truly devoted to the protection of the innocent.

I remember our single encounter with a mixture of admiration and, I must admit, a peculiar fondness. He called me "the woman," and I believe he meant it as the highest compliment he could bestow. In a world where men of his intellect rarely acknowledge the capabilities of my sex, he saw me clearly and without prejudice. For that alone, I held him in the deepest respect.

But it was more than mere respect, wasn't it, Doctor? There was something about Mr. Holmes that commanded not just admiration, but genuine affection from those privileged to know him. His fierce loyalty to you, his unexpected moments of kindness, his absolute integrity in the face of corruption and evil—these qualities made him far more than a mere consulting detective. They made him, dare I say it, a good man.

The papers describe Professor Moriarty as Holmes's intellectual equal, a criminal mastermind of the highest order. If this villain has indeed claimed our friend's life, then the world has lost not only a brilliant mind but a true guardian. I cannot help but think of all the cases that will now go unsolved, all the innocent people who might have found salvation in his remarkable abilities.

I hope you will forgive the presumption of this letter, Doctor. We have never met, yet I feel as though I know you through Mr. Holmes's evident regard for you. In this hour of grief, I find myself reaching out to the one person who might understand the peculiar sorrow I feel. It is the grief one experiences when a light goes out in the world, when something irreplaceable is lost forever.

Please know that in your mourning, you are not alone. Across the Channel, in this sun-drenched villa, a woman who knew your friend but briefly keeps vigil with you. I shall light a candle for him tonight and remember not the man who fell at Reichenbach, but the one who lived so brilliantly, who fought so courageously against the darkness that threatens to engulf us all.

Take comfort, if you can, in the knowledge that he died as he lived—in service to justice and in the company of his dearest friend. There are worse ways for a good man to meet his end.

With deepest sympathy and shared sorrow,

Irene Adler Norton

P.S. - Should you ever find yourself in need of anything—anything at all—please do not hesitate to call upon me. It would be my honor to assist the man who stood so faithfully by Sherlock Holmes's side.

To Watson from Jabez Wilson (FINA)

My Dear Dr. Watson,

I pray this letter finds you in better spirits than my own, though I confess I cannot imagine how that might be possible given the dreadful news that has reached even my humble corner of London.

When I first read the account in the newspapers of the terrible tragedy at the Reichenbach Falls, I found myself unable to believe the words before my very eyes. Surely, I thought, there must be some mistake. Not Mr. Sherlock Holmes—not the man who saw through that confounded Red-Headed League business when I myself was too simple to understand what mischief was afoot right under my very nose.

You will remember, I am certain, how I came to Baker Street that autumn day, my head full of confusion about the strange advertisement and that peculiar Mr. Duncan Ross. I was but a humble pawnbroker, Dr. Watson, with little education and even less understanding of the criminal mind. Yet Mr. Holmes listened to my tale with such attention, as though my small troubles were matters of the gravest importance to Scotland Yard itself.

How he saw through their deception! How clearly he perceived what I, in my simple way, could never have grasped! Without his intervention, those scoundrels would have made off with the gold from the City and Suburban Bank, and I would have been left none the wiser, still copying out pages of the *Encyclopædia Britannica* and congratulating myself on my good fortune.

But it was not merely his remarkable intellect that impressed me, Dr. Watson. It was his kindness to a man of modest means and understanding. He never once made me feel foolish for having been so easily deceived. Instead, he treated me with the same courtesy he might have shown to a peer of the realm.

I have spoken of Mr. Holmes many times to my customers and neighbors since that day. "There," I would say with pride, "is a man who stands between decent folk and the criminal classes. There is a man who uses his gifts not for his own enrichment, but for the protection of those who cannot protect themselves."

And now they tell me he is gone—lost to those terrible waters, locked in struggle with that Napoleon of crime, as you have called him. My heart breaks, Dr. Watson, not only for the loss of such a man, but for you, his faithful companion, who must bear a grief far heavier than mine.

Please know that in this humble shop in Coburg Square, the name of Mr. Sherlock Holmes will always be spoken with reverence and gratitude. I am but one small man whose life he touched, but I suspect there are hundreds—nay, thousands—like me, scattered across London and beyond, who owe him debts that can never be repaid.

Should you find yourself in need of any service, however small, that a simple pawnbroker might provide, I hope you will not hesitate to call upon me. It would be my honor to serve the man who stood so faithfully beside the greatest detective this world has ever known.

With deepest sympathy and highest regard,

Your humble servant,

Jabez Wilson

P.S. - I have enclosed a small token—a watch chain that passed through my shop some years ago. It belonged to a gentleman of learning, though he never returned to claim it. I thought perhaps Mr. Holmes might have appreciated such an item, and it pains me to think he will never have the opportunity to examine its curious markings. I hope you might accept it as a small memorial to his extraordinary life.

To Watson from John Clay (FINA)

My Dear Dr. Watson,

I trust this letter finds you in the depths of mourning, though I confess it finds me in the most extraordinary spirits. Word has reached even these dreary stone walls here at Pentonville Prison of the delicious events at Reichenbach Falls, and I simply could not contain my jubilation without sharing it with the one person who knew that insufferable consulting detective as intimately as I.

How utterly fitting that your precious Holmes should meet his end tumbling through the air like a common criminal fleeing justice! The man who took such perverse pleasure in unraveling the carefully laid plans of his intellectual superiors has finally been unraveled himself. Professor Moriarty—now there was a mind worthy of admiration! That he should be the instrument of Holmes's destruction is poetry of the highest order.

I remember our encounter in Saxe-Coburg Square as if it were yesterday. The arrogance! The theatrical flourishes! The way Holmes preened as he explained how he had "deduced" what any fool with eyes could observe. And you, dear Watson, hanging on his every word like a lovesick schoolboy. How it grated to watch such mediocrity celebrated as genius!

But the wheel has turned, hasn't it? The great Sherlock Holmes, terror of the criminal classes, has been reduced to fish food in a Swiss waterfall. I do hope you'll forgive me if I've ordered a bottle of the governor's finest brandy to toast this magnificent news. In fact, I've shared the delightful tidings with several of my fellow residents here in Pentonville, and I can report that there has been quite the celebration. Why, even Sikes in the next cell managed a smile—the first I've seen from him in months!

I trust you understand that this correspondence springs not from cruelty, but from simple justice. Your friend made his career on the misery of others, breaking up enterprises that required months or even years of careful planning. How many brilliant minds did he send to places like this? How many promising careers in our... profession... did he cut short with his meddling?

Please don't think I hold any personal animosity toward you, Doctor. You were, after all, merely the chronicler of his exploits—the Boswell to his Johnson, as it were. Perhaps now you might find more worthy subjects for your literary talents. I understand the mortality rate among crossing-sweepers is quite fascinating.

Do give my regards to Mrs. Hudson. I always rather liked her.

With the deepest satisfaction at your loss,

John Clay
Fourth son of a royal duke, Oxford graduate
Formerly of the Millbank Prison
Currently enjoying accommodations courtesy of Her Majesty

P.S. I do hope this letter provides some small comfort in your time of grief. After all, you can take solace in knowing that your friend died as he lived—dramatically and with complete disregard for common sense.

To Watson from John Rance (FINA)

Dear Dr. Watson,

I hope you will forgive the liberty I take in writing to you during what must be a time of profound grief. Though we have met but briefly, the news of Mr. Sherlock Holmes's tragic end has moved me to put pen to paper.

You may recall our encounter some years past at No. 3 Lauriston Gardens, during that dreadful business with the American gentleman found dead in the empty house. I was the constable on duty that morning when you and Mr. Holmes arrived at the scene. I confess that at the time, I thought your companion rather an odd sort of fellow, with his peculiar questions about my movements and his keen interest in matters that seemed, to my mind, quite beside the point.

How wrong I was in that assessment! It was not many days before the newspapers were full of Mr. Holmes's remarkable solution to that baffling case. The way he unraveled the mystery of those strange circumstances—the wedding ring, the word "RACHE" upon the wall, and all the rest—showed me that I had been in the presence of a truly extraordinary mind.

Please accept my sincere condolences on the loss of your dear friend and colleague. Though I knew Mr. Holmes only slightly, I could see even in our brief acquaintance the deep bond of friendship and mutual respect that existed between you. That he had such a loyal companion as yourself must have been a great comfort to him in his dangerous work.

I remain, dear sir, with deepest sympathy for your loss, Your humble servant,

John Rance
Police Constable 426H
Metropolitan Police

To Watson from Kate Whitney (FINA)

My Dear Dr. Watson,

I write to you with the heaviest of hearts, having only recently learned through the newspapers of the terrible tragedy that befell Mr. Holmes at the Reichenbach Falls. Words seem woefully inadequate to express the profound sorrow I feel for your loss, and indeed, for the loss that all of London—nay, all of England—has suffered.

Though my acquaintance with Mr. Holmes was brief, the memory of his extraordinary kindness and capability remains vivid in my mind. When I came to you in desperation that dreadful night, fearing for my poor Isa's safety and knowing not where to turn, Mr. Holmes took up our cause without hesitation. His remarkable deductive powers and unwavering determination led him into the very depths of that terrible opium den, where he secured my husband's safe return to me.

I shall never forget the mixture of authority and compassion with which he handled that delicate situation. He could have easily dismissed the troubles of a woman unknown to him, yet he treated our predicament with the same gravity and attention he might have afforded to matters of national importance. That night, Mr. Holmes was nothing short of our salvation.

From that encounter, I witnessed firsthand the extraordinary partnership you and he shared. The implicit trust between you, the seamless way you worked together, and the obvious depth of your mutual regard spoke to a friendship that transcended the merely professional. I can only imagine the magnitude of the void his absence has created in your life.

Please know that in our household, Mr. Sherlock Holmes will always be remembered as a guardian angel who appeared in our darkest hour. My children have been taught to speak his name with reverence, and they shall grow up knowing that there once walked among us a man who dedicated his remarkable gifts to the protection of the innocent and the pursuit of justice.

The papers speak of Professor Moriarty as a criminal of extraordinary cunning, and if the reports are true that Mr. Holmes perished in ensuring this villain could no longer prey upon society, then his final act was entirely consistent with the noble character I was privileged to witness. That he should have made such a sacrifice speaks to the greatness of his spirit and his devotion to the greater good.

I pray that in time, the sharp edge of your grief may be softened by pride in having been the closest companion to such an exceptional man. The world may have lost Sherlock Holmes, but the good he accomplished, the lives he touched, and the evil he prevented will echo through the years to come.

If there is any service I might render to you during this difficult period, or if you should ever have need of a friend's ear, please do not hesitate to call upon us. It would be a small opportunity to repay, in some measure, the enormous debt of gratitude we owe to Mr. Holmes's memory.

With deepest sympathy and warmest regards,

Mrs. Kate Whitney

To Watson from The Langham Hotel (FINA)

Dear Dr. Watson,

It is with the deepest sorrow and profound shock that I write to express my most sincere condolences upon learning of the tragic loss of your dear friend and colleague, Mr. Sherlock Holmes. The news of the dreadful events at Reichenbach Falls has cast a pall of grief not only over myself and the entire staff of the Langham Hotel, but indeed over all of London's most distinguished citizens who have had the privilege of witnessing Mr. Holmes's extraordinary talents.

I am compelled to share with you that several of our most esteemed patrons have expressed their own profound grief upon learning of this tragedy. Lady Frances Carfax, who had occasion to benefit from Mr. Holmes's protective services, wept openly when I conveyed the news, declaring that "the world has lost its greatest guardian of justice." Sir Henry Baskerville, whose very life was preserved through Mr. Holmes's intervention in that most harrowing affair on the moors, has written from Devonshire to say that he considers himself forever in debt to your friend's memory.

I understand, dear Doctor, that no words can adequately console you for the loss of so devoted a friend and brilliant a companion. Yet I hope it may provide some small comfort to know that Mr. Holmes's memory shall be preserved with the highest honour at the Langham Hotel. We shall always remember him not merely as London's greatest consulting detective, but as a gentleman whose nobility of character was matched only by his remarkable gifts of observation and deduction.

With the utmost respect and sincere condolences,

Charles Morrison
General Manager, The Langham Hotel

"The game may be up, but the memory of the greatest player shall endure forever."

To Watson From Lord Saint Simon (FINA)

My Dear Dr. Watson,

It is with the most profound sorrow that I have learned of the tragic circumstances at Reichenbach Falls, and the loss of your esteemed colleague and dearest friend, Mr. Sherlock Holmes. Though our acquaintance was brief, formed during that rather peculiar affair surrounding my wedding day, I was deeply impressed by both his extraordinary abilities and the remarkable partnership you two gentlemen shared.

I confess that during our initial meeting, I found Mr. Holmes's methods somewhat... unconventional. However, I came to appreciate not only his singular genius but also the deep loyalty and steadfast friendship you showed him throughout his investigations. It was evident to any observer that your association transcended the merely professional—yours was a bond forged by mutual respect, shared adventures, and genuine affection.

The nation has lost a defender against the darkest criminal minds, but you, my dear Watson, have lost something far more precious—a friend whose like we shall not see again.

Please know that you have the sympathy of all decent men who value justice and admire courage. Mr. Holmes's sacrifice in ridding the world of Professor Moriarty, though it cost us dearly, stands as a testament to his unwavering dedication to the cause of right.

Should there be any service I might render during this dark hour, or in the days to come, please do not hesitate to call upon me.

I remain, with deepest condolences and highest regard, Your most obedient servant,

Robert Saint Simon

To Watson from Mary Sutherland (FINA)

My Dear Dr. Watson,

I hope you will forgive the liberty I take in writing to you during what must be the darkest of times. Though we met but once, under circumstances I shall never forget, I feel compelled to express my most sincere condolences upon hearing the dreadful news of Mr. Sherlock Holmes's passing.

I often think of that afternoon when I came to Baker Street in such distress over my dear Hosmer Angel's disappearance. How patient Mr. Holmes was with my tears, how methodically he examined my typewriter samples and questioned me about every detail. Even when the truth proved so painful—that my own stepfather had deceived me so cruelly—Mr. Holmes delivered it with such consideration for my feelings.

You must know, Dr. Watson, that his kindness to a foolish woman like myself revealed the true measure of his character. Beneath that sharp intellect and sometimes brusque manner lay a heart that truly cared for justice and the protection of the innocent. That he died in service of ridding the world of such evil as Professor Moriarty only confirms what I learned that day—that Mr. Holmes was not merely a brilliant detective, but a truly good man.

Should you ever find yourself in need of a quiet place for reflection, or simply a friendly cup of tea and a sympathetic ear, please do not hesitate to call upon me.

With deepest sympathy and respect,

Mary Sutherland

P.S. - I have kept the typewriter samples and my stepfather's letters that Mr. Holmes examined. Should they ever be of service to his memory or your work in preserving his methods, they remain at your disposal.

To Watson from Nancy Barclay (FINA)

My Dear Doctor Watson,

It is with the heaviest of hearts that I take up my pen to write to you in this, your darkest hour. The news of Mr. Holmes's tragic fate at the Reichenbach Falls has reached even our quiet corner of Aldershot, and I felt compelled to express my deepest sympathies for your immeasurable loss.

Though our acquaintance was brief during that unfortunate business with poor Colonel Barclay, I could not help but observe the extraordinary bond between you and your remarkable friend. The devotion and admiration you showed for Mr. Holmes was evident in your every word and gesture, just as his profound respect and affection for you shone through his manner, despite his often austere demeanor.

I have read with great interest your published accounts of Mr. Holmes's adventures, and through them, I have come to understand something of the noble work you both undertook together. How many lives were saved, how many wrongs were righted, how much evil was prevented through your partnership! The world has lost not merely a brilliant detective, but a champion of justice, and you have lost far more than a colleague—you have lost a brother in all but blood.

Please know that in our household, we remember Mr. Holmes not only for his extraordinary intellect, but for the compassion he showed during our family's trials. His methods may have seemed cold to some, but I witnessed firsthand the gentle consideration he extended to those in pain. That such a man should meet his end in combat with the forces of darkness seems both fitting and utterly heartbreaking.

I cannot pretend to know the depths of your grief, nor would I insult you with hollow consolations. But I would offer this: the light that Mr. Holmes brought to this world continues to shine through the chronicles you have so faithfully recorded. His name will live on, his methods will inspire others, and his victories over evil will not be forgotten. In this way, though his mortal form may be lost, his spirit endures.

My husband joins me in extending our sincere condolences, and we both hope that in time, the sharp edge of your sorrow may be softened by treasured memories of your years together in Baker Street. Should you ever find yourself in our county and in need of quiet companionship or simply a peaceful place to rest, you would be most welcome at our home.

Please accept the enclosed pressed flowers from our garden—forget-me-nots seemed appropriate, for indeed, neither you nor the world shall ever forget Sherlock Holmes.

With deepest sympathy and warmest regards,

Nancy Barclay

P.S. I have taken the liberty of lighting a candle in our parish church for both Mr. Holmes and Professor Moriarty. Though the latter was surely a villain of the highest order, even the darkest soul may find redemption in the next world, and perhaps there, these two brilliant minds might find peace.

To Watson from Percy Phelps (FINA)

My Dear Dr. Watson,

I have only this morning received word through the Foreign Office channels of the most dreadful and incomprehensible tragedy that has befallen you and, indeed, all of England. The news of Mr. Sherlock Holmes's death at the Reichenbach Falls has left me in a state of profound shock and disbelief from which I fear I shall not soon recover.

I confess that upon first hearing the report, I dismissed it entirely as some cruel fabrication or misunderstanding. Surely, I reasoned, the man who solved the mystery of the Naval Treaty with such brilliant deduction—who saw through the most intricate web of deceit as though it were mere child's play—could not simply have perished in such a manner. The very notion seems to defy the natural order of things.

Yet as the hours have passed and the terrible reality has begun to settle upon my mind, I find myself compelled to write to you, knowing as I do that your grief must exceed my own a thousandfold. For while I had the privilege of witnessing Mr. Holmes's extraordinary abilities on but one occasion, you were his constant companion, his chronicler, and—if I may be so presumptuous—his dearest friend.

I shall never forget our first meeting at my home, when my career and reputation were hanging by the merest thread. My nerves were shattered, my health broken, and my faith in justice all but extinguished. Yet under Mr. Holmes's penetrating gaze, I found not only hope restored but witnessed a mind at work that seemed to transcend the limitations of ordinary human reasoning.

The manner in which he unraveled the mystery—seeing connections where others saw only confusion, perceiving truth where others found only shadows—it was nothing short of miraculous. In those moments, I understood that I was in the presence of a man whose intellectual gifts were perhaps unparalleled in our age.

And now to learn that such a mind has been silenced forever, that those keen eyes shall never again pierce through deception, that those long, thin fingers shall never again demonstrate some crucial detail that had escaped lesser mortals—it seems an immeasurable loss not merely to you and to his other friends, but to the cause of justice itself.

I am told that this Professor Moriarty—this Napoleon of Crime as Holmes termed him—perished alongside our friend in that dreadful cascade. While there may be some comfort in knowing that such a villain can no longer plague society, the price paid seems impossibly dear. What manner of criminal could be worth the sacrifice of Sherlock Holmes? What evil so great as to demand the life of our greatest detective?

Please know, my dear Doctor, that in these dark hours you are not alone in your sorrow. Though my acquaintance with Mr. Holmes was brief, the impression he made upon me was indelible. I shall carry with me always the memory of his kindness in my hour of need, his unwavering commitment to truth, and the remarkable gift he possessed for bringing order from chaos.

I pray that time will ease your grief, though I suspect that for one who shared so much with so extraordinary a man, the wound may never fully heal. Should you ever find yourself in need of any service that I might render, please do not hesitate to call upon me. It would be my honor to assist the partner of Sherlock Holmes in whatever small way I might.

With deepest sympathy and profound respect,

Percy Phelps
Foreign Office

P.S. - I have taken the liberty of ensuring that within the Foreign Office, the story of how Mr. Holmes recovered the Naval Treaty shall be preserved in our most secure files, that future generations might know something of the debt our nation owes to his memory.

To Watson from Percy Trevelyan (FINA)

My Dear Dr. Watson,

It is with the heaviest of hearts that I take up my pen to write to you in this, your darkest hour. The news of Mr. Holmes's tragic fate at the Reichenbach Falls has reached me through the morning papers, and I find myself quite unable to comprehend that so brilliant a mind, so keen an intellect, should be forever stilled.

Though my own acquaintance with your remarkable friend was but brief, centered as it was around that most disturbing affair at my residence, I shall never forget the extraordinary manner in which he unraveled the web of deception that had so thoroughly ensnared me. His methods seemed almost supernatural in their precision, yet I came to understand that they were grounded in the most rigorous application of scientific observation and deductive reasoning.

As a medical man myself, I can appreciate perhaps better than most the unique partnership you shared with Mr. Holmes. I witnessed firsthand how his analytical brilliance was perfectly complemented by your steadfast loyalty and practical wisdom.

In my own small way, I remain forever in his debt. The resolution of my case freed me from a web of terror that had nearly claimed my sanity. For this deliverance, and for the privilege of witnessing genius at work, I shall always be grateful.

Please know that you have my deepest sympathy in this trying time. Should you ever find yourself in need of companionship or simply wish to speak with someone who, however briefly, shared in the experience of witnessing Mr. Holmes's extraordinary abilities, I hope you will not hesitate to call upon me.

With profound respect and heartfelt condolences,

Dr. Percy Trevelyan

To Watson from Peter Steiler (FINA)

My Dear Dr. Watson,

It is with the heaviest of hearts that I take up my pen to write to you in these most terrible circumstances. The events that have transpired at our beloved Reichenbach Falls have shaken me to my very core, and I find myself struggling to comprehend how such tragedy could befall our peaceful valley.

Never, in all my years as proprietor of the Englischer Hof, have I witnessed anything approaching the horror of what occurred yesterday. Our little corner of Switzerland has always been a haven of tranquility, where the most excitement we might expect would be the arrival of a party of enthusiastic botanists or perhaps a group of alpine climbers. The thunderous roar of those falls, which has provided such a soothing backdrop to countless peaceful evenings, now seems to mock us with its terrible secret.

I cannot begin to express my profound sorrow at the loss of your dear friend, Mr. Sherlock Holmes. In the brief time that you both graced our establishment with your presence, it became abundantly clear that he was a gentleman of the most extraordinary caliber. My entire staff spoke of him with the greatest admiration—from young Franz, who was so delighted by Mr. Holmes's keen observations about the local flora, to our cook, who was thoroughly charmed when your friend complimented her *Älplermagronen* and requested the recipe for what he termed "Mrs. Hudson's benefit."

Your friend possessed such a remarkable vitality, such a sharp and penetrating intelligence, that it seems almost impossible that someone so vibrantly alive could be taken from us in such a sudden and violent manner. I recall how he stood at our front terrace that first evening, his keen eyes surveying our valley with what seemed to be genuine appreciation for its natural beauty. "A perfect retreat from the clamor of London," he remarked to you, and how prophetic those words now seem.

The constabulary and I have searched every conceivable spot along the falls and the torrent below, but as you know, the power of those waters is beyond imagination. I fear that both your friend and his adversary have been claimed by forces far greater than any mortal man might hope to overcome.

Please know that you have our most sincere condolences during this time of unimaginable grief. Should you find yourself able to return to our region under happier circumstances, you will always be most welcome at the Englischer Hof. We shall never forget the honor of hosting two such distinguished English gentlemen, nor shall we forget the sacrifice that Mr. Holmes has made in his noble pursuit of justice.

I remain, with the deepest sympathy and respect,

Your most humble servant,

Peter Steiler
Proprietor, Englischer Hof Hotel

P.S. - I have taken the liberty of preserving Mr. Holmes's few personal effects that remained in his room. They await your instruction, though I understand if you are not yet ready to address such matters.

To Watson from Pinkerton's (FINA)

My Dear Dr. Watson,

It is with the heaviest of hearts that we at Pinkerton's National Detective Agency write to express our most sincere condolences upon learning of the tragic loss of your dear friend and colleague, Mr. Sherlock Holmes. The news of his heroic sacrifice at Reichenbach Falls, along with the demise of the infamous Professor Moriarty, has reached us here across the Atlantic, and we find ourselves united in grief with you and all who knew and respected the great detective.

From our founder, Allan Pinkerton himself, to every operative in our employ, we wish you to know that Mr. Holmes was held in the highest esteem by our Agency. His remarkable deductive abilities, his unwavering commitment to justice, and his invaluable assistance in matters of international concern—particularly in the affair involving Mr. Birdy Edwards and the Scowrers—demonstrated a level of professional excellence that commanded our deepest admiration.

Our operative Edwards, now safely relocated thanks in no small part to Mr. Holmes's intervention, has asked that we convey his personal gratitude for the detective's role in bringing the Vermissa Valley criminals to justice. Edwards often spoke of Holmes's brilliant analysis of the case and his crucial support during those dangerous months in Pennsylvania.

The criminal underworld has lost its greatest adversary, and the cause of justice has lost one of its most dedicated champions. Yet we take comfort in knowing that Professor Moriarty, that "Napoleon of Crime" as Holmes so aptly termed him, has been stopped once and for all. That Mr. Holmes chose to sacrifice himself to rid the world of such a menace speaks to the nobility of character that defined him throughout his career.

We have followed, with great interest and admiration, your chronicling of Mr. Holmes's cases. Your faithful documentation has allowed those of us in the detective profession, both here in America and throughout the world, to learn from his methods and be inspired by his dedication. We hope that you will continue this important work, ensuring that Holmes's legacy and his contributions to the science of detection will endure for future generations.

Please know that you have friends and colleagues here at Pinkerton's who share in your sorrow. Should you ever find yourself in America, or should you require any assistance in your future endeavors, our Agency stands ready to aid you in any way possible. The bond forged between Mr. Holmes and our organization transcends national boundaries and will not be forgotten.

We understand that no words can ease the pain of losing such a remarkable friend and partner. Yet we hope you will find some small comfort in knowing that across the ocean, fellow detectives honor his memory and mourn his passing alongside you.

Mr. Holmes's methods, his brilliance, and his unwavering moral compass will continue to guide and inspire those of us who have dedicated our lives to the pursuit of justice. Though he is gone, his influence on the art of detection will live on forever.

With our deepest sympathy and highest respect,

Robert A. Pinkerton
General Superintendent
William A. Pinkerton
Assistant General Superintendent
On behalf of all operatives and staff of
Pinkerton's National Detective Agency

"We Never Sleep"

To Watson from Reginald Musgrave (FINA)

My Dear Dr. Watson,

It is with the heaviest of hearts that I take pen to paper today, having learned through the most distressing accounts in the newspapers of the terrible tragedy that has befallen our mutual friend, Mr. Sherlock Holmes. Though words seem inadequate to express the profound shock and sorrow I feel upon hearing of his loss, I felt compelled to write to you, knowing as I do the deep bond of friendship and partnership that existed between you.

I confess that when I first read the accounts of that dreadful business at the Reichenbach Falls, I could scarcely credit what my eyes beheld. That such a brilliant mind—one that had illuminated the darkest corners of criminal enterprise with such singular clarity—should be extinguished in so violent and sudden a manner seems almost beyond comprehension.

My own acquaintance with Mr. Holmes, though perhaps not as intimate as yours, stretches back to our days at university, where even then his remarkable powers of observation and deduction marked him as extraordinary among our peers.

When circumstances later brought him to Hurlstone to resolve that peculiar matter of our ancient family ritual, I was struck anew by his exceptional abilities. The methodical precision with which he unraveled centuries-old mysteries, transforming what had seemed mere antiquarian curiosity into a matter of life and death, demonstrated once again why his reputation had grown to such remarkable heights.

But beyond his professional accomplishments, I was impressed by his fundamental decency—his genuine concern for justice and his determination to protect the innocent, qualities that I know you witnessed daily in your shared adventures. That such a man should meet his end in combat with one so thoroughly evil as Professor Moriarty seems, in some terrible way, fitting—though no less tragic for it.

I can only imagine the depths of your own grief, having lost not merely a colleague but a dear friend and the closest of companions. The world has lost a singular detective, but you have lost far more. Please know that in these dark hours, you have the sincere sympathy and respect of all who knew Mr. Holmes, however briefly.

Should you ever find yourself in Yorkshire and in need of quiet refuge to collect your thoughts, please know that the doors of Hurlstone remain open to you. The peaceful countryside might provide some small comfort during this most difficult period.

I remain, with deepest sympathy and highest regard,

Your obedient servant,

Reginald Musgrave

To Watson from the King (FINA)

My Dear Doctor Watson,

It is with the profoundest grief and heaviest of hearts that I take up my
pen to address you upon this most sorrowful occasion. Word has reached
us here in Prague of the tragic loss of your esteemed colleague and
dearest friend, Mr. Sherlock Holmes, at the Reichenbach Falls. Though
the news arrived some days past, I confess that I have been unable to
compose myself sufficiently to write until this moment, so deeply has this
intelligence affected me.

I am acutely aware that no words of mine can adequately express the
magnitude of your loss, nor can they provide true solace for the grief that
must now overwhelm you. Yet I feel compelled to share with you the
profound respect and admiration which I, despite our brief acquaintance,
came to hold for your remarkable friend.

You will recall, I am certain, that circumstance brought Mr. Holmes and
myself together during what I can only describe as the most delicate and
perilous moment of my reign. The affair of the photograph—that matter
which threatened not merely my personal happiness but the very stability
of my kingdom—required the services of a man of extraordinary
capabilities. I had heard whispers of Mr. Holmes's reputation, but I
confess I was unprepared for the singular brilliance I encountered.

What struck me most profoundly was not merely his intellectual
supremacy—though that was evident from our first meeting—but his
uncompromising integrity. When I offered him rewards befitting his
service to the Crown, he declined them all, asking only for that which
held no monetary value: the photograph of the lady who had so
thoroughly outwitted us both. In that moment, I recognized that I was in
the presence of a man whose character was as remarkable as his mind.

Though Miss Adler proved herself more than equal to Mr. Holmes's
considerable talents—a fact which seemed to delight rather than vex
him—I observed in your friend a quality rarely found among men of
genius: the capacity for genuine admiration of another's superior wit. His

request for her photograph was not, I believe, mere sentiment, but rather the tribute of one exceptional mind to another.

I have often reflected upon our encounter in the years since, and I have come to understand that in Mr. Holmes, England possessed not merely a great detective, but a guardian of justice whose like may never be seen again. His methods were unconventional, his manner sometimes brusque, yet his dedication to truth and his protection of the innocent were absolute.

That such a man should meet his end in the service of humanity, battling against the forces of evil, seems both tragic and yet somehow fitting. For I cannot imagine Mr. Holmes choosing any path but one that placed duty above personal safety.

To you, Dr. Watson, who stood beside him through countless adventures, who chronicled his achievements, and who knew better than any other the true nobility of his spirit, I extend my deepest and most heartfelt sympathies. Your loyalty to your friend was legendary even in the courts of Europe, and I know that his loss leaves a void that can never be filled.

Please know that in the Kingdom of Bohemia, the name of Sherlock Holmes will always be spoken with the utmost reverence, and that our prayers are with you in this dark hour.

I remain, with the greatest respect and sympathy, your most humble and devoted servant,

Wilhelm Gottsreich Sigismond von Ormstein
Grand Duke of Cassel-Felstein
Hereditary King of Bohemia

Post Scriptum: I have enclosed a small token—a medal of the Order of the Golden Fleece—which I had intended to present to Mr. Holmes should our paths have crossed again. Perhaps you might find it fitting to place it with whatever memorial you choose to establish in his honor.

To Watson from Violet Hunter (FINA)

My Dear Dr. Watson,

I have only just learned through the morning papers of the terrible tragedy that has befallen both you and the world at large. The news of Mr. Holmes's heroic sacrifice at the Reichenbach Falls has left me quite overcome with grief, and I felt compelled to write to you immediately.

Though my acquaintance with your remarkable friend was brief, the impression he made upon me during that singular affair at the Copper Beeches remains as vivid today as it was those months ago. His keen intellect, his unwavering dedication to justice, and his genuine concern for those in peril—qualities I witnessed firsthand when he came to my aid—mark him as a man whose loss will be felt by countless souls he has touched.

I cannot pretend to comprehend the depth of your sorrow, dear Doctor, for it is evident to anyone who has observed you both that your friendship transcended the ordinary bonds between companions.

Please know that you are in my thoughts and prayers during this most difficult time. Mr. Holmes's sacrifice in ridding the world of the odious Professor Moriarty serves as testament to his noble character—he has given his life that others might live in safety.

Should you ever find yourself in need of a friend's company or simply wish to speak with someone who understood, even briefly, the extraordinary nature of the man we mourn, please do not hesitate to call upon me.

With deepest sympathy and warmest regards,

Miss Violet Hunter

P.S. - I have enclosed a small nosegay of forget-me-nots from my garden. Though modest, they seemed fitting, for truly, Mr. Sherlock Holmes shall never be forgotten.

To Watson from Victor Trevor (FINA)

My Dear Dr. Watson,

I write to you with the heaviest of hearts, having just learned through the morning papers of the terrible tragedy that has befallen our dear friend Sherlock Holmes. Though the years have passed since we were last in correspondence, the shock of this news has struck me as profoundly as if I had spoken with Holmes only yesterday.

You will perhaps remember me as Victor Trevor—Holmes mentioned me in connection with the Gloria Scott affair, though I suspect he was characteristically modest in his account. What he may not have told you is that I was his only friend during our university days, when his extraordinary mind was already beginning to show its remarkable powers of observation and deduction. Even then, I recognized that I was in the presence of someone quite exceptional, though I could never have imagined the heights of detection he would achieve, nor the service he would render to our nation and to justice itself.

I cannot pretend to comprehend the depth of your loss, my dear Watson. While I knew Holmes in his youth, you were his constant companion through the years of his greatest triumphs. You alone witnessed his methods, shared in his adventures, and understood the true nobility of his character. The partnership between you was, I believe, one of the finest friendships I have ever observed—each complementing the other in ways that made both stronger.

I find myself thinking of Holmes as he was in those early days at university—already possessed of that sharp wit and penetrating gaze, yet still young enough to be surprised by his own deductions. He was a singular man even then, often lonely despite his brilliance, or perhaps because of it. How fortunate he was to find in you not only a collaborator but a true friend who could appreciate both his genius and his humanity.

The papers speak of Professor Moriarty as Holmes's intellectual equal, and perhaps in the realm of pure mental capacity this was so. But what they cannot convey—what only those who knew Holmes truly understand—is that his greatest strength lay not merely in his analytical powers, but in his unwavering commitment to right and justice.

That Holmes chose to face this final confrontation, knowing full well the likely outcome, speaks to the courage that always lay beneath his sometimes cold exterior. He could not permit such a criminal to continue his work, even at the cost of his own life. There is something almost noble in the manner of his passing—locked in combat with his greatest adversary, ensuring that neither could continue to menace the world.

Please know, Dr. Watson, that though we may not have met often, I hold you in the highest regard for your loyalty and devotion to our friend. Your published accounts have given the world a true picture of Holmes's greatness, and for this, those of us who knew and loved him are deeply grateful. You have ensured that his memory and methods will live on, inspiring others to follow the path of reason and justice he illuminated so brilliantly.

If there is any comfort to be found in this dark hour, it may be in knowing that Holmes's work was not in vain. Should you find yourself in Norfolk and in need of quiet companionship or simply a change of scene, please know that you would be most welcome at Donnithorpe. Sometimes the countryside can provide a balm for grief that the city cannot offer.

Until that time, please accept my deepest sympathies and know that Holmes's memory is cherished by all who were fortunate enough to know him.
With profound respect and shared sorrow,

Victor Trevor

P.S. — I have taken the liberty of enclosing a small momento that Holmes left behind after his visit here years ago—a pipe he was fond of during our university days. I thought you might wish to have it as a remembrance.

To Irene Adler Norton from Holmes (EMPT)

My Dear Mrs. Norton,

It is with considerable emotion that I take pen to paper to address you, having learned from my dear friend Watson of the gracious letter of condolence you sent upon hearing the erroneous reports of my demise at Reichenbach Falls. That you, among all people, should have taken the time to express sympathy for my supposed passing moves me more deeply than I can adequately convey in mere words.

I write now with the dual purpose of expressing my profound gratitude for your kindness and of offering what I fear must seem an inadequate apology for the necessary deception that has caused you—and indeed all those who honored me with their regard—such unwarranted grief.

The circumstances that led to my feigned death were, I confess, as extraordinary as they were dire. Professor Moriarty, that Napoleon of crime whose malevolent influence you may recall from our past correspondence regarding certain continental affairs, had indeed cornered me at those fatal falls.

However, through a combination of preparation, mathematical calculation, and what I must honestly acknowledge was considerable fortune, I was able to survive our final encounter while allowing the world—including the criminal network that served him—to believe me dead.

This deception, painful as it was to maintain, proved essential to the dismantling of Moriarty's extensive organization. For three years, I traveled the globe under various disguises, pursuing his lieutenants and accomplices from Tibet to France, from the back alleys of Montpelier to the bazaars of Khartoum. Only recently did I return to London, drawn back by the murder of young Ronald Adair—a case that could only have been perpetrated by Colonel Sebastian Moran, Moriarty's second-in-command and the most dangerous man in London.

I understand that no explanation can fully justify the anguish my apparent death must have caused to those who knew me. To discover that someone you believed dead has in fact been alive and active in the world, choosing to remain hidden, must feel like a betrayal of the worst sort. I can only say that every day of my exile was marked by the knowledge that good people like yourself mourned unnecessarily, and this knowledge was perhaps the heaviest burden I carried during those years of wandering.

Your letter to Watson, which he showed me upon my return, revealed a warmth and generosity of spirit that I have always associated with your character. That you should remember our brief but memorable acquaintance with such regard, despite the rather unusual circumstances of our first meeting, speaks to the nobility that has always distinguished you among the remarkable individuals I have been privileged to encounter in my career.

I hope you will find it in your heart to forgive this elaborate deception, understanding that it was born not of callousness toward those who cared for my welfare, but of absolute necessity in bringing dangerous criminals to justice.

Should you find yourself in London at any future time, I would be deeply honored to receive you at Baker Street. Mrs. Hudson would be delighted to prepare tea, and I confess I would welcome the opportunity to apologize in person and to hear news of your life in France, which I trust continues to bring you the happiness and fulfillment you so richly deserve.

I remain, your most humble and penitent servant,

Sherlock Holmes
Consulting Detective

P.S. Watson sends his warmest regards and asks me to convey his hope that you will not judge him too harshly for his role in perpetuating this necessary fiction. His loyalty, though it demanded he maintain a painful silence, ultimately served the cause of justice—as, indeed, your own discretion and grace continue to do.

Letter to Holmes from Colonel Moran (EMPT)

My Dear Holmes,

How gratifying it must be for you to believe that these stone walls and iron bars have rendered me as harmless as a declawed cat. I write to you from my cell not in defeat, but in contemplation of the delicious irony that your greatest triumph shall prove to be the architect of your ultimate downfall.

You played your hand admirably, I confess. The ruse with the wax bust was particularly clever—though I suspect you learned such theatrical deceptions from your late nemesis, Professor Moriarty. How fitting that his methods should serve to ensnare his most devoted lieutenant. Yet in your moment of victory, dear Holmes, you have made a most fundamental error: you have assumed that my influence died with my imprisonment.

The Professor built an empire that stretched far beyond the gaslit streets of London, into the shadows of every great city from Calcutta to Constantinople. Did you truly believe that his organization would simply crumble because you eliminated its head? That my own network of associates would abandon their commitments merely because I now wear prison stripes?

You caught me red-handed with that air-gun of Von Herder's manufacture—a weapon that served me well in Afghanistan and served me better still in disposing of that troublesome young Adair. The boy was a fool to threaten exposure over a few hands of whist, but his death served a greater purpose: it brought you out of hiding. For that, at least, I am grateful.

But here is what you have failed to comprehend in your analytical mind: fear is a far more potent weapon than any air-gun. Every shadow that falls across your path, every footstep that echoes behind you in the fog, every knock upon your door at an unexpected hour—all will remind you that Sebastian Moran's reach extends far beyond these prison walls.

I have associates who owe me debts that transcend loyalty, Holmes. Men whose very survival depends upon my continued goodwill, even from within these confines. The underworld does not forget its debts, nor does it forgive those who consign its princes to cages.

Sleep well in your Baker Street lodgings, detective. Examine every letter that arrives by post. Question every new client who seeks your services. Wonder, each time you light your pipe, whether this breath might be your last. You have won this battle, but the war between us has only begun.

The Professor once said that you were the one man in London worthy of his steel. I find myself in complete agreement. You are indeed worthy— worthy of a death far more elaborate and lingering than the swift bullet I granted young Adair.

I remain, with the deepest professional respect and the most sincere personal enmity,

Colonel Sebastian Moran
Late of Her Majesty's Indian Army
Former Chief of Staff to Professor James Moriarty

P.S. - Do give my regards to the good Doctor Watson. I trust he recovered adequately from our brief encounter in that empty house. I should hate for him to suffer unnecessarily when my associates finally call upon you both.

To Holmes from John McFarlane (NORW)

Dear Mr. Holmes,

I find myself at a loss for words adequate to express the depth of my gratitude for your extraordinary intervention in what appeared to be my certain doom. When I burst into your chambers that morning, a desperate man convinced of his imminent arrest for murder, I could never have imagined that within mere days you would not only secure my freedom but expose one of the most diabolical schemes of revenge I have ever encountered in my legal practice.

Your immediate recognition that something was amiss with Oldacre's hastily written will—noting its careless composition as if written aboard a moving train—was the first ray of hope in what had seemed an utterly hopeless situation. While Inspector Lestrade and the entire Metropolitan Police were convinced of my guilt, you alone perceived the inconsistencies that would prove my salvation.

The discovery of those substantial payments to one "Mr. Cornelius" was, as you so astutely observed, indeed a "curious little point"—one that proved to be the key to unraveling Oldacre's elaborate masquerade. Your deduction that this mysterious beneficiary was none other than Oldacre himself, preparing for a new life under an assumed identity, demonstrated the remarkable powers of observation and reasoning for which you are so justly celebrated.

I confess that when Inspector Lestrade presented what appeared to be damning evidence—my own thumbprint upon the wall—even I began to doubt my own innocence for a terrifying moment. Yet your certainty that the print had not been present during your previous examination of the premises, and your brilliant stratagem of forcing Oldacre from his hiding place by means of a carefully controlled fire, revealed not only the man's survival but the full extent of his vengeful plot against my dear mother.

To think that this entire elaborate scheme—the false bequest, the staged murder, even the planted evidence—was orchestrated merely to satisfy an old grudge against a woman who had the wisdom to reject his advances decades ago! It chills me to consider how close such petty malice came to destroying my life and career entirely.

Your methods, though unorthodox, have restored not only my freedom but my faith in justice itself. Where conventional police work would have seen me hanged for a crime I did not commit, your unique approach to detection has revealed the truth in all its shocking complexity.

I am eternally grateful not only for your professional expertise but for your willingness to take on a case when all seemed lost. Your reputation for championing the innocent, even in the face of overwhelming evidence to the contrary, is well-deserved indeed.

Please know that should you ever require legal assistance, you need only call upon me. It would be my honor to serve you as you have so magnificently served me.

With the deepest respect and gratitude,

John Hector McFarlane
Solicitor

P.S. — I have taken the liberty of enclosing a small token of my appreciation, though I know no material gift could ever adequately reflect the magnitude of the service you have rendered me.

To Holmes from McFarlane's Mother (NORW)

My Dear Mr. Holmes,

No words can adequately express a mother's gratitude when her child has been snatched from the very jaws of destruction, yet I must attempt to convey the profound debt our family owes to your extraordinary abilities.

When my dear John came to us in such distress, proclaiming his innocence while all evidence seemed to point to his guilt, my heart was torn between absolute faith in my son's character and the terrible fear that justice might fail him. That you alone perceived the truth beneath Jonas Oldacre's elaborate deception is a testament to powers of observation that I can only regard as providential.

I must confess, Mr. Holmes, that learning of Oldacre's true motivation has filled me with a horror I can scarcely describe. To discover that my son nearly paid with his life for a grievance that has festered in that man's heart for more than two decades is almost beyond comprehension. That Jonas should harbor such malice over a broken engagement—one I terminated for reasons that time has only proven wise—speaks to a darkness of character that I failed utterly to perceive in my youth.

I was barely nineteen when Jonas first paid his attentions to me, and though he was considered by many to be a suitable match, something in his nature—a coldness, perhaps, or a hardness about the eyes when crossed—made me uneasy. My dear mother, God rest her soul, counseled me to trust my instincts, and I broke the engagement despite considerable social pressure to proceed. Jonas appeared to accept the decision with good grace at the time, even wishing me well in my future endeavors. How little I knew the depths of resentment that simple act would plant in his heart!

To think that he should wait all these years, watching my family from afar, waiting for an opportunity to strike at me through the person I hold most dear—it is a calculated cruelty that chills me to the bone. Had you not intervened with your brilliant deductions, my innocent boy would have been destroyed to satisfy this twisted desire for revenge against me.

The knowledge that my past judgment, however sound it may have been, led to such danger for my beloved son has weighed heavily upon my conscience. Your intervention has not only saved John but has also revealed the true character of a man I once thought merely unsuitable, showing him to be capable of the most heinous deception and malice.

Please know that you will always be welcome in our home, and that the prayers of a grateful mother will follow you in all your endeavors. Should you ever require anything within our modest power to provide, you need only ask.
With the deepest gratitude and highest regard,

Mrs. McFarlane

P.S. — I have instructed my cook to prepare a hamper of her finest preserves and baked goods, which John will deliver along with his own correspondence. It is but a trifling token of appreciation, yet it comes from a heart overflowing with thankfulness.

To Holmes from Elsie Cubitt (DANC)

Dear Mr. Holmes,

I hope this letter finds you and Dr. Watson in good health. I trust you will forgive my long silence, but I confess that these past months have been necessary for both my physical recovery and, perhaps more importantly, for the restoration of my troubled mind.

As I write these words in the very study where my dear Hilton once sat puzzling over those dreadful dancing figures, I am compelled to address the grave injustice I did you during our brief but tragic acquaintance. Though you solved the mystery with your usual brilliance and likely saved my life in doing so, I fear I must shoulder the burden of knowing that my deception—however well-intentioned—contributed to the very tragedy I had sought so desperately to prevent.

You see, Mr. Holmes, in the months that have passed since that terrible night, I have come to understand the full magnitude of my folly. My silence, born of shame and a misguided desire to protect my husband from the darkness of my past, ultimately became the very instrument of his destruction. Had I been forthright from the beginning, perhaps dear Hilton would still be alive today.

I realize now that when Hilton first contacted you, I should have overcome my pride and fear to tell you everything. I should have explained that the dancing men were no mere childish prank, but the sinister calling card of Abe Slaney and the Chicago gang from which I had fled. I should have told you of my father's criminal empire, of the blood money that had paid for my childhood comforts, and of my desperate escape from a world I could no longer bear to inhabit.

I have spent many sleepless nights wondering if Hilton might have understood, had I found the courage to confess my past to him. He was such a good man, Mr. Holmes—kind and gentle, with a heart large enough to forgive even the gravest sins. Perhaps he would have forgiven mine, just as he had already forgiven so much by marrying a woman whose origins he agreed never to question.

The irony is not lost on me that in my attempt to protect him from my shameful history, I instead delivered him directly into harm's way. My silence became complicity in his murder, and this knowledge weighs more heavily upon my soul than the bullet wound I inflicted upon myself in my moment of despair.

I understand from Inspector Martin that Abe Slaney has been changed to hard labor—a punishment that seems almost merciful when I consider the life sentence of guilt I have imposed upon myself. Yet I take some small comfort in knowing that he will never again terrorize another woman as he did me, and that the dancing men code will die with him behind prison walls.

I have decided to remain at Riding Thorpe Manor, Mr. Holmes. Many have suggested that I sell the estate and begin anew elsewhere, but I find I cannot abandon the place where Hilton was happiest.

In closing, I wish to express my profound gratitude for your extraordinary efforts on my behalf, despite my shameful lack of cooperation. Your brilliant deduction that led to Slaney's capture prevented him from escaping justice, and your careful examination of the crime scene ensured that I was not wrongly convicted of my husband's murder—though I remain guilty of causing it through my silence.

I hope that someday I may prove worthy of the second chance your intervention has afforded me. Until then, I remain,

Your most humble and eternally grateful servant,

Mrs. Elsie Cubitt
née Patrick

P.S. I have enclosed a small donation for your favorite charity, with the hope that some good might yet come from the fortune I inherited from my father's ill-gotten gains.

To Holmes from Inspector Martin (DANC)

Dear Mr. Holmes,

I trust you will pardon the liberty of a country inspector writing to you unsolicited, but I find myself compelled to set pen to paper regarding the extraordinary case of the Cubitt shooting, which you so brilliantly resolved some weeks ago.

In my twenty-three years of service with the Norfolk Constabulary, I have investigated murders, thefts, and all manner of criminal enterprise, and I confess I thought myself a reasonably competent officer of the law. Your demonstration at Riding Thorpe Manor, however, has shown me that there are depths to the science of detection that I had never imagined possible.

When I first arrived at the scene and saw poor Mr. Cubitt dead and his wife gravely wounded in that locked study, the case seemed as plain as daylight—a tragic murder-suicide born of domestic discord. Every man in my station would have sworn to it, and indeed, I was preparing the necessary paperwork to formally charge Mrs. Cubitt pending her recovery.

Then you arrived, Mr. Holmes, and within minutes of examining the scene, you had spotted that third bullet hole in the window sill—the one that none of us, despite our careful examination, had noticed. I have gone over that moment again and again in my mind, wondering how we could have missed such a crucial piece of evidence. It was right there before our eyes, yet it took your trained observation to recognize its significance.

But even more remarkable than your powers of observation was your deciphering of those dancing men symbols. When you first showed me the code and explained how you had broken it down—identifying the frequency patterns, recognizing that the flags indicated the ends of words, determining that "E" must be the most common letter—I confess I was utterly bewildered.

The manner in which you used that same code to lure Abe Slaney to his capture was nothing short of genius. To compose a message in the very cipher that had terrorized Mrs. Cubitt, knowing that only Slaney would understand it, demonstrated a mastery not just of deduction but of practical criminal psychology that left me speechless.

I have since shared your methods with my colleagues here at the station, and we have all resolved to be more thorough in our examination of crime scenes. You have taught us that what appears obvious may be merely the surface of a deeper truth, and that careful observation and logical analysis can reveal facts that escape even experienced eyes.

The successful resolution of this case has not gone unnoticed by my superiors. Chief Constable Bradshaw has asked me to convey his compliments and to extend an invitation for you to lecture to our officers should you ever find yourself in Norfolk again. We would be honored to learn from your methods, and I believe it would greatly improve the standard of detective work in our county.

I hope you will not think me presumptuous in saying that should your investigations ever bring you to Norfolk again, you will find the full cooperation and assistance of this office at your disposal. It would be both an honor and an education to work alongside you once more.

Please give my regards to Dr. Watson, whose detailed notes of the case have already become required reading among the detective staff here. I remain, with the greatest professional respect and admiration,

Your obedient servant,

Inspector Frederick Martin
Norfolk Constabulary

P.S. I have taken the liberty of sending along a bottle of Norfolk's finest ale, brewed locally here in Great Yarmouth. A small token of appreciation for opening this country inspector's eyes to the true art of detection.

To Holmes from Mrs. Violet Morton (SOLI)

My Dear Mr. Holmes,

I trust this letter finds you and Dr. Watson in excellent health and spirits. As the autumn leaves begin to turn, I find myself reflecting upon the extraordinary events of last April, and I feel compelled to write to you both with news of how my life has progressed since that dreadful business in Farnham.

I am delighted to inform you that Cyril and I were married in June, in a beautiful ceremony at St. Mary's Church in Kensington. The contrast between that joyous occasion and the horrible mockery of a marriage forced upon me by that villainous Woodley could not have been more pronounced. Thanks to your swift intervention and brilliant deductions, that shameful union was indeed annulled without difficulty, just as you assured me it would be.

Cyril and I have established ourselves in a charming little house not far from Hyde Park, where I continue to give music lessons to several pupils. The income, while modest, is perfectly adequate for our needs, and I find great satisfaction in my work. More importantly, I am now able to pursue my profession in complete safety and peace of mind, knowing that those who sought to harm me are no longer able to do so.

I was profoundly relieved to learn that both Williamson and Woodley have received substantial prison sentences for their crimes. Justice has been served, and I sleep soundly knowing that Woodley's brutish advances and Williamson's corrupt assistance in that forced ceremony have been properly punished by the law. I confess that I sometimes think of poor Mr. Carruthers with a mixture of pity and gratitude—while his initial intentions were certainly mercenary, his genuine affection ultimately led him to attempt my protection, albeit in that rather mysterious manner which caused me such distress at the time.

I cannot adequately express my gratitude to you both for your heroic efforts in my case. Your remarkable ability to unravel the truth behind Uncle Ralph's friends from South Africa, and to deduce the real motive behind the inheritance scheme, likely saved me from a fate far worse than I care to imagine. Dr. Watson's diligent investigation in Farnham provided crucial intelligence, while your own brilliant reasoning illuminated the entire sordid plot.

Had you not acted with such speed and determination, I shudder to think what my circumstances might be today. Instead, I write to you as a happily married woman, secure in the knowledge that truth and justice have prevailed through your efforts.

Please convey my warmest regards and eternal gratitude to Dr. Watson. I hope that you both continue to use your extraordinary talents to help others who find themselves in similar predicaments.

Your most grateful and devoted friend,

Mrs. Violet Smith Morton
(Formerly Miss Violet Smith)

To Carruthers from Violet Morton (SOLI)

Dear Mr. Carruthers,

I hope this letter finds you well and that you have found some measure of peace following the troubling events of last spring. I have debated for some time whether it would be appropriate to write to you, but I feel I must acknowledge the service you rendered me, despite the complicated circumstances that brought us together.

I am writing to inform you that I was married to Mr. Cyril Morton in June. We have established ourselves happily in London, where I continue to teach music and where we both feel blessed to have found such contentment together. I hope you will understand that it brings me great joy to share this news, as it represents the fulfillment of hopes that seemed so imperiled during those dark days in Farnham.

I must confess that I have given considerable thought to your role in the entire affair. While I cannot forget that your initial approach to my mother and myself was born of mercenary motives, I have come to understand that your feelings toward me became genuine, and that this transformation led you to act as my protector rather than my exploiter. The mysterious cyclist who so frightened me was, I now know, a guardian rather than a threat.

Your assistance to Mr. Holmes and Dr. Watson in locating me after that dreadful abduction was instrumental in my rescue. Without your knowledge of Woodley's haunts and Williamson's character, I shudder to think how much longer I might have remained in that terrible situation. For this service, I am truly grateful.

I hope you will forgive me for the necessity of refusing your proposal of marriage. I trust you understand that my heart had already been given to another, and that no consideration of fortune or security could have altered that fundamental truth. I believe you would not have wished me to accept you without the affection that such a union deserves.

I pray that you have found it in your heart to forgive Woodley's betrayal of your partnership, though I confess I am grateful that his treachery led to the exposure of the entire scheme. Perhaps there is some providence in how events unfolded, bringing justice to light while preventing greater harm to all concerned.

I hope that your daughter is well and that you have found a suitable music teacher to continue her education. Children are such a blessing and deserve every advantage we can provide them.

Please know that I hold no ill will toward you, and that I shall remember with gratitude your ultimate desire to protect rather than harm me. I wish you happiness and success in all your future endeavors.
With sincere regards,

Mrs. Violet Smith Morton
(Formerly Miss Violet Smith)

To Duke of Holdernesse from Hayes (PRIO)

Your Grace,

I write to you from my cell, where I await the hangman's rope for crimes that, while I committed them with my own hands, were set in motion by another's design. You know well of whom I speak, though his name shall not stain this page—not yet, at any rate.

The constables and that meddlesome detective Holmes believe they have unraveled the full truth of Lord Saltire's disappearance and poor Heidegger's death. But you and I both know there are threads still hidden in this tangled skein—threads that could destroy more than just a common innkeeper like myself.

I am not a learned man, Your Grace, but I am not fool enough to go quietly to my grave while my family starves and the true architect of this scheme continues to enjoy your protection and patronage. My Martha has been turned out of her position since my arrest, and my three young ones face the workhouse. This weighs heavier on my conscience than the German teacher's blood on my hands.

I propose a bargain, Your Grace—one that benefits us both. You know I could tell a different story to the magistrates, one that would see another man standing beside me on the scaffold. But I am prepared to hold my tongue and let the full weight of justice fall upon me alone, provided you show Christian mercy to my innocent family.

See that my Martha receives employment on one of your estates— something befitting her station, perhaps as cook or housekeeper. Ensure my children receive proper schooling and apprenticeships when they come of age. A modest pension for my widow would not be beyond your considerable means, and would purchase my eternal silence.

However, Your Grace, I am not so naive as to trust entirely in the honor of nobility. I have committed to paper a full and detailed account of recent events—names, dates, and the true sequence of who ordered what and when. This document resides in hands unknown to you, with strict instructions for its delivery to the proper authorities should any misfortune befall my family, or should they find themselves abandoned to poverty after my death.

I await your response, though I understand it cannot come directly. A word to my Martha that she has found new employment will suffice as your agreement. Should I hear nothing within a fortnight, I shall have no choice but to unburden my conscience fully to the authorities.

I remain, with necessary respect,

Reuben Hayes
The Fighting Cock Inn (formerly)

P.S. — I bear you no personal ill will, Your Grace. In your position, faced with such circumstances, I might well have made similar choices. But a man must look after his own, as I'm certain you understand.

To Duke of Holdernesse from Holmes (PRIO)

Your Grace,

I trust you will find it advisable to consign this letter to the flames immediately upon reading it, as its contents are of a nature that would be better left unrecorded in any permanent form.

The matter of your son's disappearance has been resolved to the satisfaction of all concerned parties, and I have no intention of disturbing the arrangements we have made. However, as a student of human nature—a necessary qualification in my profession—I feel compelled to offer you one final observation.

You have chosen to shield James Wilder from the consequences of his actions, sending him to the colonies where he might, as you put it, "start afresh." This decision springs from paternal affection, and I do not presume to judge it. Yet I would be remiss if I did not point out certain... probabilities that may arise from this course of action.

Young men transported to distant shores under such circumstances often carry with them not gratitude, but resentment. The weight of secrets, particularly those involving violence and deception, has a curious way of growing heavier with time rather than lighter. Australia is far from England, but it is not beyond the reach of confession, remorse, or—dare I say it—revenge.

Consider this: should James Wilder, in some future moment of desperation, disillusionment, or simple human weakness, choose to unburden himself of this affair, you will have no control over the manner or timing of such a revelation. The story that emerges may be colored by bitterness, distorted by memory, or sensationalized by whatever publication chooses to print it. Your legitimate heir, Lord Saltire, may find himself reading of his father's shame in some colonial newspaper, far from your protective influence.

Whereas, should you choose to address this matter now—quietly, through proper channels, with dignity intact—you retain agency over your own narrative. A man who acknowledges his mistakes, particularly when they spring from human failings rather than malice, often finds society more forgiving than he anticipated.

I make no prescriptions, Your Grace. The choice remains entirely your own. I merely suggest that truth, like water, has a tendency to find its way to the surface eventually. The question is whether it emerges as a controlled spring or an unpredictable flood.

Your son showed remarkable courage during his ordeal. Perhaps he has inherited more of your strength than either of you realize.

I remain, as always, your most obedient servant,

Sherlock Holmes
Consulting Detective

P.S. - Watson reminds me to mention that our fireplace draws particularly well at this time of year, should you require its services upon finishing this correspondence.

To Holmes from Inspector Hopkins (BLAC)

My Dear Mr. Holmes,

I trust this letter finds you in good health and spirits. I write to you now, some six weeks after the conclusion of the curious affair at Forest Row, to apprise you of the final resolution of the Black Peter case and to express once again my profound gratitude for your invaluable assistance.

As you predicted with your characteristic prescience, the trial of Patrick Cairns proceeded quite differently than I had initially anticipated. Your testimony, which I had fully expected would be required to establish the chain of evidence leading to Cairns' capture, proved entirely unnecessary. The harpooner, when faced with competent legal counsel, elected to plead self-defence rather than maintain his initial confession of murder.

The proceedings, I must report, were remarkably swift. Cairns' barrister painted a compelling picture of a man who had witnessed a heinous crime in 1883 and had spent years seeking justice for the murdered banker Neligan. When confronted with the brutal Captain Carey in that garden shed, Cairns claimed he had merely sought his rightful share of the stolen securities as compensation for his silence—a morally questionable position, perhaps, but one the jury seemed to understand given the circumstances of the original crime.

The defence argued most eloquently that when Carey became violent and threatening, Cairns acted purely in self-preservation, seizing the nearest weapon—ironically, the very harpoon that had served as decoration in Carey's macabre shrine to his whaling days. The jury, comprised largely of working men who seemed to sympathize with Cairns' position, deliberated for less than two hours.

Their verdict was both judicious and, I believe, just: guilty of attempted blackmail, but not guilty of murder. His Honour sentenced Cairns to six months' imprisonment for the blackmail charge—a sentence which, given the circumstances and the twelve years the man spent seeking to right a terrible wrong, seems quite reasonable.

I am pleased to report that young Neligan has been entirely vindicated and has, through his solicitors, begun the process of recovering what remains of his father's estate. The securities that Carey had not yet disposed of have been restored to their rightful ownership, providing the young man with at least some measure of financial security to begin rebuilding his life.

I must confess, Mr. Holmes, that this case has taught me a valuable lesson about the dangers of hasty judgment. Had I proceeded with charging Neligan based solely on the circumstantial evidence at hand, a grave injustice would have been perpetrated.

Your method of unmasking the true culprit—advertising for sailors under your assumed identity of Captain Basil—was nothing short of brilliant. I have studied your technique in this matter with great interest and hope to apply similar principles of deduction in future cases. The speed with which you identified Cairns among the respondents and secured his confession was truly remarkable to witness.

I am also grateful for your discretion regarding my initial arrest of young Neligan. While the Commissioner was naturally pleased with the successful resolution of the case, I am aware that your recommendation carried significant weight in ensuring that my professional reputation remained intact despite my earlier misjudgment. The case has enhanced my standing considerably within the Yard, though I am keenly aware that the credit belongs entirely to you.

With the highest regard and sincere gratitude, I remain, your obedient servant,

Stanley Hopkins
Inspector, Criminal Investigation Department
Metropolitan Police

P.S. - I have taken the liberty of ensuring that the evidence room maintains complete records of this case for your future reference, should you ever wish to review the particulars for your chronicles or professional studies.

To Holmes from John Neligan (BLAC)

My Dear Mr. Holmes,

I find myself at a complete loss for words adequate to express the depth of my gratitude for your extraordinary intervention in what Inspector Hopkins was pleased to call "the Black Peter affair." When I was led away in shackles, accused of a murder I did not commit, I feared that justice had abandoned me entirely. How wrong I was to despair, for justice had merely donned a deerstalker hat and taken residence at 221B Baker Street.

Your brilliant deduction that a man of my slight frame could never have driven a harpoon through the formidable chest of Captain Carey was the first ray of hope to penetrate the darkness that had enveloped my life. While Inspector Hopkins—though well-meaning—seemed content to close his case with my arrest, you saw what others could not: that the truth lay buried deeper than surface appearances would suggest.

I confess that when you appeared at Scotland Yard with Patrick Cairns in custody, I could scarcely believe my eyes. To learn that this harpooner had not only murdered Carey but had witnessed that blackguard's killing of my dear father was both a vindication and a revelation that shook me to my very core. For three long years, I have lived with the uncertainty of my father's fate, clinging to the faint hope that he might yet return from that ill-fated voyage to Norway. Your investigation has at last provided the closure I had almost ceased to believe possible.

The knowledge that Captain Carey murdered my father for those securities—securities that rightfully belonged to my father's creditors and might have restored some small measure of honor to our family name— fills me with a righteous anger. Yet I am profoundly grateful that the truth has emerged, however dark it may be. A painful truth is infinitely preferable to a comfortable lie.

I must also express my admiration for the ingenious method by which you apprehended Cairns. Your masquerade as "Captain Basil" seeking to recruit sailors was nothing short of inspired. That you could so quickly identify the guilty party from among the respondents speaks to powers of observation and deduction that are nothing less than miraculous to those of us possessed of more ordinary faculties.

Inspector Hopkins has since expressed his own gratitude for your assistance, though I suspect his professional pride may have suffered somewhat in the process. I hope you will not judge him too harshly—he is a dedicated officer, even if his methods lack your extraordinary insight.

As for myself, I find that I can now begin to rebuild my life with the weight of suspicion finally lifted from my shoulders. The scandal of the murder charge had made it impossible for me to secure employment in the banking profession, but your clearing of my name has restored possibilities I had thought forever lost.

I should very much like to call upon you at Baker Street at your convenience, both to thank you in person and to discuss the small matter of a fee for your services. I know that you do not undertake such cases for monetary gain, but I would be deeply honored if you would accept some token of my appreciation for the immeasurable service you have rendered.

Until such time as we may meet again, I remain, sir, with the utmost respect and gratitude,

Your most obliged and humble servant,

John Hopley Neligan

P.S. I have taken the liberty of sending a small case of port to your lodgings—a vintage that I believe you will find acceptable. It seems little enough recompense for a man who has given me back my freedom and my future.

To Holmes from Agatha (MILV)

Mr. Holmes (if that is even your true name),

I write this letter with hands that shake not from the cold of this December morning, but from the rage and sorrow that consume me. I know now who you are. I know what you have done. And I know that every tender word you spoke to me, every gentle touch, every promise of our future together was nothing more than the calculated performance of a man who sees other human beings as mere instruments to be used and discarded.

You made me love you. Do you understand the cruelty of that? You studied me as you might study a lock you intended to pick, learning exactly which words would make my heart flutter, which gestures would lower my defenses. You discovered that I dreamed of a small cottage with roses climbing the walls, and so you painted that very picture for me with your lies. You learned that I had grown up without a father's protection, and so you became my gentle guardian, promising me the security I had always craved.

When you took my hand in the garden behind the servants' quarters and asked me to be your wife, I felt as though my life was finally beginning. I, a mere maid, had somehow captured the heart of a kind and educated gentleman. I thanked God for this miracle every night in my prayers. I began planning our wedding in secret, choosing flowers, imagining the dress I might wear if I could afford such luxuries.

But it was all performance, wasn't it? Every stolen kiss, every whispered endearment, every moment when you gazed into my eyes with what I foolishly mistook for genuine affection—it was all just your method of ensuring I would grant you access to Mr. Milverton's study.

The night Mr. Milverton was murdered, I waited for you by the garden gate as we had arranged. I waited until dawn, sick with worry that some harm had befallen my beloved. When I learned of my employer's death, my first thought was fear for your safety. My second was how we might comfort each other through such a terrible time. I never imagined that you were the cause of it all. It was the cook who recognized your name when it appeared in the papers.

"That's your young man," she said, showing me the article that praised the famous detective Sherlock Holmes for his role in exposing Milverton's blackmail schemes. I laughed at first, thinking it impossible. But as I read on, the terrible truth crystallized. The man I had agreed to marry, the man who had held me in his arms and promised me a future, was the same cold, calculating detective who had needed entry to a blackmailer's house and found in me the perfect, willing accomplice.

I have always been a practical woman, Mr. Holmes. I understand that servants like myself are not the heroines of grand romances. But I believed—fool that I was—that love might still find me in some modest way. I believed that a man might see worth in me beyond my usefulness. You have taught me how thoroughly I was mistaken.

There have been dark moments since learning the truth, moments when the pain seemed too great to bear, when the future stretched before me like an endless corridor of loneliness and shame. You have taken from me not just my heart, but my ability to trust it. How am I ever to believe in love again, when I was so thoroughly deceived by its counterfeit?

I do not ask for your apology, for I doubt you are capable of genuine remorse. Men like you see the world as a vast chess board, and people like me as pawns to be moved and sacrificed as strategy demands. But I wanted you to know that your pawn was a human being, with a human heart that you broke as casually as you might snap a twig underfoot.

I hope your stolen papers were worth it, Mr. Holmes. I hope the satisfaction of your solved case compensates you for the knowledge that you purchased your success with a woman's love and trust. And I hope that someday, someone treats your heart with the same casual cruelty you showed mine, so that you might understand what you have done.

I remain, though no longer yours in any capacity,

Agatha

To Holmes from Lady Brackwell (CHAS)

My Dear Mr. Holmes,

I have just this morning read in The Times the most extraordinary and, I must say, welcome news of the untimely demise of that odious creature Charles Augustus Milverton. The report states that he was murdered in his own home at Appledore Towers under most mysterious circumstances. I cannot pretend to feel any sorrow at this development—indeed, quite the contrary.

As you will readily understand, Mr. Holmes, this turn of events has rendered your services in my particular matter entirely unnecessary. I am, of course, most sensible of the efforts you made on my behalf in attempting to negotiate with that blackguard. Though your mission was unsuccessful through no fault of your own, I recognize that you devoted both time and considerable personal risk to my cause. Pray inform me of whatever fee is appropriate for the services you rendered, and I shall see that it is forwarded to you immediately.

If I may be permitted one final observation, Mr. Holmes—and I trust you will understand the sentiment behind it—I confess that if it were within my power, I should very much like to shake the hand of whatever bold soul put an end to Milverton's career of villainy. Whoever this person may be, they have done a service not merely to myself, but to countless others who have suffered under that monster's cruel dominion. I pray they are never discovered, and that they know they have the gratitude of more victims than they could possibly imagine.

I remain, with the deepest appreciation for your discretion and professionalism in this delicate matter, sincerely yours,

Lady Eva Brackwell

P.S. I trust this letter finds Dr. Watson in good health as well. Please convey my regards to your faithful companion.

To Holmes from Lestrade (SIXN)

Dear Holmes,

I trust this letter finds you and Dr. Watson in good health following our rather eventful conclusion to the Napoleon bust affair. I confess that in all the excitement of apprehending Beppo and solving the mystery of poor Venucci's murder, a most important matter escaped my immediate attention.

Upon returning to the Yard and filing my report, it has been brought to my attention by the Commissioner himself that the Black Pearl of the Borgias, now in your possession, remains stolen property. While I have no doubt that your methods of recovery were both brilliant and entirely within the bounds of justice, the law requires that we return the pearl to its rightful owner through proper channels.

I am therefore writing to request that you bring the pearl to Scotland Yard at your earliest convenience, where we may ensure its safe transfer to the appropriate authorities. The Italian Embassy has already been contacted regarding the matter, and they are most eager to see this historic artifact restored to where it belongs.

I must say, Holmes, your ability to perceive the connection between Beppo's criminal history, the factory records, and the pearl's concealment continues to astound both myself and my colleagues. The Yard owes you a considerable debt of gratitude for solving this perplexing mystery.

You know, Mr. Holmes, this entire affair brings to mind a passage from the Good Book that my dear mother was fond of quoting. In the Gospel of Matthew, chapter thirteen, verse forty-four, it is written: "The kingdom of heaven is like treasure hidden in a field. When a man found it, he hid it again, and then in his joy went and sold all he had and bought that field."

How remarkably similar was your situation, Holmes! You knew of the treasure hidden within one of six busts, yet you could not simply claim it outright. Instead, like the man in the parable, you were compelled to seek out each "field"—each location where a bust resided—until you could lawfully acquire the final one and claim your prize. And indeed, like the righteous man in Scripture, your methods were entirely proper and Christian in nature, for you purchased that last bust with your own coin before breaking it open to reveal what lay within.

Please do call round when convenient—I shall ensure that the paperwork is handled with all due efficiency and that proper recognition is given to your invaluable assistance in this matter.

With sincere appreciation and respect,

G. Lestrade
Inspector, Criminal Investigation Department
Scotland Yard

P.S. — The Commissioner has asked me to extend his personal thanks for your continued cooperation with the Metropolitan Police. Your assistance in matters both great and small has not gone unnoticed in the highest quarters.

To Holmes from Mr. Sandeford (SIXN)

Dear Mr. Holmes,

I write to you in a state of considerable indignation and with the gravest accusations regarding your recent conduct in the matter of the Napoleon bust which you purchased from my residence. Having since learned the true circumstances surrounding your visit and subsequent acquisition of my property, I find myself compelled to address what I can only describe as a most unconscionable deception.

You presented yourself at my door under the pretense of being a collector with a particular fondness for such artifacts. Yet I now understand that you acted with full knowledge—knowledge gained through your official association with Scotland Yard and Inspector Lestrade—that my seemingly worthless plaster cast contained the famous black pearl of the Borgias. In essence, sir, you engaged in what the financial markets would term "insider trading," utilizing privileged information obtained through your quasi-official capacity to defraud me of valuable property.

Your conduct, Mr. Holmes, represents a gross violation of the trust placed in you by the Metropolitan Police and an unconscionable abuse of your position. You knowingly allowed me to part with an item worth thousands of pounds for a mere pittance, all while possessing information that was wholly unavailable to me as a private citizen. This constitutes nothing short of fraud, perpetrated under color of official authority.

I have consulted with my solicitor, Mr. Pemberton of Gray's Inn, who confirms that your actions may well constitute criminal fraud. The fact that you operated with knowledge obtained through police channels while presenting yourself as a private collector seeking to purchase my property under false pretenses establishes both the deceptive nature of the transaction and your abuse of privileged information.

Therefore, I demand the following remedy: You shall immediately arrange for the sale of the recovered pearl through proper channels and divide the proceeds equally between us. This represents the only equitable resolution to your duplicitous conduct. Should you fail to accede to this reasonable demand within fourteen days of receipt of this letter, I shall have no recourse but to pursue the matter through both civil and criminal proceedings.

I had heard tell of your reputation for brilliance, Mr. Holmes, but I confess I had not anticipated such a capacity for deception and self-enrichment at the expense of innocent parties. Your conduct in this matter falls far short of the standards one would expect from a gentleman, let alone one who trades upon his reputation for justice and fair dealing.

I await your immediate response and compliance with my demands. Your most displeased correspondent,

Mr. Harold Sandeford

P.S. - I trust you will not insult my intelligence by claiming ignorance of the pearl's presence, given the methodical nature with which you tracked and acquired each bust in the series. Your actions demonstrate clear premeditation and calculated exploitation of your privileged position.

To Bannister from Professor Soames (3STU)

My Dear Bannister,

I write to you this evening following the resolution of the unfortunate affair regarding the Fortescue Scholarship examination, and I feel it necessary that we speak plainly about the events that have transpired and their implications for our continued association.

I wish you to understand, first and foremost, that I do not write from a position of anger or vindictiveness. Mr. Holmes' investigation has made clear to me the circumstances that led to your actions, and I am not insensible to the difficult position in which you found yourself. Your long acquaintance with young Gilchrist and his family, stretching back as it does to his childhood, naturally created bonds of affection and loyalty that I cannot and do not condemn.

However, Bannister, we must address the matter directly: your assistance in concealing young Gilchrist's transgression represented a fundamental breach of the trust that exists between us as employer and servant. When you discovered the true nature of the disturbance in my study, your first duty was to inform me immediately, regardless of your personal feelings toward the perpetrator.

I have given considerable thought to this matter, and I believe I understand the conflict that must have raged within your conscience. You saw a young man of promise about to ruin his future through a moment of weakness, and your natural impulse was to protect him from the consequences of his folly. This speaks well of your character, even as it speaks poorly of your judgment in the circumstances.

The question now before us is whether we can continue our professional relationship, and under what terms. I am prepared to retain your services, Bannister, for you have served me faithfully in all other respects for many years. Your knowledge of my habits and requirements, your careful attention to the maintenance of my chambers and the organization of my academic materials, and your general competence in household matters are not easily replaced. Moreover, I recognize that this situation presented you with an almost impossible choice between competing loyalties.

However, if you are to remain in my employ, we must establish a clear understanding: your primary loyalty must be to me and to your duties as my assistant. I do not ask you to be heartless or to abandon your natural sympathies for those you have known and cared for over the years. What I do require is that you recognize the distinction between your private sentiments and your professional duties, and that when these come into conflict, you choose your responsibilities to your employer above all other considerations.

Young Gilchrist's decision to remove himself from the university and seek service with the colonial police suggests that he has accepted the consequences of his actions with some measure of dignity. In this, perhaps, your counsel to him proved beneficial. But you must understand that it was not your place to determine what those consequences should be, nor to shield him from the natural results of his choices through deception.

I trust that this frank discussion will serve to clarify our mutual expectations going forward. You are welcome to continue in my service under these conditions, but I must have your assurance that you understand and accept them completely.

I await your response, and I hope that we may continue our association on this clearer foundation. The work we do here at the college is important, and it requires that all of us—faculty, staff, and students alike—maintain the highest standards of integrity and loyalty to our shared mission.

With continued regard, though tempered by necessary firmness,

Professor Hilton Soames
The College of St Luke's

Written in confidence, for your consideration alone.

To Holmes from Hilton Soames (3STU)

My Dear Mr. Holmes,

I find myself compelled to take pen to paper this evening to express my most sincere gratitude for your exceptional service in resolving the distressing matter of the Fortescue Scholarship examination. Your discretion and remarkable deductive abilities have saved not only the integrity of our academic institution, but have handled a most delicate situation with the sensitivity it required.

When I first approached you with this troubling affair, I confess I harboured grave concerns about the potential scandal that might befall our college. The thought that one of our students might have attempted such deception filled me with profound unease. Your methodical investigation, conducted with such careful attention to the smallest details—from pencil shavings to those peculiar balls of clay—demonstrated a thoroughness that puts even our most meticulous scholars to shame.

I must admit that your conclusion regarding young Gilchrist came as both a shock and, in some measure, a relief. A shock, naturally, to learn that such a promising student—one whose athletic prowess and academic potential had marked him as exceptional—could succumb to such temptation. His decision to seek service with the Rhodesian Police may yet prove the making of him, providing the discipline and purpose that academic life seemed unable to instill.

I must also acknowledge the wisdom of your approach regarding Bannister. The old fellow's loyalty to the boy, stemming as it does from years of acquaintance with the family, is both touching and understandable. That he chose to aid in concealing the truth rather than expose his young master immediately speaks to a divided heart—torn between duty to the institution and affection for the lad. Your decision to treat this matter with compassion rather than harsh judgment reflects both justice and mercy.

Should you ever require the resources of our university library for your research into early English charters, or should any academic matter prove useful to your investigative work, please know that you have earned both my personal gratitude and the lasting respect of this institution. The intellectual rigor you brought to bear upon this problem rivals that of our finest scholars, and your conclusions were reached with a precision that would be the envy of any researcher.

I remain, dear Mr. Holmes, your most grateful and obliged servant,

Professor Hilton Soames
Lecturer in Greek and Latin
The College of St Luke's

P.S. - I trust that Dr. Watson's account of these proceedings, should he choose to chronicle them, will maintain the discretion that marked your investigation. The young man deserves the chance to rebuild his character without the burden of public notoriety.

To Holmes from Student Gilchrist (3STU)

Dear Mr. Holmes,

I trust this letter finds you in good health and that your remarkable career continues to flourish. I write to you from the sun-baked veldt of Rhodesia, where I have been serving as a constable with the British South Africa Police for the better part of a year now.

You may recall our encounter at the College of St Luke's regarding the unfortunate incident surrounding the Fortescue Scholarship examination. I have often reflected upon that time, particularly in recent weeks, as your name has become something of a legend among my fellow officers here. Tales of your extraordinary deductive powers and your solutions to the most baffling mysteries have reached even this distant outpost of the Empire. Inspector Morrison, my commanding officer, speaks with genuine admiration of your methods, having read Dr. Watson's accounts in the Strand Magazine. "There's no one quite like Sherlock Holmes," he declared just last evening over dinner.

"The man sees what others cannot even imagine to look for."

I must confess, Mr. Holmes, that hearing such praise fills me with a curious mixture of pride and humility. Pride, because I was privileged to witness your genius firsthand during that difficult period at university. Humility, because I was the subject of your investigation—though I prefer to think of myself as having been caught up in circumstances rather beyond my control.

When my fellow officers ask how I came to know of you, I tell them of the case you solved at our college—though naturally, I frame the matter somewhat differently than you might. I explain that there was a concerning incident involving examination papers, and that you were called in to investigate possible academic impropriety. I mention that your powers of observation were extraordinary—how you could deduce so much from the smallest details, how you saw through the confusion to the heart of the matter.

What I do not mention, of course, is the particular nature of my own involvement. I prefer to characterize myself as having been present during your investigation rather than as its primary subject. After all, the important matter is that your methods were so effective, and that you were able to restore order and confidence to our academic community. The details of how certain individuals may have found themselves in compromising circumstances seem less relevant than the masterful way you untangled the whole affair.

The life out here has been good for me, Mr. Holmes. The responsibilities of police work, the discipline of military service, and the challenges of frontier life have provided exactly the direction I needed. I find that the physical demands suit my athletic nature, while the moral clarity required in law enforcement has helped me develop a stronger character than I possessed during my university days. Each day brings new challenges, from tracking cattle thieves to maintaining order among the miners, and I am proud to say that I have proven myself capable and reliable.

I often think of that moment when you concluded your investigation. Your understanding of human nature was as remarkable as your deductive abilities. You recognized that sometimes young men make poor choices in moments of weakness, and that such lapses need not define their entire futures. The path you helped me find—leaving university to seek honest service—has proven to be precisely what I required.

Please give my regards to Dr. Watson, whose accounts of your cases provide welcome entertainment during the long evenings on patrol. His literary skills do justice to your remarkable abilities.

I remain, with the greatest respect and gratitude,

Your obedient servant,

Constable J. Gilchrist
British South Africa Police
Rhodesia

To Holmes from Inspector Hopkins (GOLD)

My Dear Holmes,

I write to inform you of the latest developments in the Yoxley Old Place affair, which concluded so dramatically in your presence three days past.

Following your remarkable exposition of the case and the tragic death of the woman who identified herself as Anna Coram, I have this morning executed a warrant for the arrest of Professor Coram on charges of harboring a fugitive from justice. The evidence you uncovered—particularly the concealed cupboard and the professor's own admissions regarding his knowledge of the woman's identity—provides sufficient grounds for prosecution under the relevant statutes.

The professor initially maintained his innocence, claiming he acted under duress and feared for his life should he refuse his wife sanctuary. However, the Crown's position is clear: regardless of personal circumstances, he knowingly concealed a person who had confessed to homicide and was, by her own account, a fugitive from Russian justice.

I must inform you that your testimony will be required at the upcoming proceedings. The coroner's inquest into the death of Willoughby Smith has been scheduled for the 28th instant, and you will be called upon to provide evidence regarding:

- Your examination of the crime scene and the deceased
- The circumstances of your discovery of the concealed woman
- Her voluntary confession to the killing of Smith
- The manner and cause of her subsequent death by self-administered poison

Additionally, should the case against Professor Coram proceed to trial—which appears likely given the strength of evidence—the prosecution will require your testimony regarding the professor's complicity in harboring his wife.

I confess, Holmes, that this case has left me with mixed feelings. While justice must be served, one cannot help but feel sympathy for all parties involved in this tragic affair. The woman's devotion to the innocent Alexis, her husband's terrible betrayal years ago, and poor Smith's unfortunate discovery of her desperate search—it reads more like a Russian novel than a criminal matter.

The papers you mentioned—those that the woman claimed would exonerate her beloved Alexis—have been forwarded through proper diplomatic channels to the Russian authorities, as per your recommendation. I trust this was the honorable course, given the circumstances of how they came into our possession.

I shall call upon you within the fortnight to discuss the particulars of your testimony and to ensure all procedural matters are properly arranged.
As always, I remain grateful for your invaluable assistance in bringing this complex matter to its resolution.

Your colleague in the pursuit of justice,

Stanley Hopkins
Inspector
Criminal Investigation Department
Scotland Yard

P.S. I have taken the liberty of ensuring that the woman received proper burial, despite the circumstances of her death. It seemed the decent thing to do, given the tragic nature of her story.

To Godfrey Staunton from Holmes (MISS)

My Dear Mr. Staunton,

It is with the deepest regret that I write to you following the tragic circumstances which brought our paths to cross. I felt compelled to offer my sincere condolences on the loss of your beloved wife, and to clarify the nature of my involvement in what must have appeared to be an unwelcome intrusion upon your most private grief.

Please be assured that I was not, as Dr. Armstrong understandably feared, acting as an agent for your uncle, Lord Mount-James. My investigation was undertaken solely at the earnest request of your friend and teammate, Mr. Cyril Overton, whose concern for your welfare was both genuine and profound. The young man was beside himself with worry when you disappeared so suddenly on the eve of the match, fearing that some harm had befallen you. His only thought was for your safety and wellbeing.

Had I known the true nature of your absence—that you were keeping vigil beside your dying wife—I would never have pursued the matter with such determination. The revelation of your secret marriage and the terrible burden you carried these many months has moved me greatly.

Dr. Armstrong spoke truly when he called you a good man, and I hope that in time you will find solace in knowing that your wife's final hours were blessed by your presence and devotion. No uncle's fortune, however vast, could compare to the wealth of love you gave to her.

I trust that your friends, particularly Mr. Overton, will provide you with the support you need in this dark hour. Should you ever have need of my services in any matter, you may call upon me without hesitation.

With deepest sympathy and respect,

Sherlock Holmes
Consulting Detective

To Jeremy Dixon from Holmes (MISS)

My Dear Dixon,

I write to express my most sincere gratitude for your generous loan of Pompey during the recent affair concerning the missing Cambridge three-quarter. Your noble hound proved to be nothing short of indispensable in bringing the matter to its resolution.

As you may recall, Dr. Watson and I found ourselves in considerable difficulty when tracking the movements of Dr. Leslie Armstrong proved beyond conventional methods. The good doctor's intimate knowledge of Cambridge and his determination to protect his patient's privacy had rendered our usual techniques of surveillance quite futile.

The stratagem of applying aniseed to the carriage wheels, combined with Pompey's unwavering dedication to the scent, allowed us to follow Dr. Armstrong's route with precision that would have been impossible through any other means. Without your dog's assistance, I confess that young Staunton's whereabouts might have remained a mystery until it was far too late to provide him the support he so urgently needed during his wife's final hours.

Pompey conducted himself with the utmost professionalism throughout the enterprise, displaying both the intelligence and tenacity that you assured me he possessed. His contribution to this case cannot be overstated.

I trust that Pompey has returned to you in good health and spirits, and that he has received the extra portion of his favorite treats that such exemplary service surely merits.

I remain, dear Dixon, your most grateful servant,

Sherlock Holmes
Consulting Detective

To Holmes from Stanley Hopkins (MISS)

My Dear Mr. Holmes,

I trust this letter finds you and Dr. Watson in excellent health following your recent expedition to Cambridge. I write to express my profound admiration for your handling of the Staunton affair, which has left me quite speechless with wonder at your methods.

When young Overton first came to me in such distress about his missing three-quarter, I confess I was somewhat at a loss. A grown man disappearing on the eve of the Varsity match seemed more a matter for the University authorities than Scotland Yard. Yet something in the young man's earnestness compelled me to direct him to Baker Street, knowing that if anyone could unravel such a puzzle, it would be you.

What followed has reinforced my conviction that your methods, however unconventional they may appear to us mere mortals of the Yard, possess a brilliance that borders on the supernatural. Your deduction that the telegram held the key, your persistent pursuit of Dr. Armstrong despite his obvious reluctance to cooperate, and your refusal to be deterred by his attempts to throw you off the scent—all of this displayed your characteristic tenacity.

But it was your masterstroke with the aniseed that has left me quite astounded. Such elegant simplicity! To think that a few drops of that pungent substance, applied to the wheels of Armstrong's carriage, would enable you to track him across the countryside using nothing more than a keen-nosed hound. The method was so beautifully straightforward, yet I doubt a dozen of us at the Yard would have conceived of such a solution in a month of Sundays.

When I learned the true circumstances—that poor Staunton had been torn between his duty to his team and his devotion to his dying wife, that he had endured months of anguish in secret to preserve his inheritance— I was deeply moved. Your investigation revealed not a scandal or a crime, but a tragedy of the most poignant sort. The young man's character emerged not diminished but enhanced, his absence explained not by frivolity but by the most profound of human loyalties.

I particularly admire how you handled the delicate matter of Lord Mount-James. That the miserly old gentleman should have driven his nephew to such secrecy through his own avarice speaks poorly of him, yet you managed the affair with such discretion that the family's private sorrows remained private.

Your ability to see through the surface complexities to the human heart beneath continues to inspire those of us who labour in the more mundane corridors of criminal investigation. While we at the Yard pride ourselves on our methodical approach, your flashes of insight—combined with such practical innovations as your canine tracking method—remind us that detection is as much art as science.

I hope that the Varsity match proceeded despite the unfortunate circumstances, and that young Overton found a suitable replacement for his star player. Though I suspect no substitute could have matched Staunton's skill, the team surely played with extra heart knowing the noble sacrifice their missing teammate had made.

Please convey my regards to Dr. Watson, whose steadfast companionship in your adventures continues to be a source of admiration to all who know of your partnership. With the utmost respect and professional admiration,

I remain, dear Holmes, Your most obedient servant,

Stanley Hopkins
Inspector, Criminal Investigation Department
Scotland Yard

To Holmes from Stanley Hopkins (ABBE)

My Dear Holmes,

I trust this letter finds you and Dr. Watson in good health. I write to express my sincere gratitude for your assistance with the unfortunate affair at Abbey Grange. Your insights, as always, proved invaluable in bringing the matter to what appears to be a satisfactory conclusion.

The case has been officially closed, with the death of Sir Eustace Brackenstall attributed to the Randall gang during the course of their burglary. Lady Mary's testimony, corroborated by her maid Theresa, provides a clear account of events, and the evidence—the missing silverware, the wine glasses, the method of binding—all seems to support their version of that terrible night.

Yet I find myself writing to you with a peculiar sense of unease that I cannot entirely shake. Perhaps it is merely the nature of dealing with such violent crime, or the melancholy atmosphere that seemed to pervade that grand house, but something continues to niggle at the back of my mind.

You seemed particularly interested in examining those knots around Lady Mary's wrists, and I recall you making some observation about the wine glasses that I confess I did not fully appreciate at the time. There was also that rather abrupt conclusion to your investigation—quite unlike your usual thoroughness, if you'll forgive my saying so. One moment you were examining every detail with your customary precision, and the next you were declaring the case closed and making ready to depart for London.

The two ladies' testimony is, of course, entirely consistent, and I have no grounds whatsoever to doubt their word. Lady Mary struck me as a woman of obvious refinement and courage, having endured what must have been a terrifying ordeal. The maid, Theresa, clearly devoted to her mistress, provided corroborating details without contradiction.

And yet... and yet I cannot help but feel that there are aspects of this case that remain opaque to me. Call it a policeman's instinct, perhaps, but I have learned over the years to trust such feelings, even when I cannot articulate their basis.

I hope you will not think me presumptuous in asking whether you formed any different conclusions about the events at Abbey Grange than those reflected in our official report. If there are elements of this case that I have failed to perceive or properly understand, I should be most grateful for your guidance. Not for the purposes of reopening the investigation, you understand, but simply to satisfy my own professional curiosity and perhaps to improve my methods for future cases.

I realize I may be troubling you unnecessarily with what are perhaps nothing more than the shadows cast by a particularly grim case, but your opinion on these matters has always been invaluable to me.

I remain, as ever, deeply appreciative of your assistance and look forward to our next collaboration.

Your obedient servant,

Stanley Hopkins
Inspector
Criminal Investigation Department

P.S. - I trust the Randall gang will be apprehended soon. Their methods seem to be growing increasingly bold and violent.

To Stanley Hopkins from Holmes (ABBE)

My Dear Hopkins,

Your letter arrived this morning, and I must say that I find your continued thoughtfulness regarding the Abbey Grange affair both commendable and entirely unsurprising. A policeman's instinct is indeed a precious commodity, and you would be wise never to dismiss those nagging doubts that occasionally trouble the mind of a thorough investigator.

You ask whether I formed different conclusions about the events at Abbey Grange, and I can tell you quite honestly that I am entirely satisfied with how the case has been resolved. The official account provides a complete and coherent explanation of Sir Eustace Brackenstall's death, and all parties involved have found their expectations met by this conclusion.

That said, your instincts serve you well, Hopkins. If you feel there are stones left unturned, by all means continue to examine them. A detective who ignores his intuition is like a musician who refuses to trust his ear. However, I would counsel you to consider carefully what you hope to achieve through further investigation, and whether the pursuit of every last detail necessarily serves the cause of justice.

You mention that you observed my particular interest in certain physical evidence—the knots, the wine glasses. Such details are always worth noting, as they often reveal more about the character and background of those involved than might initially appear. In this instance, they served to confirm my impression that the testimony provided was... shall we say, complete in all essential particulars.

I have found, over the years, that there are occasions when the official version of events, even if it may not encompass every nuance of what transpired, nonetheless achieves the most satisfactory resolution for all concerned. The law, Hopkins, is a blunt instrument, and justice—true justice—sometimes requires a more delicate touch.

The two ladies at Abbey Grange struck me as persons of character who had endured considerable hardship. Lady Mary, in particular, seemed to me a woman who had suffered greatly and deserved whatever peace might now come to her. If their account allows them to move forward with their lives while providing the authorities with a reasonable explanation for a tragic event, perhaps that is outcome enough.

You are, of course, free to pursue whatever course your professional judgment dictates. I merely suggest that sometimes the most admirable quality in a detective is knowing when a case has reached its proper conclusion, even if a few minor mysteries remain unsolved.

I trust this addresses your concerns, though I suspect your analytical mind will continue to turn over the details as is your nature
Yours very truly,

Sherlock Holmes
Consulting Detective

P.S. - Watson sends his regards. He was particularly impressed by your handling of the initial crime scene examination.

To Lady Hilda from Holmes (SECO)

My Dear Lady Hilda,

I trust this letter finds you in restored spirits following the recent conclusion of the unfortunate affair concerning the missing correspondence. I write to express my sincere appreciation for your ultimate candour and cooperation, which proved instrumental in bringing this delicate matter to its satisfactory resolution.

Your courage in confessing the full particulars of your involvement, though it must have caused you considerable distress, demonstrated both wisdom and integrity.

If I may venture a word of counsel, gleaned from long observation of human nature and its frequent entanglements: there exists a certain peril in committing our deepest sentiments to written form. Letters, once written, become evidence—not merely of affection or admiration, but of vulnerabilities that unscrupulous individuals may exploit.

As your recent tribulation so clearly demonstrates, even the most innocent expressions of feeling can become weapons in the wrong hands. You have shown admirable strength throughout this ordeal, and I have every confidence that you will emerge from it with wisdom gained. The matter is now concluded, and you may rest assured of my continued discretion in all aspects of this affair.

I remain, with the highest regard for your courage and character,

Your most obedient servant,

Sherlock Holmes
Consulting Detective

P.S. - In the spirit of the counsel I have offered above, I would suggest that once you have read this letter and absorbed its contents, you consign it to the flames. Some communications are best preserved only in memory.
Private & Confidential

To Holmes from Beryl Stapleton (HOUN)

Dear Mr. Holmes,

I write to you with a heart heavy with shame and remorse, knowing full well that words can never undo the terrible wrongs that have been committed. The revelation of my husband's true identity and his murderous schemes has left me devastated, not only by his betrayal of my trust, but by my own complicity in his wicked plans.

I must confess to you, Mr. Holmes, that I was not entirely ignorant of Jack's intentions, though I pray you will believe me when I say I never fully comprehended the depths of his evil until it was too late. When he first revealed to me that he was a Baskerville and spoke of claiming what he called his "rightful inheritance," I was foolish enough to believe he meant to pursue some legal claim. By the time I understood the true horror of his methods—the murder of poor Sir Charles and his designs upon Sir Henry—I found myself trapped in a web of fear and intimidation.

You witnessed yourself, Mr. Holmes, how my husband controlled me through violence and threats. The bruises he left upon my arms were nothing compared to the terror he inspired in my very soul. Yet I know this is no excuse for my silence, and I am tormented by the knowledge that my cowardice may have endangered innocent lives.

I did try, in my small way, to warn Sir Henry. Do you remember when I approached him on the moor and begged him to leave this place? It was the only act of defiance I dared, knowing that Jack was watching my every move. I hoped against hope that this young man would heed my warning and escape the fate that befell his uncle. When he did not leave, I was consumed with despair, knowing I lacked the courage to speak more plainly.

The night you and Dr. Watson confronted us on the moor, when that terrible hound came charging through the fog, I felt a mixture of horror and relief—horror at seeing Jack's monstrous plan in its full, terrifying reality, and relief that finally, finally, the truth would come to light. When

I saw that poor beast fall dead, I knew that Jack's reign of terror was at an end.

I throw myself upon your mercy, Mr. Holmes, and upon the forgiveness of Sir Henry Baskerville. I know I do not deserve absolution, but I hope that my circumstances—trapped as I was in a marriage to a man I grew to fear and despise—might earn me some small measure of your understanding. I have been living as a prisoner in my own home, and now, though Jack has paid the ultimate price for his crimes, I find myself free but utterly alone.

I am making arrangements to leave Devon permanently. I cannot bear to remain in this place where so much evil was plotted and carried out. I intend to return to my native Costa Rica, where perhaps I might find some peace and attempt to rebuild my shattered life.

Please convey to Sir Henry Baskerville my deepest, most heartfelt apologies. If there is any service I can render to make amends for the terror and suffering my silence helped to cause, I am entirely at his disposal. I pray that in time, both you and he might find it in your hearts to forgive a woman who was more weak than wicked, more coward than conspirator.

I remain, with profound regret and lasting gratitude for your intervention,

Beryl Stapleton

P.S. I have left with the local constabulary all of Jack's papers and effects that might aid in any further investigation. Among them you will find his true genealogy, which confirms his Baskerville lineage and may help explain the depths of his obsession with the family inheritance.

To Holmes from Henry Baskerville (HOUN)

My Dear Mr. Holmes,

I find myself at a loss for words adequate to express my profound gratitude to both you and Dr. Watson for the extraordinary service you have rendered to me and to the memory of my poor uncle, Sir Charles. When I first arrived from Canada to claim my inheritance, I could never have imagined the web of deception and murder that surrounded this ancient estate.

Had it not been for your remarkable powers of deduction and Dr. Watson's steadfast companionship during those dark weeks at Baskerville Hall, I have no doubt that I would have suffered the same terrible fate as my uncle. The thought that I walked so unknowingly into Stapleton's trap—that I might have perished on the moor, torn apart by that phosphorus-painted beast—sends a chill through my very bones.

Your methods, Mr. Holmes, seemed almost supernatural themselves. To think that while Dr. Watson was so faithfully watching over me at the Hall, you were conducting your own investigation in secret, living rough on the moor and gradually piecing together Stapleton's heinous scheme!

The revelation that our "naturalist neighbor" was in fact a Baskerville himself, driven by greed to murder his own relations, will haunt me for years to come. And poor Miss Stapleton—how she must have suffered, knowing her husband's true nature yet feeling powerless to stop him.

Thanks to your intervention, the Baskerville curse has been revealed for what it truly was—not some ancient supernatural punishment, but the calculated malice of a living man. The moor no longer holds terror for me, and I can now take up residence at the Hall with peace of mind, knowing that the real threat has been eliminated.

I should like to invite you both to visit me here at Baskerville Hall at your earliest convenience, under far more pleasant circumstances than our last encounter. The Hall feels quite different now—the shadows seem less deep, and the very air appears clearer. I believe even the servants walk with lighter steps, knowing that the family's dark legacy has finally been laid to rest.

Please accept my enclosed check as a small token of my immense gratitude. I know that no sum could adequately repay you for preserving my life, but I hope you will allow me this gesture of appreciation.

With the deepest respect and eternal gratitude,

Sir Henry Baskerville

P.S. I have taken the liberty of having the remains of that accursed hound properly disposed of. The taxidermied head will make a fitting reminder in my study of how logic and courage can triumph over even the most elaborate deception.

To Holmes from Cecil Barker (VALL)

Dear Mr. Holmes,

I write to you from Argentina with thoughts that have been troubling me greatly since I sent that sorrowful telegram regarding poor Jack's fate aboard the Palmyra. The more I reflect upon the circumstances of his disappearance, the more I find myself wondering if we have not all been witness to yet another of Jack Douglas's masterful deceptions.

You, of all people, will appreciate the reasoning behind my suspicions. Having been intimately involved in Jack's previous staged death at Birlstone, I am perhaps uniquely positioned to recognize his methods. The man who could turn his own attempted murder into an opportunity for rebirth is certainly capable of engineering his own disappearance from a ship's deck.

I have had a chance to speak to Ivy Douglas since I sent that telegram to you, and according to her, Jack had grown increasingly anxious during our voyage, frequently scanning the passenger manifest and studying the faces of our fellow travelers. On more than one occasion, he expressed concern that even in South America, the long arm of the Scowrers might reach him. "A man can only die so many times, Cecil," he told me just two days before his supposed loss overboard.

I understand that the night of his disappearance was calm—hardly the sort of weather in which an experienced man would accidentally fall from a ship. Jack was an excellent swimmer, having spent his youth near the California coast, and was far too cautious to venture near the rails unaccompanied in darkness. Yet the crew found no trace of him, despite immediate searches.

I have made inquiries at several ports along our route, and while I found no direct evidence of Jack's survival, there were reports of a man matching his description purchasing supplies in Montevideo—supplies that would serve a man planning to disappear into the interior of the continent.

I confess, Mr. Holmes, that I am torn between grief at the loss of my dearest friend and admiration for what may be his most audacious escape yet. If Jack Douglas lives, he has achieved something remarkable—complete freedom from his past. The world believes Birdy Edwards died at Birlstone Manor, and now believes Jack Douglas died in the South Atlantic. What better protection could a hunted man devise?

I have not shared these suspicions with Ivy, for what purpose would it serve to burden her with such speculation? If Jack lives, he has chosen this path for reasons I must respect. If he is truly gone, then my theories are merely the desperate imaginings of a grieving friend.

But knowing you as I do, and knowing your remarkable ability to see through deception to truth, I felt compelled to share these observations. If any man could determine whether Jack Douglas has achieved his final and most complete escape, it would be Sherlock Holmes.

I remain, with continued respect and no small amount of hope,

Cecil James Barker

To Holmes from MacDonald (VALL)

My Dear Holmes,

Having returned to the Yard after our extraordinary adventure at Birlstone, I find myself compelled to record my thoughts on what I can only describe as a masterpiece of criminal investigation—though I suspect you would dismiss such praise with one of your characteristic waves of the hand.

When I first arrived in Sussex and surveyed that locked room, with poor Douglas apparently blown to pieces by his own shotgun, I thought we were dealing with a straightforward case of suicide, albeit one with some puzzling features. Even when the evidence began to point toward murder, I was thinking along conventional lines—a killer who had somehow managed an impossible escape.

Never in my twenty years at the Yard did I imagine that what we were looking at was not the scene of Douglas's death, but the scene of his rebirth as a free man. Your insight that the victim was actually the assassin—that Douglas had turned the tables on his would-be killer in the most dramatic fashion—was nothing short of genius.

I've worked with you before, Holmes, and I thought I understood your methods. But watching you piece together the true sequence of events from those scattered clues was like watching a master craftsman at work. The way you interpreted the significance of the missing dumbbell, the peculiar placement of the candle, the condition of the curtains—each observation built upon the last until the whole fantastic truth became clear.

But what strikes me most forcibly is how you saw through to the human element of the case. While Inspector Mason and I were focused on the physical evidence, you were reading the story of a man driven to desperate measures by twenty years of fear. Your recognition that "Birdy" Edwards would never truly be safe, that the Scowrers' reach was long indeed, led you to understand why Douglas felt compelled to stage such an elaborate deception.

The revelation of the Vermissa Valley business and Douglas's history with the Ancient Order of Freemen was like watching the last piece of an intricate puzzle fall into place. Suddenly, everything made sense—the coded warning, the strange behavior of the household, even poor Mrs. Douglas's curious reactions to our questions.

I must confess, there were moments during our investigation when your theories seemed almost fantastical. A man faking his own death using his would-be assassin's body? It reads like something from a penny dreadful! Yet your logic was unassailable, and the evidence, once properly interpreted, supported every detail of your reconstruction.

This case has reinforced my conviction that conventional police methods, valuable though they are, must sometimes yield to more imaginative approaches. Your willingness to consider the impossible, to follow the evidence into uncharted territory, has solved a case that would have baffled the Yard indefinitely.

I hope we shall have occasion to work together again, though I rather suspect the criminal classes of London would prefer otherwise.

With profound respect and gratitude,

Inspector Alec MacDonald
Criminal Investigation Department
New Scotland Yard

To Holmes from White Mason (VALL)

Dear Mr. Holmes,

Now that the dust has settled on the remarkable affair at Birlstone Manor, I feel compelled to put pen to paper and express my profound admiration for the extraordinary manner in which you unraveled what seemed to us an impossible mystery.

When I first received word of the tragedy—a man apparently shot dead in his own study, the drawbridge raised, no possible means of escape for the murderer—I confess I was entirely baffled. The physical evidence seemed to tell one story, yet something about the whole business felt wrong, though I could not for the life of me put my finger upon what troubled me so.

Your methods, Mr. Holmes, were nothing short of revelatory. Where we saw only confusion and contradiction, you perceived the elegant simplicity of truth. The missing dumbbell, the significance of the sawed-off shotgun, the curious matter of the wedding ring—each seemingly minor detail which we had noted but failed to comprehend, you wove together into a complete and compelling narrative.

But what impressed me most profoundly was not merely your powers of observation—remarkable though they are—but your ability to see beyond the immediate evidence to the human story beneath. That you should have deduced not only that John Douglas yet lived, but the entire tragic history that drove him to stage his own death, demonstrates a depth of understanding that transcends mere detection.

I have worked alongside Scotland Yard inspectors who, with all due respect to my metropolitan colleagues, too often approach a case with preconceived notions and rigid methods. Your approach—following the evidence wherever it leads, no matter how improbable the destination— has taught me lessons I shall carry throughout my career.

The revelation that "Birdy" Edwards and John Douglas were one and the same, and that the body we discovered was actually that of his would-be assassin, represents perhaps the most ingenious piece of deductive reasoning I have witnessed. That you arrived at this conclusion through careful observation and logical inference, rather than lucky guesswork, speaks to the scientific precision of your methods.

I hope you will not think it presumptuous of me to say that it has been both an honor and an education to work alongside you. The people of Sussex—and indeed all of England—are fortunate to have such a champion of justice.

I remain, with the highest respect and admiration,

Your obedient servant,

Inspector White Mason
Sussex County Constabulary

To Ivy Douglas from Holmes (VALL)

My Dear Mrs. Douglas,

It is with the deepest regret that I write to acknowledge the devastating news which Mr. Cecil Barker has conveyed to me regarding the tragic fate of your husband during the voyage of the Palmyra. Though I had hoped that Jack's departure from England would mark the beginning of a new chapter of safety and peace for you both, I find myself instead compelled to offer what meager comfort words can provide in the face of such profound loss.

Your husband was a man of remarkable courage—a quality I had occasion to observe firsthand during our brief but memorable acquaintance. That he should have successfully overcome the immediate threat of his persecutors, only to be claimed by the indifferent forces of nature, strikes me as particularly cruel. Yet I cannot help but reflect that he died as a free man, no longer hunted, having secured for you the liberty that his sacrifice has now made permanent, though at such terrible cost.

Please know that should you require any assistance in the practical matters which inevitably follow such tragedies, you need only send word. Mr. Barker speaks highly of your fortitude, and I do not doubt that you will face this ordeal with the same strength of character that sustained you through the earlier tribulations at Birlstone Manor.

I remain, with sincere condolences and respect,

Your faithful servant,

Sherlock Holmes
Consulting Detective

To Holmes from Inspector Baynes (WIST)

My Dear Mr. Holmes,

I trust this letter finds you and Dr. Watson in excellent health following our recent collaboration in the Wisteria Lodge affair. I write not merely to express my satisfaction at the case's successful conclusion, but to convey the genuine pleasure it afforded me to work alongside the most celebrated consulting detective of our age.

You cannot imagine the professional delight I experienced in having the opportunity to observe your renowned methods firsthand. To witness the rapidity with which you assimilated seemingly disparate facts, the precision of your deductions, and the elegant logic with which you approached each aspect of the mystery—it was, if I may say so, rather like watching a master craftsman at his bench. Your reputation, I can now attest from personal experience, is entirely well-deserved.

Equally gratifying, however, was the opportunity to demonstrate that the methods of the provincial police—when properly applied—need not suffer by comparison with those employed in Baker Street. I confess to no small satisfaction in having my somewhat unorthodox approach ultimately vindicate itself, particularly given your initial skepticism regarding my arrest of the cook. It is not often that a Surrey inspector finds himself in a position to surprise the great Sherlock Holmes, and I shall treasure the memory of your gracious acknowledgment that my strategy proved sound.

Indeed, I venture to suggest that this case has demonstrated something of considerable importance to both our professions: that effective detection need not follow a single prescribed pattern. Your brilliant analytical approach and my more... shall we say, theatrical methods proved quite complementary when working in concert. Where you might have proceeded directly to the solution through pure deduction, my technique of creating controlled pressure situations forced our adversaries to reveal themselves in ways they might not otherwise have done.

I am emboldened to believe that my reputation in professional circles is beginning to approach something worthy of comparison with your own. Already I have received inquiries from Scotland Yard regarding my availability for consultation on particularly challenging cases, and I find myself increasingly regarded as something more than a mere country inspector. While I would never presume to claim equality with your extraordinary talents, I do believe I am well on my way to establishing myself as a detective of considerable capability in my own right.

It is with this growing confidence that I dare to express the hope that our paths may cross again professionally in the not-too-distant future. I believe we have proven that our respective methods, far from being incompatible, actually complement each other admirably. Perhaps you would not find it entirely disagreeable to collaborate with me again should a case arise that might benefit from our combined expertise.

I have already informed my superiors of the exemplary nature of our cooperation, and I believe they would be most amenable to future joint endeavors should circumstances warrant. The criminals of England may well have cause to rue the day when Holmes and Baynes unite their efforts once more!

With the greatest professional admiration and personal regard,

Inspector Baynes
Surrey Constabulary

P.S. - I have taken the liberty of recommending your services to several of my colleagues who have expressed admiration for the methodical way in which you handled certain aspects of our investigation. I trust this presumption will not displease you.

To Holmes from Miss Burnett (WIST)

Dear Mr. Holmes,

I write to you with a heart both heavy with memory and light with gratitude. The events of these past days have left me scarcely able to comprehend that the nightmare which has consumed so many years of my life has finally reached its end, and I find myself compelled to express my deepest thanks for the role you played in bringing truth to light.

When I stumbled into your care, exhausted and barely coherent from the drugs that monster had forced upon me, I feared that my mission—indeed, the mission that had united so many of us in our quest for justice—would die with poor Garcia. How wrong I was, and how thankful I am that providence placed me in the hands of a man possessed of both your remarkable intellect and your compassionate heart.

You must understand, Mr. Holmes, that for years I have lived with but one purpose: to see that the man who destroyed my family and countless others should face the justice that had so long eluded him. When I learned that Don Murillo—that butcher who masqueraded as the respectable Mr. Henderson—had escaped to England, I knew I must follow. The position as governess was merely a means to watch, to wait, and to inform my compatriots of his movements.

But when Murillo discovered our plot and poor Garcia paid with his life, I believed all was lost. Had you not provided me sanctuary and, more importantly, had you not believed my story when I was barely capable of coherent speech, that villain might have continued his comfortable exile indefinitely. Your willingness to listen to what others might have dismissed as the ravings of a disturbed woman gave voice to truths that demanded to be heard.

The news that reached me yesterday—that Murillo and his secretary have met their end—brings a closure I had scarce dared hope for. I do not ask you to approve of the methods by which justice was ultimately served, but I pray you understand that some wounds run too deep for conventional remedies.

I shall be returning to my homeland soon, where I hope to reclaim not only my true name of Senora Durando, but also the peace that has been denied to me these many years. I carry with me the memory of your kindness and the knowledge that there are still those in this world who will fight for truth, even when it leads down dark and dangerous paths.

Please extend my gratitude to Dr. Watson as well, whose gentle ministrations helped restore my strength when I most needed it. You are both testament to the finest qualities of English gentlemen.

With profound respect and eternal gratitude,

Miss Burnett
(Senora Maria Durando)

P.S. - I have left with your landlady a small token—a cross that belonged to my mother. She wore it through Murillo's persecution until the day she died. Perhaps it will serve as a reminder that sometimes justice, though delayed, will not be denied.

To Inspector Baynes from Holmes (WIST)

My Dear Inspector Baynes,

I find myself compelled to take up my pen and offer you my most sincere congratulations on your exemplary conduct during the recent Wisteria Lodge affair. More importantly, I must tender my apologies for the grave error in judgment I committed in questioning your methods during our investigation.

When you made your arrest of the cook, I confess I was guilty of that most dangerous failing in our profession—the presumption that I alone possessed the key to unraveling the mystery. How utterly wrong I was, and how brilliantly you proved the superiority of your approach over my own hasty conclusions.

Your strategy of arresting what appeared to be the "wrong man" was, I now understand, a masterstroke of tactical brilliance. By creating the appearance of misdirection, you accomplished what my more conventional methods could not: you forced the true conspirators to reveal themselves. The pressure of your arrest compelled Henderson—or should I say, Don Murillo—to act precipitously, leading directly to Miss Burnett's escape and her subsequent revelations that broke the case wide open.

Where I saw error, there was actually elegant design. Where I perceived blundering, you had crafted a trap of remarkable sophistication. Your method demonstrated a profound understanding of criminal psychology that I fear I failed to appreciate in my initial assessment.

The art of detection, as we both know, requires not merely the observation of facts, but the ability to manipulate circumstances to one's advantage. In this case, your apparent misstep was, in reality, the very mechanism by which justice was ultimately served. Don Murillo's reign of terror was brought to its proper conclusion precisely because you understood that sometimes the indirect approach succeeds where the direct assault fails.

I have learned a valuable lesson about the dangers of professional pride
and the importance of recognizing excellence in methods that may differ
from one's own. Your work on this case stands as a testament to the fact
that there are many paths to truth, and wisdom lies not in dismissing
unfamiliar approaches, but in understanding their underlying logic.

Please accept my compliments on a case brilliantly solved, and my
gratitude for the education you have provided me in the subtleties of our
shared profession.
I remain, with the greatest respect and admiration,

Your colleague in the pursuit of justice,

Sherlock Holmes
Consulting Detective

*P.S. - Watson joins me in expressing his admiration for your work. He has reminded
me, not without some satisfaction, that he suggested your methods might prove sound
even when I was most skeptical.*

To Susan Cushing from Lestrade (CARD)

Dear Miss Cushing,

I write to you in my official capacity as Inspector of the Criminal Investigation Department regarding the most distressing matter that recently befell you. It concerns the horrific package of human ears that was delivered to your residence several days ago.

Following an investigation conducted with the invaluable assistance of Mr. Sherlock Holmes, I am compelled to inform you that you were not, in fact, the intended recipient of this gruesome parcel. The sender was one James Browner, a steward and the husband of your deceased sister, Mary.

It is my duty to explain the circumstances that led to this macabre correspondence reaching your doorstep in error. Browner has confessed that the ears belonged to two victims of his own murderous actions: one ear from your sister Mary, and the other from Mr. Alec Fairbairn, a sailor with whom Mary had formed an attachment.

According to Browner's confession, your sister Sarah had made certain advances toward him which he rejected. Subsequently, it appears Sarah influenced Mary to believe that her husband was conducting an illicit affair, which led to the dissolution of their marriage and Mary's involvement with Mr. Fairbairn. In a fit of jealous rage, Browner followed the pair to New Brighton, where he murdered them both.

Browner intended to send this ghastly token to your sister Sarah as an act of revenge, believing her to be the architect of his domestic troubles and the destruction of his marriage. However, due to his imperfect knowledge of Sarah's current residence, the package was mistakenly delivered to your address instead.

I must inform you that Browner has been taken into custody and will face the full weight of the law for his crimes. The case is now closed insofar as the murders are concerned.

Should you wish to discuss any aspect of this matter further, or require additional details regarding the investigation, I invite you to call upon me at my office here at Scotland Yard at your earliest convenience. I shall be available to receive you on any weekday between the hours of ten o'clock and four o'clock.

I remain, Madam,

Your obedient servant,

Inspector G. Lestrade
Criminal Investigation Department
Metropolitan Police

To Susan Cushing from Watson (CARD)

My Dear Miss Cushing,

I trust that Inspector Lestrade has by now provided you with the full details of the tragic resolution to the dreadful affair that began with that horrible package delivered to your door. I write to you not in my capacity as an investigator of this most distressing case, but as a medical man and, I hope, as a friend who has witnessed the courage and composure you displayed during those dark days when we knew so little of what had transpired.

Please accept my most sincere and heartfelt condolences on the loss of your dear sister Mary. Though the manner of her death was shocking beyond measure, I want you to know that those of us who worked to uncover the truth understood her to be an innocent victim of a tragedy born from passion, jealousy, and the terrible capacity for violence that can lurk within the human heart.

I am certain that Inspector Lestrade has provided you with the essential facts of James Browner's confession, but should you desire any additional details that might bring you some measure of understanding or closure, I am entirely at your service. Sometimes, in my experience, the full knowledge of events—however painful—can be preferable to the torment of unanswered questions.

I must tell you that Mr. Holmes and I both observed, throughout our investigation, that this case bore the hallmarks of a domestic situation that had spiraled far beyond anyone's control or intention. We have seen how quickly misunderstandings and wounded pride can escalate into irreversible tragedy. While nothing can restore your beloved Mary to you, I hope you might find some small comfort in knowing that justice has been served, and that Browner will answer for his crimes.

As a physician, I am acutely aware of the toll such grief and shock can take upon one's constitution. Should you find yourself in need of medical attention or simply someone to speak with who understands the weight of what has occurred, please do not hesitate to call upon me. I have arranged with my colleague Dr. Pemberton, who practices in your neighborhood, to attend to you should you require care and prefer not to travel to Baker Street.

I realize that this tragedy has affected your entire family in the most profound way, and I can only imagine the additional torment you have endured in being the unwitting recipient of Browner's vengeful act. The shock of that initial discovery, followed by the gradual revelation of its terrible meaning, would test the fortitude of anyone. Your strength throughout this ordeal has been remarkable. Please extend my sympathies to your sister Sarah as well, as I know that Mary's loss—and the circumstances surrounding it—must weigh heavily upon her heart.

Should you ever wish to discuss any aspect of this case, or if there is any service I might render to assist you or your family in the coming days, please know that you have but to send word. Mr. Holmes and I both hold the deepest respect for the dignity and strength you have shown during this most trying period.

With profound sympathy and assurance of my continued availability should you have need of assistance,

I remain, most respectfully yours,

John H. Watson, M.D.

P.S. - I have taken the liberty of speaking with Inspector Lestrade about ensuring that all evidence related to this case is handled with the utmost discretion and sensitivity to your family's privacy. The newspapers need know only the barest facts necessary for public justice.

To Holmes from Gennaro & Emilia (REDC)

My Dear Mr. Holmes,

Words seem insufficient to express the depth of our gratitude for your invaluable assistance in the matter that has so recently concluded. As we write this letter, we find ourselves, for the first time in many months, able to draw breath without fear, to sleep without starting at every sound, and to look toward our future with hope rather than dread.

Your remarkable deductive abilities not only unraveled the mystery of my seemingly strange behavior at Mrs. Warren's lodging house, but more importantly, you understood the desperate circumstances that drove us to such extreme measures of concealment. When you summoned Emilia through your own coded message that fateful night, you demonstrated not only your intellectual brilliance but your compassionate understanding of our plight.

I must confess, Mr. Holmes, that in those dark hours when Gorgiano's shadow seemed to fall across every corner of our lives, I had begun to lose hope that we would ever be free of the Red Circle's malevolent reach. The weight of my youthful foolishness in associating with such criminals had become almost unbearable, particularly as I watched my beloved Emilia suffer for my mistakes. That we fled from New York only to find that monster had followed us to London filled me with such despair.

But your intervention changed everything. Your careful observation and brilliant deduction led to that crucial moment when justice, however violent, was finally served. When Gorgiano confronted me in that empty room, I fought not just for my own life, but for Emilia's freedom and our shared future. That both Inspector Gregson and Detective Leverton, guided by your wisdom, recognized the act as one of necessary self-defense has lifted a burden from our souls that we had carried far too long.

We are now making arrangements to begin anew, this time with the blessing of knowing that the shadow of Gorgiano and the Red Circle no longer darkens our path. We plan to settle quietly somewhere in the English countryside, where we might contribute honestly to society and leave behind forever the criminal associations of my misguided youth.

Should you ever have need of our assistance, or should you simply wish to know how your kindness has borne fruit in our lives, please do not hesitate to contact us. We shall always be in your debt, not merely for your detective work, but for your humanity in recognizing that sometimes good people find themselves in terrible circumstances through no fault of their own.

With our deepest respect and eternal gratitude,

Gennaro & Emilia Lucca

P.S. - We have enclosed a small token of our appreciation - a photograph taken on our wedding day in Naples, before our troubles began. We hope that when you look upon it, you will remember not the criminals we were forced to flee, but the honest couple whose love has survived every trial, thanks in no small part to your intervention.

To Pinkerton from Leverton (REDC)

Dear Sir,

I write to inform you of the successful conclusion of my assignment to apprehend or neutralize the fugitive Giuseppe Gorgiano, known associate of "The Red Circle" criminal organization.

CASE SUMMARY:

After weeks of surveillance in London, the subject Gorgiano was located in a building near Great Orme Street. Working in cooperation with Inspector Gregson of Scotland Yard and the consulting detective Mr. Sherlock Holmes of 221B Baker Street, we entered the premises on the evening in question.

Upon entry, we discovered Gorgiano deceased in an empty room on the upper floor. The cause of death was determined to be knife wounds sustained during what appears to have been a violent struggle.

CIRCUMSTANCES OF DEATH:

Through subsequent investigation, we determined that Gorgiano had been killed by one Gennaro Lucca, an Italian immigrant whom Gorgiano had been pursuing on behalf of The Red Circle organization. Mr. Lucca and his wife Emilia had fled first from Italy to New York, and subsequently to London, to escape the criminal organization's threats and demands.

According to Mrs. Lucca's testimony, Gorgiano had tracked her husband to the building and confronted him with the intention of compelling him to commit murder on behalf of The Red Circle. When Mr. Lucca refused, a physical altercation ensued, resulting in Gorgiano's death.

DISPOSITION:

After careful review of all evidence and testimony, Inspector Gregson, Mr. Holmes, and myself are in unanimous agreement that Mr. Lucca's actions constituted clear self-defense against a known criminal who posed imminent mortal danger. We are confident that no English court would find grounds for prosecution in this matter.

The threat posed by Gorgiano to American citizens residing in London has been permanently neutralized. The Red Circle organization has lost one of its most dangerous enforcers.

ACKNOWLEDGMENTS:

I must commend the exceptional cooperation provided by Inspector Gregson of Scotland Yard, whose knowledge of London criminal elements proved invaluable. Special recognition must also be given to Mr. Sherlock Holmes, whose analytical methods and investigative insights were instrumental in bringing this case to a swift conclusion.

CONCLUSION:

With Gorgiano deceased and the immediate threat to the Lucca family resolved, I consider this assignment complete. I shall be departing London on the next available steamship and expect to arrive in New York within the week.
All expenses incurred during this assignment are documented and will be submitted separately for reimbursement.

I remain, sir, Your obedient servant,

J. Leverton
Detective
Pinkerton National Detective Agency

This report contains sensitive information and should be filed under the highest security protocols.

To Violet Westbury from Watson (BRUC)

My Dear Miss Westbury,

It is with the heaviest of hearts that I write to you today, on behalf of both myself and my dear friend, Mr. Sherlock Holmes. We wish to express our most sincere and profound condolences upon the tragic loss of your beloved fiancé, Mr. Arthur Cadogan West.

Having had the solemn duty of investigating the circumstances surrounding Mr. West's untimely death, I can say with absolute certainty that he was a man of unimpeachable character and honour. The suspicions that were initially cast upon his name have been entirely dispelled, and his reputation stands unsullied. Indeed, it was his very loyalty and sense of duty that led to his tragic end, as he sought to prevent a most serious breach of our nation's security.

Holmes has asked me to convey his particular admiration for Mr. West's courage. In following Colonel Walter that fateful evening, your fiancé demonstrated the highest principles of patriotism and moral fortitude. Though it cost him his life, his actions ultimately prevented vital state secrets from falling into foreign hands.

Please know that justice has been served. Both Colonel Walter and the foreign agent Oberstein have been apprehended and will answer for their crimes. While this cannot restore your dear Arthur to you, we hope it may provide some measure of solace to know that his death was not in vain, and that those responsible will face the full consequences of their actions.

With deepest sympathy and respectful condolences, I remain, your most obedient servant,

Dr. John H. Watson, M.D.

On behalf of Mr. Sherlock Holmes and myself

To Holmes from Inspector Morton (DYIN)

Dear Mr. Holmes,

I write to express my most sincere gratitude for your extraordinary assistance in the matter of Victor Savage's untimely death and the subsequent apprehension of Mr. Culverton Smith.

When I first learned of your involvement in this case, I confess I was skeptical of your methods. Reports of your apparent grave illness and your insistence on keeping even Dr. Watson at arm's length struck me as most peculiar. Your elaborate deception—feigning mortal illness to draw out Smith—was nothing short of brilliant. To witness you transform from what appeared to be a man on death's door into your usual sharp, commanding self was remarkable indeed. The way you manipulated Smith into confessing his heinous crime against poor Savage was a masterclass in psychological strategy.

The evidence we have now secured, thanks to your machinations and the confession you extracted, should ensure that Smith faces the full weight of justice for his calculated murder. The exotic disease he employed as his weapon might have remained undetected indefinitely had it not been for your keen insight and theatrical prowess.

I must also commend your foresight in having Inspector Baynes and myself positioned as witnesses to Smith's confession. Your attention to the legal requirements of evidence gathering, even while orchestrating such an elaborate ruse, speaks to your thoroughness and professionalism.

The Yard recognizes that this case could not have been solved through conventional means. Smith's method was too sophisticated, too unusual for our standard procedures.

Most respectfully yours,

Inspector Morton
Metropolitan Police

To Holmes from Philip Green (LADY)

My Dear Mr. Holmes,

I find myself at a loss for words adequate to express my profound gratitude for your extraordinary efforts in the rescue of Lady Frances Carfax. As I sit here in the quiet of my hotel room, the events of these past weeks seem almost too incredible to have been real, yet the blessed relief of knowing Frances is safe and recovering reminds me that we have indeed lived through what might well have been the most harrowing chapter of both our lives.

When I first returned to England, driven by a desperate hope to make amends for my past follies and to lay my heart before Frances once more, I never imagined that my pursuit of her would cast me in the role of a suspected villain. I confess that your initial wariness of my motives, though it stung my pride, was perhaps not entirely unwarranted given my chequered history. A man who has made the mistakes I have made must expect to face suspicion before trust.

How mortifying it was to learn that my clumsy attempts at investigation—following the same trail as Dr. Watson, asking the same questions—had marked me as a threat rather than as one who sought only to protect the woman I have never ceased to love. Yet I cannot fault your caution, for it was precisely this thoroughness and refusal to accept easy answers that ultimately saved Frances from a fate too terrible to contemplate.

Your brilliant deduction regarding the true nature of Dr. Schlessinger— or rather, that villain Holy Peters—fills me with both admiration and horror. To think that while I fumbled about Baden and Montpellier like some amateur sleuth, Frances was already in the clutches of such a calculating predator! The cunning with which Peters and his confederate had ensnared her, using the guise of Christian charity and missionary work, speaks to a sophistication of evil that chills my very soul.

I must particularly commend your remarkable insight regarding the funeral arrangements. When you roused Dr. Watson in those early hours and insisted we attend what appeared to be a perfectly ordinary burial service, I confess I feared the strain of the case had perhaps affected your usually impeccable judgment. How wrong I was! Your intuition that Peters would attempt to dispose of Frances by concealing her in the very coffin meant for his accomplice's grandmother was nothing short of genius.

The moment when you forced open that coffin and we saw Frances lying unconscious but breathing in that horrible hidden compartment will remain burned in my memory forever. Dr. Watson's immediate attention to Frances's condition was a mercy, for I was trembling too violently to be of any practical assistance.

I am pleased to report that Frances has made a remarkable recovery from her ordeal. The physician attending her assures me that while the chloral hydrate Peters used to keep her unconscious was dangerous, she suffered no permanent harm.

As for the personal matter that first brought me back to England—I am happy to say that Frances has accepted my proposal. She has been gracious enough to forgive the indiscretions of my youth and sees fit to believe in my reformation. We plan to marry quietly in the spring, and I hope that you and Dr. Watson might honor us with your presence at the ceremony.

In closing, allow me to say that England is fortunate indeed to have a man of your extraordinary abilities dedicated to the protection of the innocent.

I remain, with the deepest respect and gratitude, your most obliged and humble servant,

Philip Green

P.S. - Should you ever have need of assistance in any matter where a reformed wastrel might prove useful, you have only to call upon me. After what you have done for Frances and me, my life is entirely at your service.

To Doctor Agar from Holmes (DEVI)

My Dear Dr. Agar,

I write to you from the familiar confines of my Baker Street lodgings, having recently returned from the Cornish holiday you so emphatically prescribed for my alleged "complete breakdown from exhaustion." I must confess that your medical counsel proved most sound—Watson and I did indeed benefit from the bracing sea air of Poldhu Bay, though I fear the rest you envisioned was rather more elusive than either of us anticipated.

You will no doubt be amused, though perhaps not entirely surprised, to learn that even in the remote wilds of Cornwall, criminal enterprise managed to seek me out with its customary persistence. It would appear that my reputation precedes me even to the furthest reaches of the peninsula, or perhaps, as Watson more cynically suggests, trouble simply follows in my wake like some malevolent shadow.

The case that interrupted our peaceful respite was of the most singular and tragic nature. A local family, the Tregennises, fell victim to what the parish priest and local inhabitants attributed to supernatural malevolence—though you know my views on such explanations. Three siblings were found dead or driven to madness around their card table, with no apparent cause save what the superstitious locals termed "the Devil's work."

The mystery proved most instructive, involving as it did an exotic African poison known as "Devil's-foot root"—a substance that, when combusted, produces vapours of extraordinary toxicity. I must admit that my investigative enthusiasm nearly cost both Watson and myself our lives when I attempted to replicate the murderous method. Only Watson's quick thinking in dragging us both from that accursed cottage saved us from sharing the fate of our unfortunate victims.

The resolution, while satisfying from a purely intellectual standpoint, was rather more complex from a moral perspective. The perpetrator of the original murders met his own end through an act of vigilante justice, carried out by one whose motives, while legally questionable, were emotionally comprehensible. I found myself in the unusual position of allowing justice to take its own course rather than that prescribed by Her Majesty's courts.

Watson sends his regards and wishes me to assure you that he kept a most vigilant eye on my health throughout our sojourn, though I suspect he would agree that preventing me from involving myself in criminal investigation is rather like attempting to prevent the tide from reaching the shore.

I remain, with gratitude for your medical wisdom and friendship,

Your obedient servant,

Sherlock Holmes
Consulting Detective

P.S. - I trust this account will not discourage you from prescribing future holidays, though you might consider recommending destinations with lower crime rates, should such places exist in this increasingly fascinating world of ours.

To Holmes from Leon Sterndale (DEVI)

My Dear Holmes,

Six months have passed since that terrible morning in Cornwall when you confronted me with the truth of my actions, and not a day goes by that I do not reflect upon your extraordinary act of mercy. I write to you now from the sun-scorched plains of East Africa, where the roar of lions drowns out the whispered accusations that might otherwise haunt a man's conscience.

You showed me a compassion that the law never could have afforded, and for that, I am forever in your debt. Where another man might have seen only a murderer, you saw the deeper currents of justice and love that drove me to that desperate act. Your decision to let me walk free from that cottage, to disappear into the African wilderness, was perhaps the most human judgment I have ever witnessed.

I have kept my word to you, Holmes. I shall never again set foot upon English soil, nor trouble the peace of Cornwall with my presence. Africa has become my permanent exile, though I confess it feels less like punishment than redemption. Here, among the vast savannahs and beneath endless skies, I have found a kind of peace that I thought forever lost when Brenda drew her final breath.

I think often of dear Brenda, as I know I always shall. The African sunsets remind me of her smile—brilliant, warm, and gone too soon. But the crushing weight of grief has transformed into something more bearable: a constant, gentle ache that speaks of love rather than loss. Mortimer's poison may have taken her from this world, but it could not diminish what she meant to me, nor what she continues to mean.

I hope you will understand when I say that I feel no remorse for what I did to Mortimer Tregennis. The man was a monster who destroyed his own family for motives I still cannot fathom. That he met his end through the same means by which he murdered Brenda and drove his brothers to madness strikes me as the most perfect justice imaginable.

Some might call it vengeance, but I prefer to think of it as balance restored to an unbalanced world.

Your Watson, I trust, has recovered fully from your dangerous experiment with the Devil's-foot root? I confess I felt a moment's alarm when I learned of your narrow escape. The irony of the very poison that brought us together nearly claiming the life of England's greatest detective was not lost on me. I am grateful that your scientific curiosity did not prove fatal—the world would be a darker place without Sherlock Holmes.

Should you ever find yourself in need of refuge in distant lands, know that you would be welcome at my camp. I could show you wonders that would astound even your remarkable powers of observation: elephants that mourn their dead, lions that adopt orphaned cubs from rival prides, and sunrises that paint the acacia trees in colors for which no civilized language has names.

But I suspect you belong in London, among the fogs and mysteries of Baker Street, bringing order to chaos and justice to those who would otherwise escape it. You gave me the gift of choosing my own exile rather than facing the gallows, and for that mercy, I remain eternally grateful.

Until we meet again—whether in this life or the next—I remain,
Your devoted and grateful friend,

Leon Sterndale

P.S. - I have enclosed a small carved ivory lion, crafted by a Kikuyu artist whose village I helped protect from a man-eating leopard. It is a poor token for such a great debt, but I hope you will accept it as a symbol of the courage and wisdom you showed in those dark days in Cornwall.

To Holmes from Mycroft (LAST)

My Dear Sherlock,

It is with the deepest satisfaction and no small measure of pride that I write to commend you on the extraordinary success of your recent endeavours on behalf of His Majesty's Government. Your two years in the guise of that reprehensible American, Altamont, have yielded results that exceed even my most optimistic projections.

The capture of Von Bork and the recovery of his entire intelligence apparatus represents a triumph of the highest order. That you were able to maintain your cover for so lengthy a period, earning the complete trust of one of Germany's most capable operatives, speaks to abilities that extend far beyond even your considerable reputation as a consulting detective.

The documents you have secured will prove invaluable to the Admiralty in the coming months. Moreover, the comprehensive list of German agents operating within our shores—delivered so neatly into our hands through Von Bork's own meticulous record-keeping—will allow us to neutralize an entire espionage network in one decisive stroke.

I confess that when you first proposed this audacious scheme, I harbored private doubts about whether even your remarkable talents could sustain such an elaborate deception. How wrong I was. Your transformation into the crude, money-hungry Irish-American arms dealer was so complete that I myself might have been deceived had I encountered you in character.

The government's debt to you in this matter is immeasurable. At a time when the very survival of the Empire hangs in the balance, you have struck a blow against our enemies that may well prove decisive in the darker days that surely lie ahead.

Watson, I understand, played his part admirably as well. Please convey to the good doctor my appreciation for his steadfast service. Though he could not share in the years of preparation, his presence at the crucial moment provided exactly the sort of reliable support that such operations demand.

I trust you will now permit yourself a well-deserved period of rest before the next crisis inevitably calls upon your unique services. The bees of Sussex, I am told, await your attention.

With the highest regard and deepest gratitude,
Your devoted brother,

Mycroft Holmes

On behalf of His Majesty's Government

To Mycroft from Holmes (LAST)

My Dear Mycroft,

Your letter reached me this morning, and I confess that your words of commendation carry more weight than those of any minister or official whose gratitude I might otherwise have earned. The Von Bork affair is concluded, as you say, most satisfactorily.

I write now, however, on a matter of personal concern that I trust you will handle with your customary discretion and efficiency. As you have no doubt already learned through your various channels, Watson has received orders to rejoin the Army Medical Service. The old war-horse cannot resist the call to duty, despite my pointing out that he has already served his country with distinction both in Afghanistan and, more recently, in our little adventure with the German spy network.

Mycroft, I must speak plainly. Watson is no longer the young army surgeon who charged up the slopes at Maiwand thirty-four years ago. Though his spirit burns as brightly as ever, and his medical skills remain sharp, I fear that the physical demands of active service may prove... challenging for a man of his years. He is past sixty now, and while he would box my ears for saying so, I have observed that he tires more easily than he once did, and his old wound troubles him when the weather turns.

I know that your influence extends into every corner of Whitehall, and that the War Office is not immune to your particular form of gentle persuasion. Might it be possible to ensure that Watson receives a posting suited to his experience and standing? A position at a base hospital, perhaps, or attached to a headquarters staff where his wisdom and medical expertise might be better utilized than in a field dressing station?

I do not ask that he be shielded from danger entirely—he would never forgive such interference, and rightly so. But surely there are ways to deploy his considerable talents without placing unnecessary strain upon a constitution that, while still robust, is no longer that of a young man.

Your network of observation extends everywhere, Mycroft. I should be...
grateful... if you might occasionally direct that observation toward
ensuring the good doctor's welfare during the trials ahead.
The bees prosper, though they show a marked preference for the
morning hours when the Sussex air is cool and still.

Your brother,

Sherlock Holmes
Consulting Detective

*P.S. - Please do not let Watson know of this correspondence. He would view any
special consideration as an affront to his dignity, and I value our friendship too highly
to risk his knowing I regard him as anything less than indestructible.*

To Miss Kitty Winter from Holmes (ILLU)

My Dear Miss Winter,

I trust this letter finds you as well as circumstances permit. Dr. Watson has made enquiries regarding your situation, and I am informed that you are being treated with reasonable consideration, given the nature of your case. I write not merely as a matter of courtesy, but because I feel compelled to address certain matters that weigh heavily upon my mind.

First, let me say that I hold you in the highest regard for the courage you displayed throughout our recent enterprise. When others—myself included—could only work within the constraints of law and evidence, you possessed both the intimate knowledge and the resolution to act decisively. Your assistance in exposing Baron Gruner's true character was invaluable, and without your cooperation, Miss de Merville might well have proceeded to a marriage that would have destroyed her utterly.

I will not pretend to approve of violence as a solution to injustice—my methods have always relied upon reason, observation, and the proper application of legal remedies. Yet I cannot ignore the fact that conventional justice had failed utterly to address the systematic destruction of innocent women that Gruner perpetrated over many years. The law, for all its noble intentions, sometimes proves inadequate when confronting such calculated evil.

Your actions, while I cannot endorse them, arose from a moral imperative that I understand completely. You sought not personal revenge alone, but to ensure that no other woman would suffer as you and so many others had suffered. In that light, what transpired was perhaps inevitable—the natural consequence of a society that failed to protect its most vulnerable members from predators like Gruner.

Now, to practical matters. I am told that your sentence, while significant, is not without hope of reduction for good conduct. I implore you to conduct yourself with the dignity and restraint that I know you to possess. Prison authorities respond favorably to prisoners who demonstrate genuine rehabilitation and contribute positively to the institution's functioning. Your intelligence and strength of character, properly directed, could serve you well in this regard.

Additionally, I have taken the liberty of speaking with several charitable organizations that assist women in circumstances similar to your own. Upon your release, should you desire it, there will be opportunities for honest employment and the chance to begin anew. The past need not define your future, Miss Winter, and I am convinced that you possess the fortitude to build a respectable and fulfilling life.

When the time comes for your release—and I pray it will be sooner rather than later—I hope you will not hesitate to call upon me. I maintain extensive connections throughout London and beyond, and I would consider it both a privilege and a duty to assist you in establishing yourself in legitimate circumstances. You have demonstrated that you can be a formidable force for justice; imagine what you might accomplish when that force is channeled toward constructive ends.

Dr. Watson joins me in sending his regards and best wishes for your welfare. He has asked me to convey his admiration for your spirit and his confidence in your ability to emerge from this ordeal stronger and wiser.

Please know that you are not forgotten, nor are you without friends who recognize the complex circumstances that led to your present situation. Justice, though sometimes delayed and imperfect, has a way of ultimately prevailing—and you, Miss Winter, have played your part in ensuring that a dangerous man can harm no other innocent souls.

I remain, with sincere respect and best wishes for your future,

Sherlock Holmes
Consulting Detective

P.S. - I have arranged for a small monthly allowance to be credited to your prison account for necessities and correspondence. Consider it a token of gratitude for services rendered to the cause of justice.

To Holmes from Baron Gruner (ILLU)

Holmes,

I write this from the confines of my room, my face a ruin thanks to that she-devil's vitriol, and I find myself compelled to address your recent... shall we call it a "victory"? Though I suspect you understand as well as I do how hollow that victory truly is.

Your reputation precedes you, of course—the great detective, the master of observation and deduction, the man who sees what others cannot. How disappointed you must be to realize that all your vaunted methods, all your careful planning and logical reasoning, proved utterly inadequate against me. Were it not for the hysterical violence of a scorned woman, you would have achieved precisely nothing.

Let us examine the facts, shall we? Your attempts at persuasion fell upon deaf ears—Miss de Merville remained utterly devoted to me despite your warnings. Your collection of testimony from my former... acquaintances... proved meaningless in the face of my influence over her. Even your dramatic revelation of my private records failed to shake her faith in me. She would have married me still, had circumstances been different.

No, Holmes, what defeated me was not your intellect but feminine fury—the most primitive and unreasoning force in nature. That creature Winter, driven by wounded vanity and jealous rage, succeeded where all your careful deductions failed. It was not logic that stopped me, but emotion. Not reason, but violence. Not your nineteenth-century methods, but something far older and more savage.

You pride yourself on being a modern man, a man of science and observation. Yet in the end, you required the most ancient of weapons— a woman's wrath—to accomplish what your detective skills could not. How terribly revealing that must be for you.

I confess a certain admiration for the irony. Throughout my career, women have been my particular... specialty. I understood them, manipulated them, used their own desires and weaknesses against them. In the end, it was their very nature—passionate, irrational, unpredictable—that proved my undoing. Not your methods, Holmes. Theirs.

You may congratulate yourself on saving Miss de Merville, but we both know the truth. She would have come to me willingly, eagerly, had she not been shown that damning book—and even then, she wavered. It was only the shock of my disfigurement, the horror of my altered appearance, that truly turned her away. Vanity, not virtue, sealed my fate.

Your reputation will grow from this affair, no doubt. The papers will credit your brilliant detective work, your relentless pursuit of justice. Let them. We who were present know better. We know that Sherlock Holmes, for all his fame and skill, was reduced to relying on the violent impulses of a desperate woman to achieve what his intellect could not.

The world is changing, Holmes. Your methods—careful observation, logical deduction, appeals to reason and law—belong to a gentler age. The future will belong to men who understand that passion conquers logic, that force trumps reason, that the primitive drives of human nature matter more than all your careful analysis.

You won this round, I grant you. But only because you abandoned your principles and relied on something far more elemental than detection. In the end, you proved yourself no different from the rest of us—just another man who needed a woman to do his dirty work.

Nice try, Sherlock. But we both know who really deserves the credit for your "victory."

Baron Adelbert Gruner

The latest report from my doctor assures me that the damage to my face is quite permanent. How poetic.

To Holmes from Shinwell Johnson (ILLU)

My Dear Johnson,

I write to express my sincere appreciation for your invaluable assistance in the recent Gruner affair. Your contributions to the successful resolution of this most delicate case were, as always, both timely and indispensable.

Your extensive knowledge of London's underworld and your network of contacts proved crucial in gathering the preliminary intelligence we required about Baron Gruner's activities and associates. Without your insights into the less savory circles in which the Baron moved, we would have been working in considerable darkness. Your ability to navigate these treacherous waters while maintaining the discretion that such a sensitive matter demanded was exemplary.

I was particularly impressed by your persistence in tracking down corroborating witnesses and your skill in persuading certain reluctant individuals to share their knowledge of Gruner's past misdeeds. Your reformed background, rather than being a hindrance, proved to be our greatest asset—lending you a credibility among these sources that neither Watson nor I could have commanded.

The information you provided regarding Gruner's continental connections was especially valuable. Your contacts among the criminal fraternity yielded details about his activities in Prague and Vienna that ultimately helped us understand the full scope of his systematic victimization of women. This intelligence proved vital in building our case and understanding the pattern of his behavior.

The successful outcome of this case—Miss de Merville's salvation from a disastrous marriage and Gruner's permanent incapacitation—owes much to your groundwork. While others may claim the more dramatic roles in this affair, those of us who understand such matters know that solid intelligence work forms the foundation of any successful investigation.

As always, your discretion in this matter is assumed and appreciated. The reputations and welfare of several individuals depend upon our collective ability to keep certain details from public scrutiny.

Please accept the enclosed consideration as a token of gratitude for your services. Your assistance continues to be invaluable to my work, and I look forward to our continued collaboration on future matters that may require your particular expertise.

Should you require any assistance or find yourself in difficulties, you know that my door is always open to you. Your loyalty and skill have earned not merely my professional respect but my personal regard.

I remain, with sincere appreciation,

Sherlock Holmes
Consulting Detective

P.S. - Watson sends his regards and asks me to mention his admiration for the way you handled the situation with Gruner's former valet. Your approach there was masterful.

To Holmes from Violet de Merville (ILLU)

My Dear Mr. Holmes,

I write to you with a heart heavy with both gratitude and shame, knowing that words can scarcely convey the depth of my feelings or adequately express my debt to you. When I think of how rudely I dismissed you during our previous encounters, how obstinately I refused to heed your warnings, I am filled with mortification at my own blindness and foolish pride.

The book—that terrible, damning record—which you so courageously obtained has opened my eyes to truths so horrific that I can barely comprehend how thoroughly I was deceived. Page after page of that vile catalogue revealed the systematic destruction of innocent women, each entry a testament to the monster I had been prepared to marry. How could I have been so utterly blind to the true nature of Baron Adelbert Gruner?

I confess that when you first approached me with your concerns, I thought you meddlesome and presumptuous. I believed myself to be in possession of all the facts, convinced that the accusations against my former fiancé were merely the jealous fabrications of his enemies. How wrong I was! How dangerously, catastrophically wrong!

Your persistence in the face of my hostility, your willingness to risk personal danger to save a foolish young woman who treated you with nothing but disdain, speaks to a nobility of character that I can only aspire to emulate. That you continued your investigation despite my rebuffs, that you endangered yourself to obtain the evidence that would convince me, demonstrates a dedication to justice and human welfare that transcends any personal consideration.

I am haunted by the thought of what my fate might have been had you not intervened. To think that I was mere weeks away from binding myself to such a creature—a man who collected the ruin of women as other men collect butterflies or stamps—fills me with such horror that I can barely sleep. The women whose stories filled that accursed volume, their sufferings, their destruction—I might so easily have joined their ranks.

I have heard of the violent encounter that concluded this affair, and while I cannot condone violence in any form, I confess I feel little sympathy for the injuries Baron Gruner sustained. That Miss Winter, one of his victims, should be the instrument of his downfall carries with it a certain poetic justice, though I pray she will not suffer unduly for her actions.

My father, General de Merville, asks me to convey his own profound gratitude. He had grown increasingly troubled by his inability to dissuade me from the match, and the revelation of Gruner's true character has lifted a tremendous burden from his mind. We both understand now the terrible anguish you must have felt, knowing what you knew and being unable to convince us of the danger.

Please accept my deepest apologies for my previous conduct, and my most heartfelt thanks for your unwavering determination to protect me from a fate worse than death itself. I only pray that someday I might have the opportunity to repay, in some small measure, the debt I owe you.

I remain, sir, your most grateful and humbled servant,

Miss Violet de Merville

P.S. - I have instructed my solicitor to make a substantial donation to the Metropolitan Police Orphans' Fund in recognition of your services, though no sum could truly reflect the magnitude of what you have done for me.

To Holmes from Colonel Emsworth (BLAN)

My Dear Mr. Holmes,

I write to you with a heart both heavy with shame and light with profound relief. Your unwavering persistence in the matter of my son Godfrey, despite my family's regrettable attempts to obstruct your investigation, has proven to be nothing short of providential.

I must confess that when young Dodd first approached you with his concerns about Godfrey's disappearance, I viewed your involvement as an unwelcome intrusion into what I believed to be a private family tragedy of the most devastating kind. The medical opinion we had received led us to fear the worst—that terrible disease which has cast such long shadows over the history of mankind. In our terror and misguided attempt to protect both our son and our family name from the social ostracism that would surely follow, we chose the path of concealment and deception.

How wrong we were, and how grateful I am now that you refused to be deterred by our evasions and half-truths!

Dr. Kent's thorough re-examination, prompted by your astute observations and relentless pursuit of the truth, has revealed that what we feared to be leprosy is, in fact, the condition known as pseudo-leprosy or ichthyosis. While still a burden for poor Godfrey to bear, it is neither contagious nor the harbinger of the terrible fate we had imagined. The relief that floods through me as I write these words can scarcely be expressed in mere language.

You have given me back my son, Mr. Holmes—not merely his physical presence, which we had hidden away in shame, but his future, his hope, and his rightful place in our family and in society. The weeks of isolation and despair that we imposed upon him, believing we were protecting others while slowly dying inside ourselves, now seem like a nightmare from which we have been awakened by your intervention.

I am deeply conscious of how my family's behavior must have appeared to you—the locked rooms, the nervous denials, the obvious attempts to mislead your investigation. We were acting out of fear and ignorance, but I recognize now that our deception only compounded the suffering of all involved. Your patient persistence in the face of our obstruction speaks to a dedication to truth and justice that commands my highest admiration.

My wife joins me in expressing our most heartfelt gratitude. The transformation in our household since Dr. Kent's corrected diagnosis has been remarkable. Where once there was despair and furtive whispers, there is now hope and the blessed sound of normal family life resuming. Godfrey, though still bearing the marks of his condition, walks again among us with his head held high, knowing that his future need not be one of exile and progressive deterioration.

I hope you will find it in your heart to forgive our earlier conduct. We acted not from malice but from the terror that grips any parent when faced with what appears to be their child's doom. Your persistence in pursuing the truth, even when we tried to bar your way, has taught us that concealment and denial serve only to magnify suffering.

Should you ever require any service that I might render, or should your travels bring you to Bedford, please know that you will find the warmest welcome at Tuxbury Old Park. It would be our honor to receive the man who restored our son to us and our family to its proper course.

I remain, with the deepest gratitude and respect,
Your most obliged servant,

Colonel James Emsworth
Tuxbury Old Park

P.S. - Godfrey himself wishes to thank you personally, and I believe young Dodd has already called upon you to express his own relief and appreciation. We are forever in the debt of both gentlemen for their refusal to abandon a friend in need.

To Holmes from Godfrey Emsworth (BLAN)

Dear Mr. Holmes,

I write to you as a man reborn, though I scarcely know how to find words adequate to express what your intervention has meant to me. When I think of the dark despair that had settled over my life just days ago, and contrast it with the hope that now fills my heart, I am reminded that miracles do indeed occur—though they often come disguised as rigorous logic and unwavering determination.

For months, I believed myself to be facing a living death, condemned to isolation not merely from society but from everyone I held dear. The medical opinion that had been rendered seemed as final as any judge's sentence, and I had begun to reconcile myself to a future of progressive deterioration and inevitable exile. That I am now writing to you as a free man, with prospects and hope restored, seems almost too wonderful to believe.

But I would be remiss if I did not acknowledge the man whose loyalty set these events in motion. James Dodd—dear, steadfast Jimmy—refused to accept my family's evasions when I simply vanished from his life. In the trenches of South Africa, we learned to depend upon one another in ways that civilians can barely comprehend. When a man has shared your water ration during a siege, has dragged you to safety under enemy fire, has watched your back through the long, dangerous nights—well, such bonds are not easily broken by mysterious disappearances and vague explanations.

I am certain that Dr. Watson, your own stalwart companion, would understand precisely the nature of the friendship that drove Jimmy to seek you out. Jimmy could no more abandon me to an unknown fate than he could abandon his post in battle. It simply was not in his nature to do so.

When he came to you with his concerns, he was acting not merely as a worried friend, but as a brother-in-arms fulfilling an unspoken oath that we make to one another in service: that no man shall be left behind, no matter the circumstances. That you took up his cause and pursued it with such tenacity speaks to your own understanding of loyalty and duty.

I know my family's behavior must have tried your patience considerably. Their attempts to mislead and obstruct your investigation were born of love and terror, but I fear they only made your task more difficult. Yet you persisted, and in doing so, you uncovered not only the truth of my condition but also revealed the error in the medical opinion that had condemned me to despair.

You have given me back not just my life, but my dignity, my hope, and my place in the world. More than that, you have demonstrated the value of friendship—both Jimmy's unwavering loyalty in seeking you out, and your own dedication to seeing justice done and truth revealed. In a world that often seems cynical and cold, such constancy is a beacon of what is best in human nature.

Jimmy has already expressed his own gratitude, I know, but I wanted you to hear from me personally how transformative your intervention has been. You took up the cause of a man you had never met, pursued it against considerable obstacles, and saw it through to a conclusion that has restored not just my own peace of mind but that of my entire family.

Dr. Watson is indeed fortunate to have such a friend, just as I am fortunate to have found myself the beneficiary of your remarkable abilities. Military friendships may be powerful things, but the friendship of Sherlock Holmes, it seems, is more powerful still.

With deepest gratitude and highest regard,

Godfrey Emsworth
Late of the Middlesex Corps
Tuxbury Old Park

P.S. - Jimmy has suggested that we might call upon you both in London when next we are in town. I should very much like to meet Dr. Watson and thank him as well, for I suspect that his influence has helped shape the man of honor and determination who came to my rescue.

To Holmes from Ralph the Butler (BLAN)

Dear Sir,

I hope you will forgive the liberty I take in writing to you directly, and I must beg your discretion in this matter. Should the Colonel discover that I have presumed to correspond with you on family business, he would surely consider it a gross overstepping of my position. But there are some things that must be said, even if they cannot be said openly.

I have served in this household for thirty-seven years, sir, arriving when Master Godfrey was but three years old. His dear mother was often unwell during his early years, and it fell to me and my wife, in large part, to see to the young master's daily care. I taught him to tie his boots, while my wife helped him with his letters, tended his scraped knees, and was there to comfort him through childhood nightmares. In all but name and blood, we have been as much as parents to that boy as anyone could be.

You cannot imagine, sir, the agony these past months have been for one who has watched that child grow into the fine young man he became. To see him hidden away like some shameful secret, to watch the light fade from his eyes as he believed himself cursed with that terrible disease—it near broke this old heart.

I knew the family meant well, trying to protect him from the world's harsh judgment, but I also saw what the isolation was doing to the lad. He who had always been so spirited and full of life, reduced to a shadow of himself. The Colonel and his wife were beside themselves with grief, making decisions out of fear rather than hope, and I—I could only watch and tend to what little needs I was allowed to meet.

When young Mr. Dodd came looking for Master Godfrey, I must confess I wanted to tell him everything, but my position forbade it. When you arrived, sir, I sensed immediately that here was a man who would not be turned away by evasions and half-truths. Though I could not speak openly, I hoped—oh, how I hoped—that your persistence might lead to some resolution of our terrible situation.

And what a resolution it has been! When Dr. Kent delivered his new diagnosis, both my wife and I wept openly in the servants' hall. The relief was so overwhelming that I thought my old heart might give out entirely.

Master Godfrey is himself again, sir. The smile has returned to his face, and yesterday I heard him laugh—actually laugh—for the first time in months. He speaks now of his future, of plans and hopes, where before there had been only resignation to a living death. You have given him back his life, and in doing so, you have given me back the joy of seeing the boy I helped raise return to us whole.

I know the Colonel has written to thank you formally, and Master Godfrey will surely do the same, but I needed you to know what your determination has meant to someone who has loved that young man like his own flesh and blood.

There is an old saying that blood is thicker than water, but I have learned in my years that love knows no such boundaries. Master Godfrey may not be my son by birth, but he is my son by choice and care, and you, sir, have saved him as surely as if you had pulled him from a burning building.

I ask nothing in return for these words save that you know how deeply grateful one old butler can be. Should you ever find yourself in need of any service, however humble, that I might provide, you need only ask. And should you ever visit Tuxbury Old Park again, I will personally ensure that you receive the finest hospitality this house can offer.

Your most grateful and obedient servant,

Ralph
Butler, Tuxbury Old Park

P.S. - I have taken the liberty of enclosing a small tin of Mrs. Morrison's finest shortbread. The cook insisted I send it along, as she says any man who can work such miracles deserves the best we have to offer. Please destroy this letter after reading, as I value my position here, but more than that, I value the peace that has returned to this household.

To Sir James Saunders from Holmes (BLAN)

My Dear Sir James,

I trust you will permit me to express my most sincere gratitude for your invaluable assistance in the recent matter of young Godfrey Emsworth. Your willingness to accompany me to Tuxbury Old Park, despite the somewhat irregular nature of my request, proved to be the decisive factor in bringing this troubling case to its fortunate conclusion.

As you will recall, the circumstances under which I approached you were rather unusual. The family's own medical advisors had rendered a diagnosis that, while delivered with the best of intentions, had condemned a promising young man to what appeared to be a slow and inexorable decline. My own observations, while suggestive of alternative possibilities, required the confirmation that only a physician of your exceptional expertise and reputation could provide.

Your meticulous examination of Mr. Emsworth, conducted with such thoroughness and professional objectivity, revealed what I had suspected but could not definitively establish through deductive reasoning alone— that the condition presenting itself was not the dreaded Hansen's disease, but rather the far less devastating ichthyosis. The precision of your diagnosis has literally transformed a family's despair into rejoicing.

I confess that there were moments during the investigation when I questioned whether my suspicions might prove to be merely wishful thinking rather than sound deduction. The symptoms, as initially presented to the family's physicians, were indeed consistent with their original diagnosis. It required your trained eye and systematic approach to identify the subtle but crucial distinctions that differentiated between the two conditions.

The young man himself has written to thank me, but I believe the greater thanks belong to you. My role was merely to recognize that the facts as presented did not align perfectly with the family's explanation of events, and to persist until the truth could be established. Your role was to provide that truth through careful medical observation and analysis—a far more substantial contribution to the young man's salvation.

I am particularly grateful for the patience you displayed with what must have seemed like an intrusion into a private family matter. The Emsworths' initial resistance to your examination was understandable, given their belief about their son's condition and their desire to protect him from what they saw as unnecessary exposure. Your gentle but firm insistence on conducting a complete and proper examination, despite these obstacles, demonstrated both professional integrity and human compassion.

The contrast between the Emsworth household during my initial visit and its atmosphere following your diagnosis could scarcely be more dramatic. Where once there was secrecy, shame, and barely contained grief, there is now openness, hope, and the sound of normal family life resuming. Young Emsworth himself has emerged from what amounted to voluntary exile, able once again to face the world with dignity and purpose.

I hope you will not think it presumptuous if I suggest that this case demonstrates the value of collaboration between our respective disciplines. The apparent medical mystery yielded to detective work, while the detective work required medical validation to achieve its proper conclusion. Perhaps there may be occasion in the future for such cooperation again, should circumstances warrant it.

I remain, with the highest professional regard and personal gratitude,

Sherlock Holmes
Consulting Detective

P.S. - Watson joins me in extending his thanks, as he has observed the beneficial effects that successful collaborations between detection and medicine can achieve. He suggests that we would be honored to host you for dinner at Baker Street when your schedule permits, both as a gesture of thanks and as an opportunity to discuss the fascinating intersection of our professional interests.

To Holmes from Count Sylvius (MAZA)

My Dear Mr. Holmes,

How deliciously ironic that I should be writing to you from behind these dreary walls, when it is you who should be occupying this very cell. Your theatrical performance with that ridiculous wax effigy was most entertaining, I must admit—though I confess I found your ventriloquism rather more impressive than your deductive reasoning.

You will be pleased to learn that your case against me has begun to unravel with the same methodical precision you so pride yourself upon. My dear associate, Sam Merton—that simple-minded brute whose loyalty I so gravely misjudged—has seen fit to unburden his conscience to the authorities. It appears the fool believed a full confession might earn him lenient treatment. How perfectly pedestrian of him.

In his rambling statement, Merton has made it quite clear that he alone conceived and executed the theft of the Mazarin stone. I was, as I maintained throughout your insufferable interrogation, merely an unfortunate victim of circumstance—a gentleman of refined taste who happened to appreciate fine gemstones, nothing more.

My solicitor informs me that with Merton's confession and the subsequent review of evidence, my release is imminent. A matter of days, perhaps a week at most. The Crown Prosecution Service, it seems, has little appetite for pursuing charges against a man whose only crime was keeping questionable company.

When I walk free from this place, Mr. Holmes, I shall remember with perfect clarity every moment of humiliation you subjected me to. Your smug satisfaction as you orchestrated my arrest. Your theatrical pronouncements about justice and truth. That insufferable little smile you wore as they led me away in shackles.

I am a man of infinite patience and considerable resources. I do not forget slights, nor do I forgive them. You have made this personal, detective, and I assure you that I am far more creative in matters of revenge than I ever was in matters of larceny.

You fancy yourself the master of observation and deduction? Then observe this: a man wrongfully imprisoned emerges with nothing left to lose and everything to gain from settling scores. Deduce what that might mean for your future peace of mind.

I look forward to renewing our acquaintance under more... reciprocal circumstances.

Until we meet again,

Count Sylvius

P.S. — Do give my regards to Dr. Watson. I trust his nerves have quite recovered from our last encounter. He may wish to ensure his service revolver remains close at hand.

To Holmes from Isadora Klein (3GAB)

My Dear Mr. Holmes,

I trust this letter finds you in good health and occupied with cases more suited to your considerable talents than our recent, rather sordid affair. I write to confirm that our mutual acquaintance, Mrs. Maberley, has by now undoubtedly embarked upon her travels, having departed England with what I am informed was considerable enthusiasm for her forthcoming adventures.

The settlement I provided has, I believe, proven more than adequate for her purposes. My agents report that she was seen boarding a vessel bound for the Mediterranean with all the excitement of a woman half her age. One might say that our unfortunate entanglement has resulted in an unexpectedly pleasant outcome for the dear lady—certainly more agreeable than dwelling indefinitely in that rather shabby house with its painful memories.

I write primarily to remind you of our gentleman's agreement regarding the discretion you so graciously promised to maintain. As you will recall, our understanding was quite explicit: Mrs. Maberley would receive generous compensation for her troubles, and in return, certain aspects of this matter would remain permanently between us. I have fulfilled my obligations with characteristic promptness and liberality.

I trust I need not elaborate upon my expectation that you will honor your commitment with equal reliability. My position in society, as you well understand, depends upon the maintenance of certain proprieties. While I have always found your reputation for integrity to be impeccable, I confess that the temptation to share an entertaining anecdote with your chronicling friend Dr. Watson must occasionally present itself.

I am confident, however, that a man of your discernment recognizes the value of discretion—particularly when dealing with individuals who move in the highest circles of society and government. Such people, as you are no doubt aware, possess resources and influence that extend far beyond the financial compensation already provided.

Should you ever find yourself in need of assistance in matters requiring delicate handling or access to exclusive information, I hope you will remember that I am not without my own considerable network of contacts. A favor rendered is often a favor returned, as I am sure you appreciate.
I remain, as always, your obliged correspondent,

Isadora Klein

P.S. - I have heard the most fascinating rumors about certain irregularities in the recent Boscombe Valley investigation. Perhaps we might discuss them over tea sometime, should you find yourself at liberty to call upon me.

To Holmes from Mary Maberley (3GAB)

My Dear Mr. Holmes,

I write to you from aboard the *R.M.S. Oceanic* as we sail through the Mediterranean, bound for Alexandria. The azure waters and gentle sea breeze seem almost dreamlike after the terrible ordeal we endured together just a fortnight past. I confess that when I first encountered you in my ransacked drawing room, I could scarcely have imagined that our acquaintance would lead to such a remarkable turn of fortune.

Your swift resolution of that dreadful business with Miss Klein has quite literally opened the world to me. The generous settlement she provided—no doubt encouraged by your masterful handling of the situation—has afforded me opportunities I never dared contemplate during those dark days following dear Douglas's passing. I am profoundly grateful not only for your investigative brilliance, but for your compassionate understanding of a grieving mother's plight.

As I write this, I can almost hear Douglas's voice carried on the ocean breeze, and I am certain he would heartily approve of my decision to embark upon this grand adventure. You see, Mr. Holmes, my son always possessed such a wandering spirit and spoke often of distant lands and exotic ports. He would be delighted to know that his mother, at her advanced age, has finally found the courage to see something of the world beyond England's shores.

The ship's library is well-appointed, and I have been reading accounts of the ancient wonders we shall soon visit—the Pyramids, the Holy Land, and perhaps even the Far East if my constitution permits. Each page fills me with an excitement I had thought lost forever in the depths of my grief. It is as though you have not merely solved a criminal puzzle, Mr. Holmes, but restored a portion of my very soul.

I must also express my admiration for your restraint in dealing with that Klein woman. Lesser men might have been tempted by her obvious charms or cowed by her considerable influence, but you saw through her machinations with remarkable clarity. That you were able to secure both justice and compensation while preserving what remained of her reputation speaks to your singular character.

Dr. Watson's account of our case, should he choose to publish it, will no doubt focus upon the criminal elements and your deductive prowess. But I hope he will also note the human kindness you showed to an old woman who had lost her only child.

From Cairo, I shall write again to inform you of my travels. Until then, please accept my most sincere gratitude and the enclosed small token—a first edition of Winwood Reade's *The Martyrdom of Man*, which I noticed you admiring on Douglas's bookshelf. I believe he would have wanted you to have it.
With profound respect and eternal gratitude,

Mary Maberley

P.S. - Should you ever find yourself in need of a quiet retreat from the demands of Baker Street, know that The Three Gables will always welcome its most distinguished visitor.

To Holmes from Solicitor Sutro (3GAB)

Dear Mr. Holmes,

I find myself in the rather unusual position of writing to you regarding a client matter that has left me utterly perplexed. As you may recall from our brief encounter during the distressing affair at The Three Gables, I have served as legal counsel to Mrs. Mary Maberley for the better part of fifteen years, handling all manner of family business, property matters, and latterly, the sad arrangements following her son Douglas's untimely demise.

Imagine my astonishment, therefore, when I received word from Mrs. Maberley—not in person, mind you, but through a hastily scrawled note delivered by a street urchin—informing me that she has departed England for an extended journey abroad and instructing me, in her words, "not to worry about anything."

Not to worry! Good heavens, Mr. Holmes, how can a solicitor not worry when his client disappears without proper consultation, leaves no forwarding address, makes no provision for the management of her affairs, and offers no
explanation for what appears to be a most sudden change in her circumstances?

When last we spoke, following that dreadful burglary, Mrs. Maberley was in considerably reduced circumstances. The small inheritance from Douglas was modest at best, and I had been advising her on the necessity of perhaps taking in lodgers or selling The Three Gables entirely. She had seemed resigned to a quiet, rather straitened existence.

Yet now, according to the few inquiries I have been able to make, she has embarked upon what can only be described as a grand tour of the Mediterranean, complete with first-class accommodations aboard the *R.M.S. Oceanic*. The financial implications alone are staggering—such a journey would require resources far beyond anything in her previous means.

I confess, Mr. Holmes, that your involvement in resolving the matter of the burglary leads me to suspect that there are aspects of this affair of which I remain ignorant. As Mrs. Maberley's legal representative, I am naturally concerned about any arrangements that may have been made on her behalf, particularly if they involve financial settlements or agreements that could affect her legal standing.

Moreover, I am troubled by certain irregularities I have observed. The house at The Three Gables appears to have been cleaned and restored with remarkable efficiency—and expense. There are rumors in the neighborhood of workmen arriving within days of the burglary, though Mrs. Maberley never consulted me about such arrangements.

I do not wish to pry into matters that are none of my concern, but surely you can appreciate my professional anxiety. If Mrs. Maberley has come into some unexpected inheritance or settlement, there are legal formalities to be observed, documents to be filed, tax implications to consider. Her casual instruction to "not worry" strikes me as rather cavalier treatment of what could be serious legal obligations.

I would be most grateful if you could shed some light on these mysterious developments. Even a brief reassurance that Mrs. Maberley's affairs are in proper order would ease my considerable concern. As her solicitor, I have a duty of care that extends beyond mere bill-paying and property management.
I remain, with growing bewilderment,

Your obedient servant,

Sutro
Sutro & Associates, Solicitors

P.S. - I have also received an inquiry from a gentleman representing "interested parties" asking about Mrs. Maberley's whereabouts. I naturally declined to provide any information, but I confess the entire situation grows more mysterious by the day.

To Holmes from Robert Ferguson (SUSS)

My Dear Mr. Holmes,

It has been three months since you and Dr. Watson came to our aid during those dark and terrible days at Lamberley, and I feel compelled to write and express my profound gratitude for your extraordinary intervention in our family's crisis.

I confess that in the immediate aftermath of your revelations, I was overwhelmed by a mixture of relief and profound sorrow. Relief, of course, that my dear wife was not afflicted by the supernatural malady we had all feared, but sorrow that the truth proved in some ways even more disturbing—that young Jack's jealousy and resentment had driven him to such desperate and dangerous acts.

As you recommended that evening, we arranged for Jack to stay with my sister Margaret in Derbyshire immediately following your departure. The separation, though painful, has proved beneficial for all concerned. My wife has been able to recover her strength and spirits, and little baby Ferguson thrives under her devoted care, showing no ill effects from his ordeal.

I am pleased to report that Jack's time with his aunt has brought about a marked improvement in his disposition. The country air and Margaret's firm but loving guidance have done him considerable good. More importantly, he has come to understand the gravity of his actions and has expressed genuine remorse for the pain he caused our household.

It is with mixed feelings—pride tempered by natural parental concern— that I write to inform you that Jack has made the decision (at your suggestion) to enlist in the Merchant Marine. He departs next month for a year or two at sea, which his aunt and I believe will provide him with the discipline and purpose he needs to mature into the fine young man I know he can become. The sea has a way of teaching lessons that no amount of lecturing from parents can accomplish.

My wife, I am happy to say, has forgiven Jack completely and was instrumental in supporting his decision to join the Merchant Marine. Her capacity for forgiveness and understanding continues to amaze me, and I am more devoted to her than ever.

I cannot adequately express how grateful I am that you saw through the bizarre circumstances to the truth of the matter. Without your intervention, I shudder to think what might have become of our family. Your reputation for solving the impossible is well-deserved, but more than that, your discretion and compassion in handling such a delicate family matter has earned my eternal respect and gratitude.

Please extend my thanks to Dr. Watson as well. His presence provided great comfort during those trying times.

Should you ever find yourself in need of anything that I might provide, you have but to ask. I remain, Your most grateful and obedient servant,

Robert Ferguson

To Nathan Garrideb from Holmes (3GAR)

My Dear Mr. Garrideb,

It is with considerable regret that I must confirm what you have no doubt already surmised regarding the unfortunate affair of the Garrideb inheritance. As the facts have now been fully established, I feel it my duty to write to you personally to express my sincere apologies for the distressing circumstances in which you found yourself unwittingly entangled.

The individual who presented himself as John Garrideb of Kansas was, as we discovered, neither American nor possessed of that surname. He was, in fact, one James Winter, better known to Scotland Yard as "Killer" Evans—a man whose criminal enterprises have spanned counterfeiting, fraud, and considerably more violent pursuits. His elaborate charade regarding the Garrideb inheritance was merely a sophisticated ruse designed to gain access to your residence at 136 Little Ryder Street, beneath which he had reason to believe lay the counterfeiting establishment of the late Rodger Prescott.

I am acutely aware of how cruelly this deception must have struck you, given your years of dedicated collecting and the genuine excitement with which you approached the prospect of completing your remarkable assemblage of artifacts. Your enthusiasm for your collection—from your Babylonian and Assyrian antiquities to your coins and medals—was evident to both Watson and myself, and it pains me to know that what seemed a providential opportunity was nothing more than the machination of a criminal mind.

The inheritance, I must inform you definitively, has no basis in reality. There was never a Alexander Hamilton Garrideb of Chicago, nor any substantial estate awaiting claimants of your surname. The entire edifice was constructed solely to serve Evans' criminal purpose, and I deeply regret that your hopes were raised only to be so thoroughly dashed.

I trust that this experience, however disappointing, will not diminish your passion for your scholarly pursuits. Your collection, as it stands, represents years of careful curation and genuine expertise. While the promised funds will not materialize to enhance it further, the intrinsic value of your work and knowledge remains undiminished.

Should you require any assistance in the future, or should this matter have any lingering effects that concern you, please do not hesitate to call upon me. It would be my pleasure to be of service to you in legitimate endeavors, having seen how ill you were served by this false one.

I remain, with sincere regrets and best wishes for your continued collecting success, Your obedient servant,

Sherlock Holmes
Consulting Detective

P.S. - Watson has asked me to convey his particular concern for your well-being following these events, and his hope that the shock of the revelation has not been too severe.

To Holmes from Neil Gibson (THOR)

Dear Mr. Holmes,

I write to you from a heart both grateful beyond measure and broken beyond repair. Your invoice sits before me, yet no sum of money could adequately compensate you for what you have accomplished—the salvation of an innocent woman and the revelation of a truth so terrible I can scarcely comprehend it.

When I first approached you in desperation, pleading for you to prove Miss Dunbar's innocence, I believed I was asking you to overturn the evidence of a tragic crime. I never imagined you would uncover something far more sinister—that my own wife had orchestrated her death with such calculating malice as to frame the one person whose only crime was being loved by me.

The horror of it haunts me, Holmes. To think that Maria harbored such hatred, such twisted jealousy, that she would condemn an innocent soul to the gallows simply to ensure I would suffer for the remainder of my days. The woman I once married, the mother of my children, had become a creature so consumed by vengeance that she valued her own life less than her desire to destroy mine through Grace's destruction.

You have given Miss Dunbar back her freedom, her reputation, and her very life. For this, I am eternally in your debt. Yet in saving her, you have also revealed to her the full extent of the danger my affections placed her in. She now understands that loving me—or rather, being loved by me— nearly cost her everything.

Miss Dunbar has made her position abundantly clear. She will accept no communication from me, wants no reminders of the Gibson household, and seeks only to put this entire nightmare behind her. I cannot fault her for this decision. Indeed, how could I? My love for her led directly to her near-destruction. What manner of man would I be to continue pursuing someone who has suffered so much because of me?

The irony is not lost on me, Holmes. I am a man accustomed to acquiring what I desire through wealth and determination. Yet the one thing I truly wanted—Grace's affection—has been rendered forever impossible by the very circumstances that brought us together. My wife achieved in death what she could not accomplish in life: the complete separation of Grace Dunbar and myself.

The children have been told their mother died by accident. They are too young to understand the full truth, and God willing, they never shall. I have arranged for them to be educated abroad, far from the whispers and speculation that will inevitably follow this family name. Perhaps in time, the shadow of these events will fade enough that they might lead normal lives.

As for myself, I find little purpose in continuing the business that earned me the sobriquet "Gold King." What value has gold when it cannot purchase redemption? What worth has wealth when it cannot undo the harm one has caused? I am considering retiring from active business and devoting myself to charitable works—perhaps some good may yet come from this tainted fortune.

You saved an innocent woman's life, Holmes, and exposed a truth that needed telling, no matter how painful. You have my deepest gratitude and highest respect. Should you ever require anything within my power to provide, you need only ask. Though I suspect a man of your integrity would be reluctant to accept assistance from one so thoroughly disgraced.

I remain, with profound respect and eternal gratitude,

Neil Gibson

P.S. - I have heard that Miss Dunbar has accepted a position with a family in Scotland, far from Hampshire and all its painful associations. I pray she finds the peace and happiness there that my presence in her life made impossible here.

To Holmes from Sergeant Coventry (THOR)

My Dear Mr. Holmes,

I find myself compelled to put pen to paper, though I confess my modest vocabulary feels wholly inadequate to express the profound admiration and gratitude I feel following our recent collaboration on the Gibson murder case at Thor Bridge.

When we first met at the scene, I must admit I harbored the typical policeman's skepticism toward consulting detectives. The evidence seemed clear enough—Miss Grace Dunbar's revolver discovered in her very own wardrobe, that damning note clutched in poor Mrs. Gibson's lifeless fingers, and the lady's own admission of her feelings toward her employer. Any reasonable man would have concluded the case closed and the governess guilty as charged.

How wrong I was, and how magnificently you proved it!

Your examination of that curious chip in the stonework of Thor Bridge left me baffled initially. When you announced that this seemingly insignificant mark held the key to the entire mystery, I confess I wondered if perhaps your reputation had been somewhat exaggerated. But watching you work—observing the methodical way you measured distances, analyzed trajectories, and reconstructed the true sequence of events—was nothing short of revelatory.

The moment you demonstrated how Mrs. Gibson herself had engineered her own demise, using that ingenious mechanism with the stone and string to ensure the murder weapon would be found in Miss Dunbar's possession, I felt as though scales had fallen from my eyes. The diabolical cunning of it! To orchestrate one's own death so meticulously, ensuring an innocent woman would hang for the crime, simply to satisfy a twisted desire for revenge against her husband's affections—it defies comprehension, yet your proof was irrefutable.

Your patience in explaining each deduction was extraordinary. When you showed how the trajectory of the fatal shot could never have originated from the position where Miss Dunbar stood, and how the timing of events made her guilt impossible, I understood why Scotland Yard speaks of you with such reverence. You do not merely solve crimes, Mr. Holmes—you illuminate truth itself, dispelling shadows of confusion and false assumptions with the brilliant light of pure logic.

I hope I may have the honor of working alongside you again, should circumstances permit. Until then, please accept my deepest respect and admiration for your unparalleled skills as a detective and your unwavering commitment to justice.

Your most grateful servant,

Sergeant Arthur Coventry
Hampshire Constabulary

P.S. - I have taken the liberty of recommending your services to Chief Inspector Gregson, who expressed keen interest in consulting with you on a rather puzzling matter involving some missing diamonds. I trust this presumption does not offend.

To Homes from Miss Grace Dunbar (THOR)

My Dear Mr. Holmes,

I find myself quite at a loss for words adequate to express the profound gratitude that fills my heart as I take pen to paper this evening. Your remarkable intervention in what appeared to be my certain doom has restored not merely my freedom, but my very faith in justice itself.

When that dreadful revolver was discovered secreted within my wardrobe, and when the authorities presented what seemed to be such damning evidence against my character, I confess that hope had nearly abandoned me entirely. The weight of suspicion, the whispered accusations, and the seemingly inexorable march toward the gallows had reduced me to a state of near despair. Even my own solicitor seemed to regard my case as quite hopeless.

Yet you, dear Mr. Holmes, with that penetrating intellect for which you are so justly renowned, perceived what others could not—or would not—see. While the police were content to accept the obvious conclusion, you delved deeper into the shadows of Thor Bridge, uncovering truths that would have remained forever hidden but for your singular genius.

Your demonstration of how that poor, tormented woman engineered her own demise while simultaneously ensuring my destruction was nothing short of masterly. The revelation that Mrs. Gibson had fired the fatal shot herself, using that ingenious arrangement with the stone tied to the revolver's trigger-guard, was a stroke of deductive reasoning that left even Inspector MacDonald speechless. How could any of us have imagined such a diabolical scheme—that she would sacrifice her own life merely to see me hanged for a crime I did not commit?

The discovery of that chip in the stonework of the bridge, which you so astutely recognized as the key to unraveling the entire mystery, demonstrated once again your unparalleled powers of observation. Where others saw merely damaged masonry, you saw the final piece of a most complex and tragic puzzle.

I am particularly grateful for the dignity with which you treated my circumstances throughout this ordeal. Never once did you regard me with the suspicion that seemed to cloud the judgment of all others. Your unwavering belief in the pursuit of truth, regardless of how inconvenient that truth might prove to established assumptions, has quite literally saved my life.

Mr. Gibson's household was indeed a place of great unhappiness, and I fear that my presence there, innocent though my intentions were, may have contributed to the final tragedy. The knowledge that Mrs. Gibson's jealousy and desperation led her to such extremes weighs heavily upon my conscience, though I know you would counsel me that I bear no responsibility for her terrible choice.

Should you ever find yourself in need of assistance, however humble my capabilities might prove in comparison to your own remarkable talents, I remain forever at your service. The debt I owe you can never be fully repaid, but my gratitude shall endure as long as memory serves.

I remain, with the deepest respect and appreciation,
Your most grateful and obedient servant,

Miss Grace Dunbar

P.S. - I have taken the liberty of enclosing a small contribution to your household expenses, though I know that money could never adequately compensate you for the gift of life and freedom you have bestowed upon me.

To Dorak from Holmes (CREE)

Dear Mr. Dorak,

I write to you concerning a matter of the utmost gravity regarding the substance you have been supplying to Professor Presbury of Camford University. Through careful investigation, I have uncovered the devastating effects of this preparation upon the Professor's physical and mental condition.

Professor Presbury, once a man of impeccable reputation and scholarly bearing, has suffered a complete transformation under the influence of your compound. The symptoms observed include:

- Violent and unpredictable behavior toward family members and household staff
- Physical alterations resulting in an ape-like locomotion and demeanor
- Complete loss of rational thought and civilized conduct
- Aggressive tendencies that have endangered the safety of those around him
- The Professor's own faithful dog, recognizing the unnatural change in his master's scent and behavior, has been driven to attack him—a clear indication of the profound alteration this substance has wrought upon his very nature.

I must inform you that the continued distribution of this compound places you in a position of considerable legal jeopardy. Should Professor Presbury cause injury to himself or others while under its influence—which grows more likely with each dose—you may well find yourself answerable to charges of reckless endangerment, criminal negligence, or worse. The courts take a dim view of those who profit from substances that transform decent citizens into dangerous creatures.

Furthermore, your moral obligation extends beyond mere legal compliance. You have witnessed firsthand what this preparation does to the human constitution. To continue its sale knowing these effects would constitute not merely poor judgment, but a willful disregard for human welfare.

I strongly advise you to cease all distribution of this substance immediately and to cooperate fully with any forthcoming investigation into this matter. Should you possess antidotes or knowledge that might reverse the Professor's condition, I urge you to come forward without delay.

Time is of the essence. Professor Presbury's condition deteriorates with each passing day, and the danger to those around him grows correspondingly. Your prompt action in this matter may yet prevent tragedy and spare you from the full weight of the law's consequences.

I remain, sir, awaiting your immediate response and corrective action.

Most earnestly,

Sherlock Holmes
Consulting Detective

To Holmes from Chequers (CREE)

Dear Mr. Holmes and Dr. Watson,

It is with the greatest pleasure that I write to express our sincere appreciation for the honour of your recent visit to The Chequers Hotel. Your distinguished presence graced our establishment during what I understand was a most challenging investigation, and we were delighted to provide you with comfortable accommodations during your stay.

Our entire staff remarked upon your courteous demeanor and the fascinating nature of your work. Dr. Watson, your kind words to our dining room staff regarding the evening meals did not go unnoticed and brought considerable joy to our cook.

The Chequers has long prided itself on providing a haven of comfort and discretion for gentlemen engaged in matters of importance. Your reputation as London's finest consulting detective precedes you, and we would be most gratified to welcome you both back should your professional duties bring you to Camford again.

Please accept the enclosed small token of our appreciation: a bottle of our finest port, specially selected from our cellar. We hope it will provide a pleasant reminder of your stay with us. We eagerly anticipate the pleasure of your company again in the near future, and wish you continued success in your remarkable endeavours.

With the deepest respect and warmest regards,

James Whitfield
Proprietor, The Chequers Hotel

Post Scriptum: Should you ever require references regarding character or conduct for professional purposes, The Chequers Hotel would be most pleased to provide the highest possible recommendation for both gentlemen.

To Lowenstein from Watson (CREE)

Dear Mr. Lowenstein,

As a medical practitioner with considerable experience in both clinical practice and forensic investigation, I feel compelled to address serious concerns regarding your research methodologies and the conduct of what can only be described as unauthorized human experimentation.

My recent involvement in investigating the case of Professor Presbury has brought to light the catastrophic consequences of your experimental compounds. The Professor's condition represents not merely a medical curiosity, but a complete breakdown of human physiology and mental faculties that would never have been permitted under proper clinical supervision.

From a medical standpoint, your research appears to violate every principle of ethical experimentation established by our profession:

- Regarding Informed Consent: Professor Presbury was clearly not made aware of the true nature and potential consequences of your preparation. No rational individual would consent to treatment that could result in such profound behavioral and physical transformation.
- Regarding Subject Safety: The complete absence of medical monitoring during the Professor's treatment represents unconscionable negligence. Basic medical protocol demands regular examination, dosage control, and immediate intervention capability when adverse effects manifest.
- Regarding Scientific Method: True clinical trials require careful documentation, control subjects, and gradual dose escalation under medical supervision. Your apparent practice of distributing experimental compounds through correspondence, without oversight, represents pseudoscience of the most dangerous variety.

The medical consequences I have personally observed in Professor Presbury include:

- Severe neurological deterioration affecting cognitive function
- Dramatic alterations in muscular and skeletal behavior patterns
- Complete personality dissolution and loss of social inhibitions
- Physical changes detectable even to domestic animals through altered scent

Should Professor Presbury suffer permanent harm, or should he injure another person while in his altered state, you will bear direct responsibility. The medical community takes a grave view of practitioners who experiment upon unwitting subjects, and the legal ramifications could include charges of assault, administering noxious substances, and criminal endangerment.

As one medical man to another, I implore you to consider the oath we take to "first, do no harm." Your research, however well-intentioned, has violated this fundamental principle. The pursuit of scientific knowledge, no matter how promising, can never justify the endangerment of human subjects. I trust that your conscience as a researcher will compel you to take immediate corrective action.

Should you fail to respond appropriately to this warning, I am prepared to bring this matter before the Royal College of Physicians and the appropriate legal authorities.

I remain, sir, your concerned colleague in the medical sciences,

John H. Watson, M.D.
Formerly of the 5th Northumberland Fusiliers

Post Scriptum: Mr. Sherlock Holmes concurs with the contents of this letter and stands ready to provide additional evidence of the harmful effects of your compound should legal proceedings become necessary.

To Watson from Holmes (LION)

My Dear Watson,

I find myself compelled to take up my pen this evening, not merely from the solitude that these Sussex downs impose upon a retired consulting detective, but from an irrepressible desire to share with you the details of a most singular case that has recently occupied my attention. How I wished for your steady presence and keen observations during these past weeks! You would have found it, I believe, a puzzle worthy of our Baker Street days.

The affair began with the discovery of poor Fitzroy McPherson, a science master at The Gables school here in Fulworth. The man was found in the most distressing circumstances upon the beach, his body bearing the most peculiar marks I have ever encountered in my long experience with violent death. The local constabulary, good fellows though they are, were completely at sea—if you will pardon the expression, which proves more apt than intended.

McPherson had been found in a state that defied immediate explanation. His back bore welts and striations that suggested some form of savage flogging, yet no human hand could have delivered such precise and terrible punishment. The poor fellow lived just long enough to gasp a few words about "the Lion's Mane" before expiring, leaving us with what appeared to be either the ravings of a dying mind or the most cryptic of clues.

Initially, suspicion fell upon Ian Murdoch, the mathematics master, and here we encountered one of those eternal triangles that so often complicate criminal investigation. Both men had been paying court to Miss Maud Bellamy, a young woman of considerable charm who resides with her father, the local magistrate. Murdoch's jealousy was evident to all, and when McPherson was found dead after a quarrel between the two men, the case seemed straightforward enough.

But you know my methods, Watson. When the obvious presents itself so readily, I am inclined to look elsewhere. The wounds troubled me greatly—their pattern was unlike anything in my considerable experience with the varied ways in which human beings inflict harm upon one another. Moreover, Murdoch's alibi, while not ironclad, was sufficiently robust to give me pause.

The breakthrough came, as it so often does, through careful observation of seemingly insignificant details. The timing of the attack, the location, the state of the tides, and most crucially, the precise nature of those terrible welts, all pointed to a solution that was both simple and extraordinary.

The culprit, my dear fellow, was neither human jealousy nor criminal intent, but one of nature's most formidable creatures—Cyanea capillata, the Lion's Mane jellyfish. This magnificent yet deadly creature, which can trail tentacles of thirty feet or more, had been driven into our shallow cove by recent storms. Poor McPherson, taking his customary morning swim, had encountered this silent killer in the surf.

The "Lion's Mane" he gasped with his dying breath was not metaphor or delirium, but the most literal and accurate description possible. The creature's tentacles, armed with thousands of stinging cells, had embraced him in a deadly caress that left those distinctive marks upon his flesh.

I was able to locate the creature itself—a specimen of truly impressive dimensions—and ensure its removal from waters where others might fall victim to the same fate. Murdoch's name has been cleared, much to Miss Bellamy's evident relief, and the true cause of this tragedy made known.

Yet I confess, Watson, that while the intellectual satisfaction of solving such a unique puzzle cannot be denied, these Sussex evenings grow long and quiet. The sound of the waves, while soothing, cannot replace the comfort of your companionship and our familiar fireside discussions. Mrs. Hudson's ministrations, though fondly remembered, pale beside the prospect of your wife's excellent cooking and your own genial conversation.

Would it be too much to hope that you might find time for a visit to your old friend? The autumn air here is most invigorating, and I believe you would find the coastal walks beneficial to your constitution. I have secured comfortable lodgings at the local inn for any guests, and there are several interesting geological formations that might appeal to your scientific mind.

I remain, as always, your faithful friend and colleague,

Sherlock Holmes
Consulting Detective

To Mrs Merrilow from Holmes (VEIL)

Dear Mrs. Merrilow,

I trust this letter finds you in good health and spirits. I write regarding your lodger, Mrs. Ronder, who consulted with me recently concerning a matter of some personal significance.

You may set your mind entirely at ease regarding any concerns you may have harboured about the lady's welfare or intentions. Following our consultation, I am pleased to inform you that Mrs. Ronder has resolved to continue her residence under your most admirable care for the foreseeable future.

I observed during my brief acquaintance with your establishment that you have provided Mrs. Ronder with not merely lodging, but a sanctuary of remarkable discretion and kindness. Such consideration for a tenant's particular circumstances speaks well of your character.

Should any matter arise concerning Mrs. Ronder's welfare that causes you concern, you may feel free to communicate with me at the above address. I remain, with appreciation for your exemplary care of a fellow human being in distress,

Sherlock Holmes
Consulting Detecive

P.S. - Please extend my compliments to Mrs. Ronder on the excellent quality of the tea service during my recent visit. Such attention to proper hospitality, even under difficult circumstances, is a mark of true refinement.

To Eugenia Ronder from Holmes (VEIL)

My Dear Mrs. Ronder,

I write to acknowledge receipt of the small package you left with Mrs. Hudson yesterday evening. The contents—that crystalline substance which you intended as your final earthly companion—now rests safely in my possession, where it shall remain indefinitely.

Your decision to relinquish this ultimate escape speaks to a courage far greater than any you demonstrated in those dark days at Ronder's Wild Beast Show. To choose life, however diminished it may seem, over the certainty of oblivion requires a fortitude that few possess. I confess myself moved by your resolution.

You spoke of living out your remaining days naturally, and in this choice I detect not merely resignation, but perhaps the first stirrings of redemption. The terrible secret you have carried these seven years has been a poison more deadly than any chemical compound—yet in its confession, I venture to suggest, lies the antidote to your spiritual suffering.

While justice in the conventional sense may be forever beyond reach in the matter of your late husband's death, there exists yet another form of justice: that which comes from a life lived in honest acknowledgment of one's deeds.

The path ahead will not be easy, but I have confidence that the same strength which enabled you to survive these past years in solitude will serve you well in whatever days remain. You have chosen wisely, Mrs. Ronder. Live them well.

I remain, with considerable respect for your courage,

Sherlock Holmes
Consulting Detective

To Holmes from John Mason (SHOS)

Dear Mr. Holmes,

I trust this letter finds you in good health following the resolution of our recent troubles here at Shoscombe Old Place. I write to you with utmost urgency regarding a matter that has been weighing heavily upon my mind since your departure.

As you well know, my position as head trainer here depends entirely upon Sir Robert's confidence in my abilities and, more importantly, his belief in my absolute loyalty to his interests. While I remain convinced that bringing you into this affair was the only proper course of action given the peculiar and disturbing circumstances we discovered, I must confess that I am greatly concerned about the potential consequences should Sir Robert learn of my role in contacting you.

You will recall that I approached you initially through young Steve Dixie, hoping to maintain some distance from the matter. However, given the thoroughness of your investigation and the dramatic resolution in the crypt, I fear that my involvement may have become more apparent than I had hoped.

I beseech you, Mr. Holmes, and Dr. Watson as well, to exercise the utmost discretion regarding how this case came to your attention. Should Sir Robert inquire about the circumstances that led to your involvement, I would be most grateful if you could suggest that your interest was piqued through other channels—perhaps through your extensive network of informants, or through some detail that came to your attention through the racing community.

I realize this request may seem somewhat cowardly, but I hope you understand that my livelihood, and indeed the welfare of my family, depends upon my continued employment here. Sir Robert, despite his recent troubles and questionable judgment, has been a fair employer, and I have devoted many years to building the reputation of his stable.

The horses remain my primary concern, and I am pleased to report that Shoscombe Prince continues to show excellent form as we approach the Derby. Perhaps this success will help to restore Sir Robert's spirits and his fortunes.

I remain deeply grateful for your intervention in this matter, which undoubtedly prevented a far greater scandal from befalling this household. Your discretion in this small additional matter would be received with the greatest appreciation.
I remain, sir, your most obliged and humble servant,

John Mason
Head Trainer
Shoscombe Old Place

P.S. Should you ever find yourself in need of information regarding the racing world, please do not hesitate to call upon me. I would consider it an honor to assist you in any future endeavors, provided, of course, that such assistance could be rendered without compromising my position here.

To John Mason from Holmes (SHOS)

My Dear Mason,

Your recent letter has been received, and I hasten to put your mind at ease regarding the matter of your involvement in recent events at Shoscombe Old Place.

You may rest assured that neither Dr. Watson nor I have any intention of revealing the circumstances by which this case came to our attention. Professional discretion is, as you well know, fundamental to my practice, and I have never found it necessary to expose those who have acted from proper motives in bringing matters to my notice.

Moreover, I believe your concerns may be somewhat exaggerated. The official view appears to be that the unfortunate circumstances arose from grief and temporary aberration of judgment rather than any criminal intent. Given this lenient approach by the authorities, there seems little likelihood that they would concern themselves with investigating how the matter first came to light.

Your loyalty to Sir Robert, while commendable, should not blind you to the fact that your intervention likely saved him from far more serious consequences. A man who acts from conscience and genuine concern for his employer's welfare need fear no reproach from that quarter, should the truth ever emerge.

I remain, with the highest regard,

Sherlock Holmes
Consulting Detective

P.S. - Watson asks me to convey his respects and to assure you that your hospitality during our stay was much appreciated. He was particularly impressed by your knowledge of equine lineages and training methods.

To Ray Barker from Holmes (RETI)

Dear Barker,

I write to express my appreciation for your conduct during the recent Amberley affair. While our initial encounter may have begun with what I perceived as professional rivalry, I must acknowledge that your subsequent discretion and cooperation proved invaluable to the successful resolution of the case.

Your willingness to share the information you had gathered about Amberley's movements, particularly the details concerning his activities on the day in question, provided crucial corroboration for my own observations. More importantly, your restraint in not pursuing certain lines of inquiry that might have alerted our quarry to our suspicions showed both wisdom and professional judgment.

I confess that when I first learned another investigator was working the case, I may have been somewhat... territorial in my approach. However, your methodical groundwork and your keen observation regarding the inconsistencies in Amberley's financial records demonstrated that you possess genuine detective instincts. The fact that you had already begun to doubt his story, even before my own investigation commenced, speaks well of your analytical abilities.

The criminal classes of London are resourceful and numerous enough to provide ample work for all competent investigators. There is no logical reason why our paths, should they cross again, need result in professional conflict. Indeed, I have come to believe that the judicious sharing of information between practitioners of our craft can only serve to advance the cause of justice.

Should you ever find yourself working a case that intersects with one of my own investigations, I would welcome the opportunity for consultation rather than competition. Your approach, while different from mine, has proven both thorough and effective. The criminal mind is sufficiently complex that multiple perspectives can only enhance our understanding of it.

I trust that the resolution of the Amberley matter has provided you with
a satisfactory conclusion to your own inquiries on behalf of your client.
The man's elaborate deception was certainly worthy of our combined
efforts to unravel.
Please consider this letter an olive branch, if you will. London's criminal
element is challenge enough without adding unnecessary friction between
those of us committed to opposing it.

With professional respect,

Sherlock Holmes
Consulting Detective

*P.S. - Watson speaks highly of your courtesy during your brief meeting at the scene.
He was particularly impressed by your observation about the peculiar odor near
Amberley's cellar - a detail that proved quite significant in our final analysis.*

To Watson from Reverend Elman (RETI)

My Dear Dr. Watson,

I hope this letter finds you in good health and spirits. I write to you with some perplexity regarding your recent visit to our quiet parish, and I confess that I am prompted to do so by circumstances that have arisen since your departure.

When you and Mr. Amberley called upon me, you mentioned that you were researching historical records of local families for what you described as a genealogical inquiry on behalf of a client. I was, of course, most happy to assist you in examining our parish registers and discussing the various families who have resided in our district over the years.

However, I must tell you that your visit has since become something of a topic of conversation among my parishioners. Mrs. Whitmore, who assists with the church flowers, happened to mention your name to her sister in the neighboring village, who immediately recognized it. "Why, that's Dr. Watson!" she exclaimed, "The gentleman who writes those fascinating accounts of Mr. Sherlock Holmes's detective cases!"

Word of this identification spread rather quickly through our small community, as such things tend to do in country parishes. By Sunday's service, I found myself fielding numerous inquiries from my congregation about whether some dark mystery was afoot in Little Purlington, and whether the famous consulting detective himself might soon be making an appearance.

One of our older parishioners who has lived here all his eighty-three years, approached me after Evensong to express his concern that perhaps some terrible crime had been committed that required the attention of such renowned investigators. Another wondered aloud whether the recent death of poor Mrs. Blackwood might not have been as natural as we all supposed.

I assured them all that I was quite certain no such dramatic circumstances were involved, but I confess, Dr. Watson, that their questions have left me rather curious myself. Your manner during our meeting, while perfectly cordial, did strike me as somewhat more... shall I say, professionally observant than one might expect from a gentleman pursuing mere genealogical research.

I do not wish to pry into matters that are not my concern, but as the spiritual shepherd of this flock, I feel I must ask: is there indeed some matter of criminal investigation that has brought the attention of Mr. Holmes to our peaceful community? If so, I should very much like to know, both for my own peace of mind and so that I might properly address the concerns of my parishioners.

Should there be any way in which I can be of genuine assistance to you and Mr. Holmes in whatever matter has brought you to our district, please know that you may count upon my complete discretion and cooperation. The cause of justice is surely one that any servant of God must support.

I await your explanation with considerable interest, and I do hope that our little community has not unwittingly become entangled in one of those sensational affairs that seem to follow in Mr. Holmes's wake.

With Christian fellowship and sincere regards,

Reverend J.C. Elman
Vicar of St. Mary's
Little Purlington

P.S. - I should mention that young Tommy Fletcher, the blacksmith's son, has been telling anyone who will listen that he is quite certain he spotted a gentleman of consulting detective appearance examining the hedgerows near Woodman's Cottage yesterday evening. I cannot vouch for the reliability of this observation, but thought you should know that your movements may not have been as discreet as you had hoped.

About the Author

Thomas "Tom" Campbell is a Wilmington, North Carolina resident who shares his home with his dog, Watson. His diverse professional career has spanned multiple industries, including his role as an Account Executive - Industry Consultant with AT&T Information Systems. Tom has also demonstrated his entrepreneurial spirit by operating Beach PC, a local computer repair business, and serving as owner/operator of Advanced Legal Software, a statewide company that specialized in family law applications.

Beyond his professional pursuits, Tom maintains an active personal life centered around his community and interests. He is a dedicated member of the Sherlock Holmes Society of the Cape Fear, serves as a Sunday school teacher at the First Baptist Church of Carolina Beach, and treasures time spent on family vacations.

Tom can be reached through the Sherlockian website listed below:

www.SherlockHolmesSociety.com